THE NOVELLA COLLECTION

A SERIES OF SHORT STORIES FOR THE PUSHING THE LIMITS SERIES, THUNDER ROAD SERIES, AND ONLY A BREATH APART

KATIE MCGARRY

Copyright © 2020 by Katie McGarry

Cover Image and Design by and from BetiBup33 Studio Design https://thebookcoverdesigner.com/designers/betibup33

This is a work of fiction. Names, characters, places, and incidents either are the product of the author's imagination or are used fictitiously. Any resemblance to actual persons, living or dead, events, or locales is entirely coincidental.

All rights reserved. No part of this book may be reproduced or used in any form or by any electronic or mechanical means, including photocopying, recording, or by any information storage or retrieval systems without prior written permission of the copyright owner except where permitted by law or for the use of brief quotations in a book review.

First paperback edition March 2020

www.katielmcgarry.com

❀ Created with Vellum

OTHER BOOKS BY KATIE MCGARRY

The Pushing the Limits Series:

Pushing the Limits

Breaking the Rules

Crossing the Line

Dare You To

Crash Into You

Take Me On

Chasing Impossible

The Thunder Road Series:

Nowhere But Here

Walk the Edge

Long Way Home

Stand-Alone Novels:

Say You'll Remember Me

Only a Breath Apart Series:

Only a Breath Apart

Echoes Between Us

THE PROPOSAL

CHAPTER 1

ECHO

"Promise me you will not elope." Through video chat on my cell, Lila gives me her patented best-friend glare of disapproval. Her blond hair is pulled back in a ponytail and swings with the shake of her head. "I swear to God, I will never forgive you if you do. Like never. I have been your best friend for too long to be left out of a big moment like you getting married, do you understand?"

From the passenger side of my Honda Civic, I glance out the window to make sure Noah's still in line in the convenience store. He rolled down all four windows so I wouldn't wither in the August heat of Pensacola Beach, Florida, and the last thing I need is for him to walk up and hear my best friend talking about wedding-dress shopping, bachelorette parties, and what should be the something borrowed and something blue.

My car is filled with our vacation. A bag of clothes in the back that desperately needs to find a washer, printed out directions from Louisville to here that we never used since the GPS worked, a few crumpled fast-food bags and the drinks we brought along with us from the lunch we just had at the Whataburger.

"One, what makes you think Noah and I would elope?" I ask. "Two, he hasn't proposed. Three, I seriously don't think he has plans to propose."

Lila rolls her eyes and does it in such a big way that it was clearly meant as her entire response. "You'd elope because your father hates him."

True, but my father understands that Noah's not going anywhere. After regaining my memories during my senior year of high school as to why I have scars all over my arms, I forced my father into therapy with me last January.

Because we're both stubborn, we argued, we yelled, and sarcasm was used as a whip made of spiky chains. I'd get so angry I'd cry, and he'd go mute because he's my father and that's what he does when he doesn't yell. After three months of both of us being intolerable to each other and probably to the therapist, my father broke—and when I say broke, I mean he cried.

I swallow when my throat tightens with the memory. My father doesn't cry and when he cried, I cried and we were both crying and we finally talked about a lot of things. One of them being, I loved Noah and my father was going to have to deal with the fact that Noah is not a phase and would be in my life.

"I pinkie-swear to you, I am not eloping," I say, but Lila continues like I didn't speak.

"You're leaving in four days to live over a thousand miles away from Noah and the guy first asked you to marry him after you dated him for two months. You're telling me that he hasn't proposed to you while you're surrounded by white-sand beaches and tropical air? I have to admit this little game you're playing with me is starting to tick me off."

I place my hand in the air in a stop. "He took that

proposal back because he didn't really mean it. He was only seventeen! He was scared of not getting custody of his brothers and he was realizing he was falling in love with me and he just said the first thing that came to his mind as a solution, so it doesn't count. That was two years ago, and just so you know, Noah and I have absolutely no plans of getting married until we're out of college."

Because God knows we had enough complications in our personal lives before we even met each other or graduated from high school. We talk about our future together and we talk about what our lives will be like once we get married, but for now our goal is to take the next few years slow and easy.

Since we're not even halfway through college, most people would think we're too young to think about forever, but those people haven't lived my life or Noah's and they can keep their opinions to themselves.

Lila shrugs. "Whatever."

My eyes narrow as I take in my best friend since birth. There's a glint in her Glinda the Good Witch blue eyes I missed before. "What do you know?"

Her face falls. "He really hasn't asked you, has he?"

I sit up straight in the seat and ask again, "What do you know?"

She ducks. "Nothing."

Nope. Not nothing. "Too late. You know something, and you're spilling."

Lila turns her head as if there is someone else nearby. "What did you say? I'll be right there."

"Don't you dare! You're setting up your apartment and you told me your roommates aren't moving in until next week."

"Lincoln's here." She sucks at lying.

"You told me he has to work until six." Lincoln's her

boyfriend and the two of them are about to start their sophomore year at the University of Florida in Gainesville. She's super excited that she and friends of hers will be living in the same apartment complex as Lincoln and his friends.

"Our side of Florida is on a different time zone than you. Like five hours. Psh." She shakes her cell. "We have… ba….connec…tion."

I purse my lips. "You're not fooling me."

"Fine." She flops back on her already-made bed. Only Lila would have a neatly made bed on the same day she moves in. "Noah told us he was going to propose to you at the beginning of the vacation. I thought he had and you were keeping it from me. You've got so many friends now, and I'll admit I want to be the first to know."

It's weird how there's a spike of elation at the thought of him proposing and then the dip of disappointment that he and I aren't engaged. "Why do you think he hasn't proposed yet?"

Lila twists her fingers into her ponytail. "Remember when Lincoln came to Louisville and the whole group of us went to Isaiah and West's place to play cards?"

"Yes." Noah was in a foul mood when we left even though he won while playing poker. I don't play poker, so I'd spent the night sitting and talking with Lila, and I hadn't understood why Noah was angry.

"When you went to the bathroom, I heard Noah arguing with Isaiah. Noah was mad because he said everyone let him win."

My forehead furrows. "Why would they do that?" Those boys are highly competitive, especially Logan, Ryan and West.

Just thinking of them and the rest our self-made family makes me smile. To think it all started out with me meeting Noah. Eventually, I became friends with Noah's best friends,

Beth and Isaiah, and then our circle continued to beautifully expand.

"What does this have to do with a proposal?" I continue.

Lila tilts her head like I should have a massive lightbulb moment. "Noah gave all the extra money he saved this summer to Abby to help with her grandma."

"I know this." Because I gave money, too. Abby is a good friend of Noah's and Isaiah's and she became a part of our unofficial family. Her grandmother needed medical help and we all pitched in because that's what members of a real family do—love and support each other.

"Echo," she says as if saying my name slowly will help me understand. "Noah was saving that money to buy you an engagement ring. The guys let him win so he'd at least have something to give you when he proposes. Maybe he hasn't proposed because he doesn't have a diamond ring. He seemed real upset that he didn't have one to offer you."

I blink. Several times. My heart hurts and I blow out air to help with the ache. Yes, Noah and I talk about our future together, but we also talk about how we aren't in a rush to run down the aisle. "Why would Noah propose to me now?"

She offers a sheepish expression. "You're leaving—for a year. Honestly, he and I talked and he wants to propose to show you he supports you chasing your dreams while he chases his. He wants to show you that he doesn't believe distance and time are going to change how he feels about you. Noah really loves you, and I think proposing is his equivalent of making a promise to you that he'll always be by your side."

My eyes water because that sounds like Noah. He'd maybe drop an f-bomb in there because he sometimes still has a tough time with emotion, but Noah does love me and he does support me and I love him back just as much.

While Lila obviously knows things I don't, I know

hundreds of things she doesn't and one of them is that there is no extra money—not for Noah. His car broke down and even with Isaiah working on the car for free, the part needed for the repair was expensive and Noah had to pay for his car insurance and...just the normal *ands* of life.

This weeklong vacation was my birthday present to him and it was tough enough to get him to agree to it, but he did only because I am leaving for a year to study painting in Colorado while he's staying in Kentucky for college.

Tomorrow is our last day here and if he was going to ask, I bet that would be the day. He's been talking all week about doing something special on our last night, sparing no expense, and has told me to save my special dress for that night. He's talked about dinner, about dancing, about a long walk on the beach under the stars.

Last summer, when Noah and I went on a road trip to Colorado together, he did this a few times. Treated me to a special night out, so I didn't question it when he brought it up, but now I can hear the audible click as the pieces fall into place.

Noah must have told everyone he was proposing early in the trip, but he must have decided to wait.

Lila draws her ponytail over her shoulder. "You wouldn't turn him down if he didn't have a ring, would you?"

"No." Never. But it'd kill Noah to ask me without one. He struggles with the idea of being broke and is constantly telling me that someday he'll be able to take care of me like I deserve. Noah doesn't understand I'm not searching for him to take care of me as much as I want a partner. I mean, he does get it, but he doesn't. The important part is that I love him and he loves me and someday we will officially be forever.

"I didn't mean to spill." Lila glances down. "I'm sorry. I assumed he had asked already and that you were keeping it from me so you guys could announce it to everyone at once."

"I'm glad you told me. This is something I need to know. Noah's on his way, so I'll call you back when I get home, okay?"

"Okay. Love you." She blows me a kiss.

I tell her I love her back and end the chat. Truth is, Noah's on his way but not. He walks out of the convenience store and heads in my direction to pump the gas. It's the agreement we made—he'd let me cover the trip if he bought the gas and half the meals. I agreed because I wanted this time alone with him before I left.

Noah flashes me his wicked and dangerous grin as he walks past, and those mutant pterodactyls in my stomach that exist only because of him stretch their wings.

He's breathtakingly gorgeous. His shaggy brown hair is lighter due to our summer in the sun and his skin is deliciously tanned. While there's still a part of Noah, especially when he smiles at me, who is the cocky kid who made fun of my name in the counselor's office back in high school, he's definitely no longer a teen.

Any slight baby softness he had when we first met is gone. His features are a bit fuller in his face, he's grown another inch and he's gained weight in pure muscle. He was already ripped, but this past year he's become magnificent. Biceps chiseled, strong broad shoulders and his abdomen a flat hard plane. Noah is no longer a boy, but a man.

Not just physically, but emotionally, as well. Gone are the days of him working full-time as a manager at the Malt and Burger. He still works as a manager, but as part-time as he can get, just picking up extra shifts when his other job and school allow. This past spring he was offered a paid internship at an architecture firm.

He goes to class in the mornings, and in the afternoons he

works in the office with a white button-down shirt and tie. He even traded in his combat boots for a pair of black dress shoes.

My bad boy, though, is still bad. He has two more tattoos than he did in high school, one on his chest and the other on his back. One is for his brothers. The other for me. I won't lie—that tattoo is my favorite.

Noah's nonwork and nonschool hours belong to the man I originally fell for. The guy who wears jeans that slightly sag, a black T-shirt and his combat boots once again on his feet. Noah still listens to heavy metal music a little too loud, still curses sometimes a little too much and when he's hanging with his best friends on a Friday or Saturday night, still enjoys a good beer buzz.

He's still bad, but he's also good, and when it comes to me, he's very bad in all the right ways.

The car door opens, Noah drops into the driver's seat and he immediately turns on the car. The air conditioner blasts from the vents and a lock of my red curly hair blows in front of my face. Noah reaches over and with the most exquisite and soul-hugging care, he hooks the rebellious lock around his finger, gives it a slight tug, then tucks it behind my ear.

I suck in a breath as his touch creates a burning path along my cheek and I lick my lips as he tips my chin. Kissing Noah Hutchins is the closest I have been to heaven. With a simple brush of his lips to mine, he transports me to another time, another world, another place, where only the two of us belong.

He leans in; his breath is warm, and his mouth on mine causes me to melt. It's a soft press of his lips followed by a gentle and teasing nip. Every individual cell in my body begins to vibrate and Noah cups my face with one hand while his other hand tunnels into my hair. I love the sensation of his strong fingers against my face. It makes me feel small, fragile, yet loved and in control. The exchange is too short, too sweet, too enticing for this to be it.

Noah pulls away and his dark brown eyes bore into mine. "Back to the hotel?"

"I thought you wanted to go swimming," I say with a tease.

"Still the plan." The way he's currently undressing me with his eyes says he honestly has different ideas for future events.

"Are you sure about that?"

Noah straightens, puts on his seat belt and places the car into Drive. "The way I see it, if we're swimming, we're going to have to change."

"Is that so?"

"That's so. And if we're going to have to change, I'm just saying we don't have to rush. In case you forgot, there is a bed in our room."

Noah Hutchins is and will forever be so much trouble. "Wow, I guess I did forget."

"It'd be a damn shame to waste it," he says. "Damn shame."

I giggle at the implied memory of how he said those same words to me in a hospital room long ago to help me relax. "You're relentless."

"Yes, I am." Noah rests his hand on my thigh and squeezes. "But being so landed me you."

Can't argue with that.

CHAPTER 2

NOAH

Wind rushes in through the open sliding glass door of the balcony overlooking the ocean, and the breeze brings in the scent of salt and sand. The white curtain billows out and the sound of seagulls fills the hotel room. Don't want to know how much this hotel room costs. Kills my pride to let Echo pay for it. When she told me about this trip and how it was a gift for my birthday, I nearly declined.

But then, like only Echo can do, she flashed me that siren smile, brushed her fingernails along my back as she tucked herself tight to me and I belonged to her. Agreeing to whatever words she sang in that soft Southern drawl.

"I sold a painting," she whispered in my ear. Then she kissed my neck and I didn't hear words. I only heard my pulse whooshing in my temples and felt the heat seeping into my blood. "I have enough to cover the room. Let me do this. For you. For me. For us."

Somewhere between my shirt on my body, then off, I agreed.

Echo Emerson owns me. I should go ahead and have

those exact words tattooed across my chest. Hell, they're already branded on my soul.

I lean my shoulder against the wall near the bathroom and watch Echo. This is one of my favorite simple, silent moments, besides when she's painting: when Echo's getting ready and is lost in her own head.

After moving out of the apartment I shared with Isaiah to save money, I drew the lucky straw and ended up in a single-person dorm room. Echo has spent plenty of nights there; I've spent nights with her in her room, which means we've spent plenty of mornings together, too.

After my parents died when I was fourteen, I spent too many years living in a constant state of noise and chaos, but then she entered my life and she smoothed out all my rough edges.

I love her.

More than I love my own life.

Echo runs her fingers through her thick curls multiple times. Flipping them to the right, then the left and as always settling them to the same side as before. She fights with the renegade curl that constantly falls over her right eye.

She then turns to check out her outfit and brushes her fingers along the scars of her left arm, then her right. As if confirming they're still there. As if maybe one day she'll slide her fingers along her skin and the scars will be gone and maybe the worst night of her life didn't happen and was just a bad dream.

Last summer, she used to frown when she touched them, but now she doesn't react. Touching her scars has turned into subconscious movement, something she did for years and that's become muscle memory even though Echo has found a way to accept her past and her scars.

Echo straightens the top of her bikini and my gaze lingers on her curves. It's tough not to drop to my knees in worship over that bathing suit. It's royal blue, my favorite color on her, makes her fire-red hair stand out and her brilliant green eyes pop. And I have to admit, I'm a fan of Echo's body and a bigger fan of her wearing anything that shows it off.

The second she steps out of this room, every guy within a twenty-foot radius is going to be thinking of ways to hit on her, but they don't stand a chance. Echo pivots again and catches me staring. She offers a smile, the one she reserves just for me, the siren one, the one that shoots straight through my chest and awakens parts south of my belt.

Echo ties a wrap around her hips, then pins me with her gaze. "Enjoying yourself?"

Immensely. Watching her is one of my favorite hobbies. "Not my fault it takes you forever to get ready."

Not her fault all I have to do is slip into swimming trunks, and then I keep distracting her with kisses. With a roll of her eyes, she straightens the covers we tangled up.

"Housekeeping has already been through." I help with the comforter from the other side of the bed.

Echo's cheeks turn a seductive shade of crimson. "Sometimes they come back, and we wouldn't want them to think we didn't appreciate their work."

"It's a hotel. They're aware people do things in bed."

The blush spreads down her neck and onto her chest and it makes her look too damn hot. Hot enough we may mess up this bed again.

"But they don't have to know that *we* do things in the bed."

I scratch my chin to hide the smile, but with the death glare she sends me, she caught it.

"How about this, Noah Hutchins? We don't do anything for the rest of the trip and then I don't have to make the bed."

Use of my full name. I hold my hands in the air as an act

of submission. "Baby, I'll make the bed by myself every time. Army corners and you could bounce a fucking coin on it."

She tries not to, but Echo grins as she shoulders the beach bag and I grab the cooler. We've been here six days and we've settled into a routine I could live with for the rest of my life. Bed, breakfast, walk along the town, bed, lunch, bed, beach, bed, dinner, more walking and then more time in bed. We've made this bed so many times I could do it with my eyes closed.

Hate that tomorrow is our last day, hate that we're on the countdown until she'll be over a thousand miles away from me, hate that I want to propose marriage and I don't have a decent engagement ring.

But a friend of mine was in need and hurting and it was more important to give her the money. Echo will understand, she'd approve, but it still makes me feel like shit that I can't provide for her yet the way I want.

We're on the eighth floor, so it's a long ride down the elevator, especially when we stop at every floor. On the sixth we're joined by a family of five. A mom holding a chubby baby with a head full of black curls, a dad, a toddler who is ready-to-punch-someone pissed because he's being forced to carry a sand bucket, so he keeps dropping it on my foot, and another little girl, who is the oldest of the bunch, maybe eight, with the same black curls but she's wearing a pink robe.

Echo frowns and I have to admit I'm with her. This kid stares at the ground, eyes filled with tears, and her lower lip trembles. The mom and the dad both watch their oldest with a worry that causes a pain in my chest. A combination of missing having parents who would worry over me that way and my own worry over my younger brothers, who are now being taken care of by their adoptive family.

Echo takes my hand, and when I glance over at her, she flickers her eyes from me to the child.

I tilt my head to let her know I see that the kid's upset, but then Echo subtly shakes her head. She moves her arm, then inclines her head to the girl. My eyebrows draw together as I look at Echo's arm, then to the kid, and then it hits me so fast I have to quit breathing so I don't suck in air with the blow.

Everyone in that elevator would hear that intake and would know what I had seen. Being around Echo for as long as I have, I get that such a reaction is understandable but can bring pain, and that's the last thing I want to do.

The girl's leg is scarred and I'm betting a beach vacation is the last thing this kid is looking forward to.

A ding, the elevator doors open, and Echo and I let the family pile out first. They head in the direction of the pool, and Echo hesitates outside the elevator doors and watches them.

She glances up at me. "I know we were planning to go to the beach and that we're running out of time together, but do you mind if—"

"Let's go to the pool." I cut her off, and Echo falls into me for a hug. I put down the cooler so I can hold her tight and kiss the top of her head.

Echo has the biggest heart of anyone I know. She loves me, loves my friends, loves my brothers and loves strangers. Screw my pride. I don't have the ring she deserves, but regardless, I'm going to ask her to marry me. I need her to know before she drives halfway across the country that it's her I want to spend forever with.

CHAPTER 3

ECHO

Dog bite. The girl's name is Jane and she was bitten by a stray dog when she was playing in the front yard of her home. It happened a month and a half ago, the vacation was already planned and her parents had been hoping that coming to a place their daughter had loved so much in the past would help her break out of the shell she's lived in since the attack, but so far, their daughter had only seemed to further withdraw.

Little Jane sits at the edge of the pool, her legs in the water, her arms wrapped tight around her body. The pink terrycloth robe still on. The poor thing is sweating to death in the unforgiving hot August sun.

Noah and I sit on a beach chair side by side listening to Jane's mother explain the events and how they unfolded. I walked up to this woman, politely asked what happened to her daughter, and before she could tell me to go to hell for asking, she saw my arms and sank to the chair. She's been explaining things since.

In the pool, her husband plays with the toddler who was throwing a fit earlier and the two laugh and laugh often. Her husband often tries to entice Jane to play, but Jane ignores him and I understand why. Being in a shell is hard to break out of, even if you want to. Noah Hutchins helped me break out of mine. I have only a few minutes to spare, but I'd like to be a stepping-stone to help Jane break out of hers.

The woman places the chubby baby on a cushion of blanket on the ground and then hands the sitting baby some sort of biscuit. A squeal of delight and the baby begins to gnaw away. I glance over at Noah helplessly. I wouldn't have a freaking clue how to take care of one of those things on my own. The ends of Noah's mouth edge up as if he's reading my mind. He, of course, due to his younger brothers, has changed hundreds of diapers and probably knows what that hunk of cracker thing is called.

"Can you throw me the float?" her husband shouts.

Noah goes to stand. "I'll do it."

"No, let me," she says, reaching behind her to the blown-up piece of plastic and taking the few steps to the pool. Her husband talks to her in a low voice and her answers are equally quiet, but they are so close we can still hear.

He wants to know who we are, she's explaining and his expression softens when she tells him the story I told her—there was an accident and I fell through broken glass a few years ago. No one else needs to know about my mother's involvement. No one else needs to know anything at all. My therapist helped me realize that these scars belong to me. It's my decision what I want the world to know and the world can know the truth—it was a terrible, terrible tragic accident that no one could have ever predicted.

The baby drops the biscuit onto the blanket and crawls. Her big brown eyes are glued on me and her devious smile indicates I'm her destination. I fight the urge to scoot away and brace myself for when the little ball of black curls pats the top of my flip-flopped foot with her even chubbier fist.

"You've found a friend," says Noah.

"I wouldn't know what to do with one of these." My baby brother, Alexander, has been my only trip into the realm of things that cry and have no teeth, and it irritates me that Noah is better with my brother than me. Alexander laughs with Noah, blows cute baby bubbles for Noah, and Alexander spits up and poops on me.

Noah's grin is so fast and so glorious that my heart skips a beat. "Babies aren't as complicated as you think."

A phsh sound leaves my mouth. "They're plenty complicated."

"They are. Alexander is tough—babies are tough—but I'm saying when the time comes, you'll be a great mom."

A thrill runs along my veins and it's such a strong tickling sensation that I avert my gaze back to the baby. Me a mom and Noah a dad and someday we will be a real family. "I'm going to bake cookies. Chocolate chip. I want to be the mom who makes cookies with her kids."

To be the mom who makes her children a priority. I'm going to be better than my parents and I can be and I will be.

"I can live with that," Noah replies.

"Sorry." The woman returns and scoops her baby into her arms and her mini-me giggles. Maybe babies aren't so bad. That is, when Noah and I have them years and years and years from now. "My husband was curious about who you were."

"I'd be the same way," Noah admits.

He would be, and if his best friend Isaiah was around, he'd be curious, too. Thank God both of them are maturing and are finding more subtle ways of protecting the people they love, like asking for a float so they can politely ask what's going on instead of throwing people into walls for answers.

"Do you mind if I talk to Jane?" I ask. "Show her my scars?

I'm not at all suggesting that it's going to solve her problems, but maybe it will help if she knows of someone who is also scarred. Maybe it'll help that I'm not hiding them and maybe one day she'll find the strength to live her life full throttle."

Jane's mom offers me a sad smile with eyes full of moisture. "I'd like that."

I stand, Noah stands with me, and when we return to where we left our stuff, I take off the wrap around my hips and step out of my flip-flops. "Do you mind if I talk to her alone?"

"Not at all."

A rush of guilt and I bite on my lower lip. My time with Noah is dwindling so fast that it scares me, but I can't live with myself if I don't try with Jane.

"Hey," Noah says, and I look up at him.

He places a hand on my hip and gently brushes his thumb along my skin. "We've got all night tonight and all day tomorrow. You want to talk to Jane, and I want you to do this."

Relief washes through me, and I extend up on my toes and give him a fast kiss. Before he can tempt me with kissing him any more, I press off his chest with both hands and head for Jane.

CHAPTER 4

NOAH

Echo has been sitting next to Jane for twenty minutes and I had no idea, except for my younger brother, a nine-year-old could look so intense during a conversation. Echo talks, Jane talks, and they both have their feet in the pool. Echo offers Jane her arm and my heart stops as Echo nods her head in encouragement for Jane to touch.

Jane's hesitant as she reaches for Echo's skin, but she does touch and Echo smiles as if that moment wasn't huge for either of them. When I first met Echo, she wouldn't let anyone see her scars, much less touch them. Pride swells within me and I can't wait to spend the rest of my life with this woman.

The cell in my hands vibrates, and a text message pops along the top. Isaiah: *You've got problems.*

The muscles in my neck tense because the last fucking thing I need is problems. I'm done with problems, and any time Isaiah is the messenger, it means my world is about to go to hell. *What?*

Three dots as Isaiah types and the wait kills me. If something was wrong with my brothers, Carrie and Joe, their adoptive parents, would contact me, so this is an internal family problem.

Isaiah and I created a tight family of friends and my mind is racing with the possibilities of who could be in trouble and why. Did something happen to Abby, Isaiah's girl, Rachel, or West's girlfriend, Haley? West had a fight this week—did it go bad? The son of a bitch has been on a winning streak and he has a mean right hook that scares even me, but it doesn't mean he couldn't take a bad hit in the ring.

Logan's had it tough lately and we just learned about his health problems. Wouldn't shock me if it's him. He's looked like a damn zombie the past two times I've seen him, and until Abby is back home, he'll probably continue to look like a living dead man. Beth and Ryan were supposed to go to Tennessee with her uncle and aunt on a fast trip before college began. Did something happen to them?

Isaiah: *Lila contacted Rachel. Lila messed up and told Echo she thought you were going to propose on the trip. Lila thought you were doing the original plan of asking her at the beginning of the week and was fishing for Echo to tell her she was engaged. The fishing backfired. Echo now knows.*

Damn. And I bet Echo's now expecting a diamond ring. It was going to be bad enough to propose to Echo without a diamond, but at least I had the element of surprise. Bet she has guessed how the night is supposed to go—Echo in her favorite dress, me in a white shirt and tie, dinner by the ocean, dancing at the restaurant under the stars, a walk on the pier, and me down on one knee asking her to spend the rest of her life with me.

Only in her head, I'd be offering what the entire world expects. I reach into my drawstring pack in the beach bag and at the very bottom is a small black velvet box. With the box still in the beach bag, I open it.

The claddagh ring is sterling silver, and the stone in the

center is emerald colored. My father's mother had Irish roots and because of that, my father gave my mother a claddagh ring for Christmas once. At the time, they had been married for years.

When Dad got down on one knee, he gave Mom a diamond engagement ring, but I'm doing the best I can. Two months–plus of my salary isn't worth shit to begin with and what I had saved for Echo's ring is now paying for the medical care of Abby's grandmother. I don't regret it, but it still doesn't help me feel worthy of proposing to Echo.

But then I saw this ring. Dad told me people sometimes used claddagh rings as engagement rings. There are plenty of expensive claddagh rings out there with real stones instead of colored ones like the one in my hand, with real gold instead of sterling silver and that cost more than a hundred dollars, but this is what I could barely afford.

Echo says it's the thought that counts and I'm banking on that. Banking she'll listen to my story and will permit me to place this ring on her left hand with the heart toward her fingertips as a show that she's promised to spend the rest of her life with me.

A buzz from my cell. Isaiah: *You still there?*

Me: *Yeah.*

Isaiah: *You okay?*

He knows how asking Echo to marry me without a diamond ring is tearing me up. Me: *I'm going to switch it up and ask her tonight. I'll try to come up with something romantic.*

I close the ring box, shove it back into my drawstring bag, then arrange my bag so that it's at the bottom of our beach bag.

A buzz: *Rachel's with me and we want to help. And suck it up, man. We're helping, so deal. Rachel said one of Echo's favorite memories was when you put roses on a hotel room bed. Rachel's looking up a florist in town and will have roses delivered to your hotel room. Find a way to keep Echo out of the room and I'll text you when the roses are there.*

Emotions shift inside me. Isaiah isn't just my best friend; he's my brother. He and I, we don't share how we feel. We flip each other off, tell each other to go to hell and occasionally tell each other to fuck off with a well-meaning grin. But this… How do I let him know how much this means to me? *Thank you.*

Wish he understood I mean so much more than that.

Isaiah: *Anytime. Now go win over the girl.*

The sound of splashing, and I look up to see Echo and Jane kicking their legs in the water. They are still sitting on the edge and Jane is still in her pink robe, but at least the kid is smiling. Echo glances up at me, and the pure happiness radiating from her face takes my breath away.

She's the most beautiful and amazing creature on the earth, and one day, she's going to walk down the aisle and pledge forever to me.

CHAPTER 5

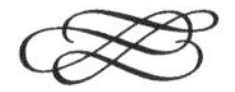

ECHO

In the surf, Noah chases me and I laugh as he tries to catch me. Waves roll in and they roll out, making the game we're playing fun and complicated. My right foot sinks in the sand, I falter and Noah is able to slip an arm around my stomach. I squeal as he lifts me in the air.

A wave crashes into us, and we fall. Water fills my ears and my body floats in the current. Noah's arm around me tightens and then we break to the surface. I gasp for air and I start laughing again. Noah spins me so we're chest to chest. One of his arms pins me to him as if I'd want to escape this embrace, and with his other hand, Noah peels my wet hair off my face.

"I gotcha," he says, and I weave both of my arms around his neck. Yes, he definitely did.

When my face is hair-free, Noah leans in and kisses me. He tastes of sea water and sand and his skin is warm from being in the sun.

Our bodies are slick and any slight movement amplifies the already-heavy edge of need that's built between us throughout the late afternoon. Throughout the day we've kissed, lips lingering and nipping. Quick brushes of hands along backs, legs and thighs. Long hugs, waking naps in his arms on the beach, his nose nuzzling my hair and a tickling blowing of breath behind my ear—this constant and delicious buildup of what's to come the moment we have four walls between us and the rest of the world.

Noah's hands wander down; he lifts me by the hips and walks us deeper into the water. I wrap my legs around him and grow lost in his kisses, in his touches, in this beautiful rhythm the two of us share.

Right when things start to become too heated, too passionate, and I'm too close to giving in and doing things that should be done only in private, I push away and smile at Noah. The game begins again.

The sky in the west blends into reds and pinks. We spent much of the afternoon playing in the pool with Jane and her family. Jane first got into the pool with her robe on when Noah and I asked her to play Marco Polo. Eventually, her parents were able to coax the robe off.

When Jane was in her bathing suit alone, her father held her. Arms wrapped around him as if he could shield her from the world, and he held her like he could be the warrior she needed. He told her he loved her, that she was okay, and eventually, she played. She played like a nine-year-old should. She played with smiles and laughter. She played as if she was loved unconditionally. She played with complete abandon and trust.

She played.

Just like Noah and I are playing now. Splashing in the water, running in the surf, laughing as if we're free and flying. Everyone in the world, regardless of age, should be able to play like this.

The wind blows, and I shiver. The gulf water is warm, the breeze cool, and goose bumps form along my arms. I slow,

Noah catches me and he immediately rubs his hands up and down my arms. The beach is deserted now except for a few lone couples walking along the sand.

Hotel rooms along the strip are lit up and the sound of music from the local bars drifts into the evening. My teeth chatter, and in a swift motion, Noah bends, swings me up in his arms and carries me to our blanket on the beach.

He wraps a towel around me before running one through his hair, then over the beads of water dripping down his chest. God, I love his chest. Like looking at it, like touching it, love kissing it. I just love him.

Noah reaches into the bag, pulls out his cell, and it lights up his face as he checks the time. His eyes dart as if he's reading. Then he drops the cell back into the bag and flashes me his wicked grin. "You ready to head to the room?"

I pull the towel around me. Am I ready for a warm shower and a night with Noah in bed? Definitely, but there's something I need to do and my foot begins to rock as anxiety tiptoes through my bloodstream. "I need to draw a picture first."

His eyebrows furrow as he scans the horizon. "It's getting dark fast. Do you want me to get the camping lantern? It's in the trunk of your car."

There's a sketch pad and pencils in the bag and he thinks that's what my canvas will be, but he's wrong. A few seconds alone, though, would be appreciated. Our car is at the front of the hotel—won't take Noah but five minutes to get there and back and that's all I need. "Do you mind?"

"I'll be right back." A swift kiss to my lips, a rummage through our bag for the keys and a T-shirt, shoes on his feet, then he's off for the lantern.

The moment he's far enough away, I pull a T-shirt over my head, yank on a pair of shorts and then begin the task of drawing a picture just for Noah in the sand.

CHAPTER 6

NOAH

A stray seagull squawks overhead as I return with the lantern in hand. The waves continuously crash against the beach and occasionally someone's laughter from the balconies drifts down. In a T-shirt and shorts, Echo's on her hands and knees in the sand next to our blanket.

She's pulled her hair into a sloppy ponytail and unruly curls have fallen away. Echo's intent on whatever she's drawing in the sand, and before I reach her, she stands, clapping her hands together to rid her fingers of the dirt. There's a soft smile on her face and it's the type that, when sent in my direction, promises very good things.

"Hey," I call out, and Echo turns her head. Her grin grows wider and she walks toward me.

"I drew you something," she says in a rush, and when I continue to try to walk past her to see what it is, she places a hand on my chest. "I drew you something."

I stop at the brush of her finger and her repeat of words. "What?"

Echo shifts her weight from one leg to another and her bare foot begins to tap against the sand. I glance around the beach, searching for what could be making her nervous. Echo rests her hand on my cheek and returns my gaze to her.

I love those green eyes. They're the reason I chose an emerald-colored stone for the ring. There's a patch of sand on her forehead, and knowing Echo, it's from when she was deep in thought about whatever she was drawing. She must have wiped at the stray curls on her forehead to brush them away, not realizing she was marking herself with sand.

Echo swipes her thumb against the evening stubble forming on my jaw, then drops her hand to take my fingers in hers. "I love you."

Before I have a chance to open my mouth and say anything back, she continues, the words stumbling out of her mouth. "The good times with you are so incredibly good and the rough times... We have faced extremely rough times and I've survived them with you right by my side. I've realized that this is life—happy times, sad times, mad and confusing times. It's up and it's down and there is no one I want with me during all of that other than you."

Echo takes the lantern from me, pulls on my hand and walks backward toward her sand drawing. "I love you, and you once asked me to marry you and I said no. I was right to say no, you were right to take the question back, but I've had that moment tucked close to my heart, thinking about the day you might ask me again. Then I realized, I don't have to wait. I realized that rules and social norms or anything normal have never and will never apply to us."

With a click, Echo turns on the light, holds it up, and in the sand is a heart. Within the heart is the question I planned on asking her.

Noah, Will you marry me? I love you, Echo

CHAPTER 7

ECHO

Noah's dragging me. My hand in his, our beach bag on his shoulder, and he left our empty cooler and blanket behind. He didn't even wait for the elevator, and I'm out of breath after practically running up eight flights of stairs. Noah is a bull, won't answer my questions, won't say a word. Just took one look at my drawing in the sand, grabbed my hand and we were gone.

We reach our room, and he releases me long enough to find the key. I suck in a breath to ask him if he's at least okay, because I'm starting to wonder if I made a terrible mistake.

Maybe Noah wasn't going to ask me to marry him. Maybe he changed his mind. Maybe he thought about how we have time left before we graduate from college. Maybe he thought about how there are so many people who don't believe that anyone under the age of thirty has a clue about what they're doing and that getting married before thirty-one is for fools.

My stomach sinks as Noah opens the door and for the first time I realize how desperate and scared he must have felt after I said no to him. He snatches my hand and we're in the room.

The door behind me shuts, Noah flicks on the light and I can't breathe. The entire room is filled with roses. Red roses, white roses, pink roses, yellow roses, orange roses, multicolored roses.

Roses.

Roses on the dresser, roses on the bedside tables, roses in vases on the floor, roses on the desk, single-stem roses on the pillows and rose petals on the made bed.

Roses.

Noah wasn't going to ask me to marry him tomorrow night. He was going to ask me to marry him tonight.

"How in the world did you do this?" I whisper.

Noah drops the beach bag, yanks out his drawstring bag and withdraws a black velvet box.

Panic floods my veins. He bought a ring. Noah bought a ring. He doesn't have money for a ring. I knot my fingers into my hair and pull until it hurts. I am not worth a loan and interest. Noah has so many other things he needs to focus on and a ring for me is insane.

I rush forward and place my hand over his. He can't give me this ring. He has to say yes to my proposal so he doesn't give me a ring he can't afford. That's why I asked him tonight —so he couldn't ask me tomorrow.

"I asked you to marry me. I want to spend the rest of my life with you and you have to answer me. You have to tell me if you want to spend the rest of your life with me and then we're engaged. Sorry about your luck, but that's how it is."

A muscle in Noah's jaw tics and I continue, "You have seen me through some of the worst moments of my life. Remembering what happened to me, the scars on my arms, my parents' involvement, working through my grief over Aries, learning how to be a big sister, and you've been there through so many highs. Selling my paintings, figuring out who I am, leaving the insecure girl behind, and becoming the woman who is strong enough to stand in front of you and ask you to spend the rest of your life with me.

"I love you, I have loved you since we sat in the hallway at Eastwick and studied math, and I will love you for the rest of my life. The question on the table is, do you love me enough to spend forever with me?"

Noah briefly closes his eyes in defeat and takes both of my hands. The small box half in my palm, half in his. "Yes."

Happiness. The fluttering in my stomach is happiness.

"Is it my turn to talk?" he asks, but even I know that really wasn't a question as much as him explaining he's going to say what he needs to say regardless.

I nod, and Noah steps closer to me. "My entire life changed the day you dropped into that chair beside me in the guidance counselor's office. You were the hot girl who I thought had it all. Two seconds with me and you were handing me shit."

"You made fun of my name," I remind him.

Noah chuckles. "If I remember correctly, you called me a stoner."

"You were a stoner."

His wicked grin is just as seductive and dangerous as the night he backed me up against the wall outside a party and came close to kissing me for the first time. And just like the night of the school Valentine's Day dance, he walks me backward into the wall. My back hits, his body presses to mine and all I can think about is kissing him.

"You challenge me, Echo," he continues. "You pushed me to use my brain, to believe I could have a future again. You taught me to trust again and you taught me it was okay to love. Since you entered my life, I have thought about you day and night. The way you smile, the way your body feels against mine and the way I feel empty whenever you aren't near.

"The next year without you is going to be hell, but we're going to make it. You and I, we're stronger than distance. We're strong enough to make this work. You want to spend forever with me, Echo, and I want to spend forever with you. You asked me to marry you and the answer is yes, but I have a question for you."

My heart beats faster when Noah drops down to one knee and opens up the small box in his hand. "Someday I'm going to be able to offer you a diamond ring, but until then, will you grant me the honor of wearing this ring? Someday, after we graduate, will you walk down the aisle and promise in front of our family and friends to be with me for the rest of our lives?"

It's the most beautiful ring I've ever seen. Tears burn my eyes and my hands tremble. My knees give, and I lower myself down to the floor along with Noah. "I don't want a diamond ring. I want this ring and this ring alone. I love it."

"It's engraved," he says and holds it so I can see the words. *I love you ~ Noah.* "Will you wear it?"

"Yes."

Noah eases the ring onto my finger, the heart toward my fingertips. He then presses his lips to the ring. "I love you, Echo Emerson. Every day for the rest of my life."

He raises his head and his dark eyes are so full of love that a tear escapes from my eye.

"You better kiss me, Noah Hutchins." Before I crawl into him and start to sob.

"I'm all about kissing you."

And I'm all about kissing him.

Noah cups my face with his hand, leans in and kisses me for the first time as my fiancé.

THE FIRST LOVES COLLECTION:

THE FIRST DAY OF SCHOOL

In *Crash into You*, Isaiah Walker, a foster kid and drag racer, meets and falls in love with Rachel Young, the youngest daughter of the wealthiest man in the state. Their love story captured the hearts of many, and I'll admit they are a favorite couple of mine. Isaiah had a rough childhood, but he found love and acceptance in Rachel. "The First Day of School" shows a glimpse of the future life Rachel and Isaiah found with each other.

CHAPTER 8

ISAIAH

The smoke alarm goes off, and I curse under my breath. I turn away from the pancakes cooking on the electric griddle on the island, and my eyes burn from the smoke rising from the beginning grease fire. I snatch the handle of the pan, and another curse word Rachel has begged me not to say in the house falls from my mouth as I burn the hell out of my hand. I drop the pan, grab a towel, and push the same pan full of bacon off the burner. A few slaps of the towel on the stove top and the fire is extinguished.

A squeal from upstairs causes me to lower my head. Rachel is going to kill me.

"Fire!" my five-year-old daughter yells. "We have to run! Stop! Drop! And Roll!"

Getting Ariel to stay still long enough to get her hair brushed on a normal day is like herding stray cats who have rabies. The fire alarm going off is only going to make life for my beautiful wife more complicated.

I head over to the fire alarm, reach up and push the button. The ear-piercing beeping ends and in its place are Ariel's complaints that having her hair brushed is killing her.

No kidding here—she makes moaning noises and declares she's about to die. The edges of my mouth tilt up as Rachel says, "You'll live."

Patient. Rachel is always patient. Not a day goes by I don't count my blessings that she and Ariel are in my life. Before the pancakes can burn, I race back over, use the spatula to slip them onto a plate and then set the plate on the kitchen table.

Footsteps echo along the hallway that leads to the front of the house, and I look up in time to see Rachel turn the corner. When I first met Rachel fourteen years ago, I thought I would never see anything as beautiful. I was wrong. Yes, Rachel was a dream at seventeen, but she's redefined beauty in her thirties.

Her blond hair is thicker, more golden, and she's filled out. Since Ariel's birth, there are more curves to her body, and I worship each and every one. She's in her work clothes of jeans and a nice button-down shirt. Her hair is pulled up into a ponytail and the ends are curled.

Rachel manages the business side of our automotive shop and occasionally still works on cars. I'm in charge of the shop, making the schedule, handling the customers and managing our employees. One of my favorite parts of the day is when she leaves her desk, shares a sandwich with me for lunch and then helps me out with a car. Rachel has always been and remains magic.

My angel pauses at the table and takes in the sight. I've made pancakes, sausage, bacon, toast, cut-up watermelon and two types of juice. Her eyebrows disappear beyond her bangs. "You remember Ariel's five, and that lately her favorite food is air?"

"It's her first day of school." Of Kindergarten. "I want her to have a good start."

Rachel eyes me warily. "At the end of the day, they give

her back. We're not sending her off for the year. It's a lot like preschool, but she goes all day instead of half-day? And they'll give her a lunch break. The state's pretty adamant about the whole five-year-olds eating thing."

"She's my baby."

"She's a big girl at five and is going to be fine."

A wave of uneasiness floods my system. Memories of my own school days haunt me. The boy who never had clean clothes. The boy who never had a stable home. The boy who didn't have many friends.

As if sensing my unease, Rachel crosses the kitchen and places her hand over my heart, where two of the many tattoos on my body that represent my wife and daughter are inked. The tattoos she's currently touching are of two sets of wings for my two angels—Rachel and Ariel.

I set my hand over hers, and her gorgeous blue eyes bore into mine. "She's loved, Isaiah. Ariel's going to be okay. She's going to have good days and she's going to have bad days, and whichever one she has today, she's going to come back to this house and be loved."

So far, Ariel's life hasn't been anything like mine. She has two doting parents, a home, and she *is* loved. Loved not only by me, but by Rachel's brothers, Rachel's parents, my family I hadn't found until after I graduated from high school, and the expanded set of nonblood uncles and aunts Rachel and I have become friends with along the way.

Rachel reaches up and kisses my lips, and what I know was meant to be a swift embrace to calm my demons turns into something more as I weave my arms around her. One hand skims along her back, the other cups her face, and I tilt her head and deepen the kiss. Doesn't take long for my blood to run warm. Doesn't take much for me to get lost in my bride.

My body shifts to the side as something solid hits my leg,

and when I look down, I'm met by gray eyes identical to my own and a head full of blond curls. I smile, because she's dressed herself. Purple shirt with a glittery black cat on it, black leggings, a pink tutu and cowboy boots. She's a ball of fire and a combination of everything good about me and Rachel.

She grins up at me, proud of her fashion choices, proud we let her dress herself, proud I'm her father—as if I'm the man who pulls the sun up in the morning and hangs the moon at night. "Hi, Daddy."

Daddy. The title hits me each and every time straight in the heart—in a good way. In the best way. Rachel kisses my cheek before walking away. In less than a heartbeat, I scoop up my daughter and a peace descends upon me when her arms wrap around my neck.

I start for the table and just as I lean down to put her in her chair, I tickle her side and she breaks out into giggles. Ariel spots the pancakes and hops onto her knees so she can reach over for more than she'll eat.

Rachel takes her seat at our small round breakfast table, and I take mine. We smile at each other then at our daughter, who pours too much syrup on her overly large stack of pancakes, and we listen to her chatter about first days, tying her own shoes and how she wants a puppy.

Rachel and I aren't the only parents parking their cars to walk their children into school. Cars of all makes and models fill the lot, and I choose a spot in the back. First day of school is driving me slowly insane—and I survived foster care. If I'm feeling this way, then so are the other parents and I won't have their nerves wrecking my car.

Owning a car shop that not only repairs cars but

remodels and restores them, Rachel and I have several cars, most of which we fixed up together. This car is Ariel's favorite—a 2004 Mustang SVT Cobra Supercharger. As we pull up, the engine growls because it's technically not street legal with the cutouts Rachel and I installed, but it did fine for the five miles of my smallest angel's first ride to school.

I turn off the car, slide out and grab Ariel's race car backpack, which has pink ribbons tied to the handle. Rachel unhooks Ariel from her car seat in the back and she springs out of the car, bright eyed and full of energy for the day. Maybe the extra syrup wasn't a good idea.

She holds Rachel's hand, and I don't believe Ariel takes a breath as she talks about who she hopes will be in her class, how she hopes she gets to take the class guinea pig she learned about at orientation home first and that maybe she should have worn her tap shoes.

Rachel laughs at the last part, and I crack a grin. Tap shoes in school. Rachel and I would have been called into the principal's office on the first day. That probably would have been a record. But because my daughter is precocious, I do a quick check of her backpack to make sure she didn't drop in her tap shoes as a back-up pair for later.

I don't find them, but I do find the ballet slippers and I leave those in there. Don't see the harm in them, but then again, I'm probably not the best judge.

At the entrance, several school officials greet parents and students with big smiles. They're explaining how, for school security, this is as far as the parents can go. We heard about this at orientation, and we respect it, but there's a part of me that would feel better if I could see my daughter in her seat instead of just setting her free into the building.

"Isaiah," Rachel says. "Watch Ariel while I pick up her transportation stickers."

They're stickers they'll put on Ariel's backpack and back,

along with a plastic bracelet they'll put around her wrist that informs anyone looking how she's heading home and who will be picking her up. Better believe I'll be out here waiting for my baby when the clock strikes three forty-five. I'll give the school a few minutes grace, but I better see that smile soon after the bell rings.

Ariel finds a friend from preschool and the two talk. Or if I'm being honest, Ariel talks and the other girl listens. My daughter could talk fleas off a dog, has never met a stranger, and I admire her love of life. God help anyone who ever tries to snuff that light out.

I glance around, and it's a familiar scene. Staring at me like I don't belong are a few parents in suits for their corporate work life or stay-at-home moms with a boxed in view of what a dad should be. Whispering to one another as they glare at me, because in their mind, talking about me in hushed tones is somehow polite. With sleeves of tattoos on both arms, earrings in my ears, a T-shirt, jeans and steel-toed boots for work, I'm not their definition of a parent.

I'm well-schooled on judgmental stares and gave up caring about anyone else's opinion of me years ago. What they don't know is that Rachel and I make more money than five of these well-off families combined. What they don't know, because we chose to remain anonymous, is that the new playground the school unveiled on orientation day was thanks to me, my wife and our friends, because our friends are doing just as well in their jobs as Rachel and I.

I don't care what the other parents think of me, but I do care how they treat my daughter. Because of that, I keep my mouth shut and focus only on Ariel.

Rachel returns, calls Ariel over, and Ariel is a constant jumping jack as Rachel places the stickers on her backpack and back and slides the bracelet on her wrist. My daughter's eyes are trained on the school and on her next new adventure.

"Okay," Rachel says and plants a fast kiss on her forehead. "You listen to your teacher, have a good day, and your daddy and I will be right here to take you home after school. We love you."

"Okay," Ariel replies, and she bolts for the front door.

"Ariel," I call out, and hold her backpack out to her. She blinks as she looks at me as if wondering why I said her name and then recognition dawns on her face.

She runs back at full throttle, and as I lower her pack so she can grab it, she runs right past it and into me. My heart stutters as I crouch and accept her hug.

"I love you, Daddy," she whispers in my ear, and then gives me a kiss on my cheek. She pulls back and all I see is that love. Yes, she's loved and I'm loved in return.

"You forgot your backpack," I say, and she smiles as she realizes that's why I called her back. "Have a good day, baby girl. I love you."

"You, too." And then she's gone, past the double doors, and after she greets her teacher on the other side, she turns back to wave at us.

I wave, Rachel waves and then I wrap my arm around my wife's shoulder. She leans into me, and I kiss her temple.

"We did something right in this world," Rachel says.

"Yeah," I answer. "We did."

THE FIRST LOVES COLLECTION:

THE FIRST MEETING

Nowhere but Here, the first book in the Thunder Road series, is the story of Emily, a girl who is forced to spend the summer with her biological father, the head of a motorcycle club, and Oz, a soon-to-be member of the club. When a rival club places Emily in danger, Oz is assigned to help protect her. They spend the summer getting to know each other, falling in love and figuring out the secrets of Emily's parents' past.

My original idea for the Thunder Road series involved Eli and Meg, Emily's biological parents. But once I played Eli and Meg's story out in my head, I realized that it would end in a sad place. Being a happily-ever-after type of girl, I decided to take a different look at Eli and Meg's story and tell it through the eyes of their daughter.

After reading *Nowhere but Here* many, many readers contacted me, asking for Eli's story. This may not be his full story, but I thought my readers would enjoy seeing how Eli and Meg met.

CHAPTER 9

ELI

Assholes. The world is filled with them, and unfortunately my hometown of Snowflake, Kentucky, has more than its share. Not fair when we're one of the least-populated counties in the state, but I guess even assholes need a capital. Of course, there are some girls who would throw me into that category, and I probably deserve the label.

But I'm not a grade-A asshole. I'm just the garden-variety type that rides a motorcycle, falls asleep in class, says too many curse words at the wrong time, and has a father who is the head of a motorcycle club.

What I do that other assholes in this town don't do? Treat girls with respect. If I ever talked badly to a girl, my mother would cut off my balls with a dull kitchen knife and that's not hyperbole. My mother is as badass as they come.

And if I ever touched a girl without permission? My father would end my life. Don't get me wrong, my parents love me, but they expect me to be a human being—to be a man. There are lines, and I'm expected to know them, see them and never cross.

The problem with all that tonight? I'm being me, and doing what I need to be doing, and the clean-cut looking asshole guys, the ones from the rich side of town whose daddies have too much money, are doing what they normally do with a girl who is new to town and isn't aware that these are the type of guys no one should be around.

It's Friday night, halfway through October, and we're in an abandoned field a few miles from town. There are two bonfires going at the party, and there's an unwritten rule about who hangs at which one. The bonfire my best friend started crackles, pops and warms my cold hands. The air temperature has dropped, and the ride over here on my motorcycle was a lot cooler than I thought it would be. I love riding my bike, love the wind in my face, but I should have worn gloves. Frozen hands suck.

The bonfire I'm near is for people associated with the Reign of Terror and for those who are tired of being ridiculed by anyone who thinks they own our school. The other bonfire is for the people doing the ridiculing.

"You okay?" My best friend's girlfriend, Rebecca, comes up beside me and sits on the tailgate of a friend's truck. "Charlie's been trying to get your attention."

I glance over to the right, and sure enough, Charlie is standing there with the other guys from school who don't automatically think anyone associated with the Terror are murderers. Charlie has a football in his hands and he spins it as he raises his eyebrows. He's asking if I want to play by the light of the moon and the bonfire. I shake my head no, as I can't be distracted. There's a situation I've got to watch. A dove has wandered off to the wrong bonfire.

The girl is new to town, and by looks, she probably thinks she's made the right call by standing near the fire with the preppy-clothes-wearing, sticks-up-their asses sacks of shit, but she is wrong. We would have been the better choice.

"You don't want to play football?" Rebecca says. "Then something has to be terribly wrong, so spill."

Rebecca, Charlie and I have been friends for as long as I can remember. Charlie and Rebecca have been a couple since before they graduated from high school. They're older than me, but not by much, and Charlie is already patched-in to the club. They call him Man 'O War, but to me, he's Charlie. The moment I graduate from high school this spring and turn eighteen, I'm joining the Reign of Terror MC. Then Charlie and I won't just be best friends, but brothers.

Charlie could hang out at the clubhouse if he wanted, but because I can't due to my age, he chooses to hang with me. I gotta love him for that.

Across the field, the new girl stands next to the fire and stares into it like she's lost. I don't know who she came with, and don't know how she's getting home. Honestly, besides the fact that she moved to Snowflake this week, started at our school, is in my English and math classes, and has blond hair, blue eyes and a body made for sin, I don't know much about her. Name included.

What I do know is that the guy chatting her up is bad news. Very bad news. He's not the type to ask for permission. He's the type that needs to be six feet under or locked in a jail cell for life. "What do you know about the new girl?"

Rebecca side-eyes me. "Leave her alone. She's new, she's quiet and the last thing she needs is you hitting on her."

"When did you become my block?"

"Since you started kissing girls," she answers like she's bored. "Go hit on the girls who want to be kissed. Linda Glade has been staring at you all night like you're an entrée on a menu."

I turn my head in Linda's direction. She smiles. I nod back. That I will keep in mind. But later. "I'm not going to hit on the new girl."

I want to ask her if anyone has warned the new girl off Ron yet. I don't, because the mention of Ron makes Rebecca nauseous. He cornered her once, and it was a mistake. While he didn't get far, it was far enough to freak Rebecca out, and far enough that Charlie beat the hell out of the bastard. But that's the thing about bastards like Ron—they don't learn.

"What's your take on the new girl?" I'm fishing to see if they've spoken. Fishing to see if I need to keep an eye on her for the rest of the night.

"She's not exactly friendly. I tried talking to her the first time she came to the diner. I was working, gave her free pie, and she sort of blew me off."

"Sort of?"

"She was pleasant to me until Charlie swung by to pick me up on his motorcycle. She asked if he was part of the MC in town, and I said yes, then Meg made up some excuse to leave, and when she sees me now, she walks the other way. While I don't have physical evidence, I'm betting she has some very wrong preconceived ideas about motorcycle clubs. Which is fantastic, because that's all this town needs—one more hater."

All Rebecca says is true, but I don't focus on that. Instead, I try to think of a way to work Meg's name into the conversation because I want to hear how it rolls off my lips. Meg. Her name is Meg.

"Izzy," Charlie calls out, using his nickname for Rebecca. "Are you playing?"

"Damn straight I am." Rebecca smacks my arm. "Come play with us. My team is lacking talent, and I seriously want to beat Charlie. If he wins, he gloats, and I want to punch him in the nose when he gloats."

I chuckle. "Maybe later."

"Whatever, but I meant what I said. Stay away from Meg. Besides the fact she's quiet and she obviously doesn't like

MCs, I get the feeling she's here to heal from something. So if you want to kiss a girl, kiss somebody else."

"If she dissed you, then why are you defending her?"

Rebecca slips off the tailgate and shoves her hands into her front pockets. Her shoulders hunch, and she loses some of the color in her face. There's an ache in my chest for her. Rebecca and I are close because Rebecca's dad is Satan, and she spends a lot of time at my house to hide from him. That look she has on her face is the same one she gets after the two of them have a rough run-in. "I understand ghosts."

That rumbles through me. "Meg told you she has ghosts?"

She shakes her head. "When you live in a haunted house, sometimes it's easy to spot other people's demented spirits."

I nod to let her know I understand. I may not have real life experience with those sorts of ghosts, but I've seen enough of the aftermath of living with Rebecca's and Charlie's parents that I can empathize. "No kissing the new girl. I got it."

Rebecca's smile is weak, and she tries to play off the hurt with a wink. She walks into the night, closer to the trucks that have turned on their headlights to create a playing field.

Ron's still talking to Meg, and Meg's still staring at the bonfire. He's zeroed in on her for the evening even though she hasn't given him much indication she's interested, but a girl's consent has never been his thing. Sweet-talking them until he gets them alone is his MO.

Truth is, I'd like to play football and hang with my friends, not be an unpaid babysitter for the night. I got three choices. One—I can walk away, because she's not my responsibility. Two—I can play guardian angel all night from a distance and then hop in if he makes a move on her. Three—I can go over now and tell her what's up.

Option one won't work. I couldn't live with it if something happened to her. I'm not patient enough for two, so that leaves me with three.

Ron jacks his thumb over his shoulder, pointing at the keg. That's all this girl needs, a drink brought to her from this asshole. Meg looks at him for the first time with an air of contempt. Takes everything I have not to laugh. Good girl, not buying what he's selling, but Ron is the ultimate dirty used car salesman. He keeps up that smile and pretends not to read her body language.

Hell, maybe the bastard can't read her body language. Maybe there's a short circuit in his brain—but that doesn't give him an excuse. Just gives more credence to my theory that he needs to be locked in a cage at the zoo.

Ron leaves, and I take my opportunity do to my public service announcement. Whatever she decides to do after she's been warned won't be on my conscience.

I'm off the tailgate, nodding my head at people who greet me along the way, even pause for a few beats to accept handshakes and one fast hug from an old friend. Once I get past the unseen barrier between my side of town and the other, the greetings aren't as warm, when there are any at all.

Gotta admit, Meg is a sight. She wears expensive jeans that look tailored to her and a blue sweater that against the bonfire gives her a soft glow, and her blond hair spills over her shoulders. Upon closer examination, her face leaves me breathless. She has a face I could stare at for a very long time.

A few more steps until I'm in her space, and a stick cracks under the weight of my foot. Meg jumps, a shudder running through her body, and her head snaps in my direction. I stop in my tracks and put my hands in the air to show I come in peace. She wraps her arms around herself at the sight of me, and I slowly breathe out. I don't live in a haunted house and even I can see her ghosts.

"I didn't mean to scare you."

Her blue eyes narrow. "You didn't scare me."

All right. If that's how we're going to play then that's how we're going to play. I lower my hands and walk up to her, but leave a few feet between us for her comfort. "My bad then. We haven't had a chance to talk yet. I'm Eli McKinley. We have math and English together."

Damn, same glare of contempt she gave Ron. "And?"

I blink. There are a lot of things she could have said that I would have comebacks for, but that wasn't one of them. "And I wanted to introduce myself."

"You have." Meg returns to staring at the bonfire.

Good thing I had already decided against kissing her. Otherwise, my ego would be shredded to bloody pieces. "You always this friendly?"

"No, I used to be nice. But nice didn't work out so well for me."

That brings me up short, and I glance around as if someone will give me a clue as to how to continue the conversation. "You met my friend Rebecca earlier this week. She said you were nice."

Meg's face screws up, and internally I'm wincing. *She said you were nice*. What the hell is wrong with me?

"Your dad is Cyrus McKinley, the head of the Reign of Terror, right?"

Why do I feel like I'm being set up? "Yeah."

"And from what I understand, the Reign of Terror are a relatively new and small club. You have a few chapters in-state. Some in Tennessee, Ohio and Indiana. Nothing huge, and for your sake, I hope it stays small, because flying under the radar is working for you now. But regardless of all that, you're MC, correct?"

My eyebrows draw together. Granted, she's been in town

a few days and all that information is public knowledge, but it's not the type of information normally given to a new girl. "That's right."

"I'm going to make this easier on both of us. I don't do MCs. Not anymore. Rebecca seems like a great girl, but it appears she's on the fast track to being someone's old lady. That's her decision, and I'm all for her living her life as she wants to, but I don't travel those roads anymore. While I'm in this town, I won't give you a hard time, so how about you guys don't give me one?"

I'm dazed, as if someone hit me in the head. She's well-versed in the MC lifestyle, as if she wrote the poem herself, which means she has connections to a club. Question is, which one, and why is she now in my town? "What club are you from?"

"Not answering. And this is my second request for you to please leave me alone."

Fine. I get it. The ice beneath my feet is thin and cracking and if I don't leave soon, she's going to stomp it open and push me into dark, cold waters. "Believe me, don't believe me, but I didn't come over to hit on you. I came by because that guy who was talking to you is a bastard in the first degree. His name is Ron and he likes to use girls in the worst way. I wasn't sure if anyone had gotten around to warning you yet. I didn't want to see you get hurt, and your only crime is that you're new to town."

Her face and eyes soften, and her pure beauty in that moment takes my breath away. Meg's throat moves as she swallows and slowly exhales. "Thank you then…for the warning."

I didn't know there'd been such a weight on my chest at the idea of her not knowing the dangers that lie ahead until now. "You're welcome."

I should leave her be and walk away, but I can't. Not with how small and defenseless she appears. "It looks like you don't want to be here, and I'm not stupid enough to think you'd take a ride from me, but if you want a ride home, I know plenty of girls who'd give you one."

Meg scans the area, her gaze darting from one person to the next as if she's searching for someone. "I came with my cousin, and I can't go home without her. Our grandmother would only let her come here if I came too, and considering I have to share a bedroom and small bathroom with her for an indefinite amount of time, I'm doing my best to play along."

"Who's your cousin?" I ask.

"Jana Silverman."

That sucks for her. Jana has a drinking problem, and from the expression on Meg's face, she's aware of it.

"Do you have her keys?" I ask.

She reaches into her jeans and pulls them out. "Lifted them when we first pulled up."

"Lifted them?"

"Nine out of ten times, I can take care of myself."

Gotta give the girl credit, she's smart.

"Look," she says. "You seem nice, and I appreciate the warning, but I need you to understand that while you can take it as a disrespect, I mean the following as no disrespect at all. Your lifestyle is your choice, and my lifestyle is my choice, and I'm choosing to stay away from guys on motorcycles. It's what will work best for everyone. So I'm fine with us ignoring each other, but I want you to understand me keeping my distance is a matter of survival, okay?"

I came over here to give her a heads up about the bastard known as Ron, but talking with Meg has made me curious. Like a damn itch in the back of my brain. "I don't know what your experience is with MCs, but the Reign of Terror isn't a one percent club, if that's what you're concerned about."

She rolls her eyes. Rolls. Her. Eyes. That pisses me off while amusing me at the same time.

"That's what they all say. In fact, I think it's required when talking with someone outside the MC. You know, you're all Boy Scouts, help old ladies across streets, feed the homeless, give lollipops to babies and all that jazz."

A smile spreads across my lips. "I was a Cub Scout. Have the uniform and more than a few patches as proof."

Her mouth twitches and her eyes dance, and I'm hungry for more.

"I'll hand it to you." She releases a fraction of a blinding smile, and I have a feeling her full smile would be like staring into the sun. "You're smooth."

If she was any other girl, I'd slide in close, but out of respect for her, I keep the distance between us. "Is that a bad thing?"

She laughs then—a gorgeous sound. "Yes."

I laugh with her because I'm pretty sure she just called me on my bullshit. But I sober up because what I'm about to say is the honest to God truth. "I'm serious about our club being legit. I understand your concern, but at least think about it before passing judgement on me. We could be friends. Hang out. Talk. Not once will I bring you around the clubhouse. If you're MC or were MC, you and I both know that means you're a different breed than Jana and Rob, and you're not going to feel comfortable hanging with the likes of them. You've gotta admit that with being new to town, it would be nice to make friends."

"I never said I was part of an MC. In fact, I clearly remember not answering."

She hadn't. "But you know about us, and while a hundred guys have tried talking to you tonight, I'm the only guy you've said a word to."

"That's because you're more annoying than the rest."

I smile because that's probably true. "All the same, the offer to hang stands."

Meg rubs her hands along her arms, and those eyes that had been dancing in laughter become empty. "Thank you, but no thanks."

Do I plan on giving up on Meg? No. She's piqued my curiosity and that rarely happens. Do I plan on giving her some space? Definitely. Rebecca's right. She has ghosts, and I need to give her some breathing room. Even though the urge is to stay, to make her smile and laugh again, it's time for me to give her that space she asked for. "If things get hairy tonight and you change your mind about needing a ride, come find me and I'll hook you up."

"I'm sure you will." Heavy on the sarcasm, but at least there's the return of a slight upward tilt of her lips. I'll add that to the "win" column.

"See you around," I say.

She inclines her head and then returns to staring at the fire. I head back to my side of the party, glancing over my shoulder a few times, and never once do I catch her looking back at me.

To the right, the football game is going strong. Rebecca's team is lacking talent and on the losing end. Any other night, I'd jump into the game to help her out, but tonight, I hop back up onto the tailgate and settle in.

Meg's still standing near the fire, still staring at it like she's looking at some other time, some other place and wherever that place is, it's causing her pain. A pit forms in my stomach. Even with the denial, she's MC and I can't help but wonder if her being here is going to cause problems for the Reign of Terror. I also can't help but feel protective of her, too. If an MC hurt her and she's here to heal, she'll need a friend and she's not going to find one on that side of the bonfire.

I'm curious. Nothing more. Nothing less. And my parents raised me to treat girls with respect. She's new, she's vulnerable, so tonight I'll sit here and make sure no other asshole gives her a hard time. Tomorrow she'll become somebody else's problem. But tonight, I don't mind being her lookout.

THE FIRST LOVES COLLECTION:

THE FIRST UNDERSTANDING

Dare You To, the second book in the Pushing the Limits series, is possibly one of the most personal stories I've written. I have an emotional connection with Beth's character, and twenty years ago, I met and married my own Ryan (Beth's love interest in *Dare You To*).

A character that struck a chord with my readers in *Dare You To* was Beth's uncle Scott. He and Beth shared a very special and complicated relationship. Even though he was just a teenager, he raised her from the time she was a toddler until the day he left to pursue his dreams. He returned to Beth's life when he was in his thirties and Beth was seventeen.

The pair shared so much love from their past, but Beth had lived a terrible life with a mother who was a heroin addict. Scott had hoped that his reappearance in Beth's life would go smoothly, but with her huge trust issues, their road to reconciliation was extremely bumpy.

Writing the breakfast scene from Beth's point of view was

one of my favorite moments involving Scott. Because so many other people also loved Beth and Scott's relationship, I decided to show the scene between Scott and his wife, Ashley, before the breakfast scene, and then the breakfast scene from Scott's point of view.

CHAPTER 10

SCOTT

Blond hair. Blue eyes. A smile that healed every cut and bruise on my body that I got protecting her from my father—her grandfather. My niece. Elisabeth. In my office, I lean on my desk and stare at a picture of us. She's five in the photo, and she looks at me in it as if I'm the center of her universe.

Considering the other options in her life back then for center of the universe contention, I'm guessing I was the best and only pick. She lived with me, my father, my brother—her father—and her mom in a two bedroom trailer. Her grandfather was a sloppy drunk who liked to hit, her father was on the road to repeating the pathetic drunk genetics and her mother was so sad all the time that she would put anything in her body that would wipe her memory clean.

That left me. A teenage boy who didn't have a penny to his name or enough common sense to think half of his decisions through.

I read somewhere once that a boy's brain doesn't develop the ability to understand the consequences of actions until later in his teen years. Part of me wants to believe it's true. If it is—there's a reason I was a bastard. If it's not true, then I'm just a bastard.

The latter is probably my truth whether I want it to be or not, and it's the reason I don't sleep at night.

At eighteen, I had limited and straightforward thoughts and they went like this:

Baseball.

Playing in the minors.

Playing in the majors.

Becoming a star.

Getting out of town.

Getting out of the state.

Running as far away from my family as possible.

Running from my brother.

Running from his girlfriend.

Running from my father.

Just plain running.

Here's the thing. I succeeded...at all of it. Excelled at running. I'm now in my thirties and recently retired from playing major-league baseball. I have more money than even God would know what to do with. I have investments and portfolios and a cushy job as a sales rep to keep myself occupied, because staying still drives me insane.

Staying still means I have time to listen to those annoying voices in my head. Means I have to live with demons who like to remind me of the past.

I used to lay in bed at night in my room in our trailer and as the wind shook the thin walls, I would imagine living the life I have now. I own a house that's big enough that voices echo inside it. I have fast cars. I have enough land that I could farm it and feed a small nation. I have a beautiful wife who I love, who loves me and is my best friend.

I have it all.

It. All.

Because I ran. Because I stayed single-minded. Because I acted and didn't give a damn about any consequences, any fallout, any hurt. I ran and I won...and I traded Elisabeth's life for mine.

I left her behind by lying to myself and to her, saying that I'd be back as soon as I could. A lie. One I made myself believe as she hugged me goodbye. One she also believed as she kissed my cheek one last time.

Now she's dying. Not a physical death, an emotional one, and from the first eighteen years of my life I know that an emotional death is the worst kind there is. It's the least humane, the most painful, and if it goes on for too long there's no cure.

And now I've fooled myself again by believing that if I finally kept that promise, I could save her—but really I wanted to save myself. I wanted the nightmares to go away. I wanted the demon in my head to cease chattering. I wanted peace and stillness and silence, but got none of it. Instead, failing my niece has created an explosion of anarchy.

Simple truth—I screwed up and I don't know how to make us right, especially when everything I do is wrong.

The door to my office opens. Just a turn of the knob and a slight push in. Centimeter by centimeter, my wife, Allison, peeks in. I put down the picture frame and meet her eyes. There's hesitancy in them. There's also pain, and that causes a ripple of an ache in my chest. I'm a bastard, I don't deserve her, yet in spite of all that, in her eyes, there's also love.

In a white nightgown and with her blond hair pulled up into messy bun, she crosses the room. When she reaches me, she brushes her fingers along my jaw, the pads of her fingers soft against the stubble on my chin. "Come back to bed. It's cold there without you."

I left our bed so that my tossing and turning wouldn't wake her. Another fail. I capture her hand, kiss it then draw her into me. Hug her tight. Allison is the one woman in all my years that has fit perfectly, her body into mine. Her laughter sweet in my ears. Her warmth countering my cold. Her heart filling my holes.

"I'm sorry," I say. Sorry is all I say anymore. Apologies to my wife. Apologies to my niece. By trying to do right by one, I let down the other.

She squeezes and then lets me go. Allison frowns at the picture of me and Elisabeth on my desk. Taking it in her hand, she wanders over to the long table full of pictures and returns it to its rightful spot in the middle. "May I be blunt with you?"

Blunt is better, but blunt can also be the equivalent of a baseball bat to the groin. I take a deep breath and brace myself for impact. "Yeah."

Allison looks me over as she forms the words and sentences in her head. My wife is a million times smarter than me. I play ball. I can throw a ball. I can hit a ball. I can run fast. My wife has brain cells that do productive things—things that can change and save the world. Not a day goes by that I don't question why she's with me. Her family has money. She had a million guys more put together than me to choose from, but it's my wedding ring she wears.

"When we were dating, you talked about Beth, but you never once said a word about finding her and forcing her to live with us."

I shift as a rumble of anger goes through me, and I have to work to keep my mouth shut. One, because she's right. Two, because I hate the use of the word *force*. Elisabeth may not be happy here, but this *is* the best place for her. It's better than living with a heroin-addict mother who prostitutes herself for the next hit. But what really got under my skin was... "Her name's Elisabeth."

"The five-year-old that you took care of when you were

barely past being a child yourself was Elisabeth. The close-to-adult living in my spare bedroom is Beth. That's what she calls herself. Even she knows that what you are trying to make her into is a ghost of a person who no longer exists."

I roll my neck. "Elisabeth is seventeen and doesn't know who she is. I agree, she's not six, but she's not an adult. She's scared and she's confused and she's lived in hell her entire life. I know she's rough around the edges, but so was I when I first left my family. When you grow up like Elisabeth and I did, you don't trust."

Allison wipes a few strands of hair away from her face. "Scott, I don't want to argue about Beth. I want to talk about you."

My mind swims. "You're the one who brought up Elisabeth."

"I brought up that you never mentioned wanting to take on custody of your niece. Over the years, you mentioned that you'd sent money to her mother to help. You mentioned a very small possibility of wanting to see her again someday. You talked about possibly paying for her college education. But you never once talked about forcing her mother to sign custody over to you and moving her into our house. Since we met, you've been a planner. You have goals and you are relentless in working toward them. Beth was never part of the plan."

"I didn't know then how she was living."

"You knew how she was living this past summer, but she wasn't living with us then."

"Her mom said she ran away, and I hired a private detective. You said then if I found her she could live with us."

"I said it because I didn't actually believe you would find her. I didn't believe you honestly *wanted* to find her."

My head whips up so quickly that my eyesight goes red.

"You think I wanted her on her own? You think I wanted her to live in garbage? In filth?"

Allison meets my eyes, and the anger pulsating out of them strikes me in the chest. "I love you, and because of that, I've kept myself from saying this, but after living the past few weeks with your niece who is bound and determined to mess up our lives, I will not stay silent anymore."

The brief pause as she sucks in a breath shakes me to the core, because I don't know if I'm strong enough to hear what she has to say. Not sure how many more simple truths I can stomach.

"Scott…you knew how she was living."

I open my mouth to argue and she holds up her hand. "You knew. You may not have seen it yourself or had someone in your ear telling you, but you knew. That's why you sent the money and it's why you turned a blind eye for years. You knew if you faced how Beth was living, you would have had to alter your life to save her, and there was a good chance that in doing so, you would have been sucked right back down into that black hole you were living in before. So please stop trying to make yourself feel better and me feel bad about bringing Beth into our lives, as if you're the hero who just discovered how bad her life was. We both know that's a lie."

I glance down to see if her truth has pierced my flesh, and while there's pain in my chest, there's no blood dripping out of the wound. "What was I supposed to do? When I got that phone call saying she was in jail because Beth went after some asshole who hurt her mother, what did you want me to do? Continue to her ignore her?"

Allison tilts her head in the most sympathetic way, and I can't find the nerve to look at her anymore. Her bare feet pad against the wooden floor, and when she touches my arm, I shake my head from the agony.

"No, I never expected you to ignore her, but I didn't expect you to ignore me, either."

"I didn't ignore you."

"We lost a baby."

Her words tear through me, shattering walls I had thrown up, and my throat becomes thick. "The miscarriage doesn't have anything to do with Beth."

"We saw a heartbeat and we were filled with joy," she continues as if she doesn't see the pain on my face. "But then there wasn't a heartbeat and that hurt us. We didn't dodge the bullet that time. We were hit and we bled and it hurt."

Hurt. Such a simple word, but it doesn't explain this feeling inside me. This feeling like a million knives are slicing all at once along my skin. Doesn't describe the strangling of my heart. Doesn't describe the withering of my soul.

I cross my arms over my chest as if that can hold me together. "None of that has anything to do with Elisabeth."

Allison places her hand over mine. Warmth against my cold. "You couldn't save our baby so you decided to save the baby you took care of before. And that's fine, Scott. I admire you for this. I respect you for this. I love you for this, but you aren't saving her. You're trying to change her. You're trying to force her into our world and force her to be this memory you hold on to of that small child who loved you. You two are strangers. Accept that, and then maybe you can get past it. And maybe while you try to figure her out, maybe you can stop shutting me out. Maybe you can try to love and get to know me once again, too."

Tears burn my eyes, and because Allison is an angel bent on saving my soul, she leans into me, fitting once again perfectly against my body. Making the cold less cold, making the pain less painful, making me better than I should ever be.

"You're my world," I whisper into her hair. "And I love you."

~

OUTSIDE ELISABETH'S DOOR, I take a deep breath. It's six in the morning and Elisabeth and Allison are asleep. Last night, after I talked with Allison, I left the house, but this time I wasn't running away from my problems. At least I hope I wasn't. Now, I'm listening. As much as it hurts, my niece and I are strangers, and that's not good enough.

I'm still in the same clothes as yesterday—jeans and a T-shirt. Once I returned from my trip to Beth's old home, I slipped right into bed to hold my wife and it felt right as she cuddled in close to me, but I didn't sleep. Instead, I watched her sleep. She's my gift, and so is Elisabeth. I don't know how to make us all work, but the first step is to stop running from my wife and the next is to make Elisabeth feel like we're a family.

A family. A twist in my gut. The only family Elisabeth and I had known had included pain. We've got to do better. Both of us deserve better.

Another deep breath and I steady myself for battle. My niece will come out swinging, especially after the fight we had last night. I scared her. I didn't mean to, but I did, and scaring her isn't going to make her trust me.

I raise my fist and knock on the door. "Elisabeth. Wake up."

Movement from behind the door, footsteps against the carpet and the sound of the lock on the doorknob being undone. I roll my neck to ease the tension. Yeah, I guess I deserved to be locked out. A squeak as the door opens and my niece stands in front of me with bedhead and barely cracked-open eyelids.

I shove the bag of her clothing and personal items that I grabbed from her aunt's last night into her hands. "Here. I got your stuff."

Elisabeth wipes the sleep from her eyes. "What stuff?"

Once upon a time, I had only to narrow my eyes and tilt my head to get her to do what needed to be done. Right now, I need her to accept this bag and not make a big deal out of it. This type of trying is awkward as hell, so I drop the same look as I did when she was four and throwing a fit.

The bag becomes lighter as she takes it into her hands, and I might be hallucinating, because I think she might have smiled slightly. Well, I'll be damned. Maybe this will work. "I went by your aunt's and picked up your clothes. That Noah guy was there and he showed me what was yours. I'm sorry if I left anything behind. If there's something specific missing, maybe I can swing by one day after work and get it."

Elisabeth blinks several times, looking as if she is trying to translate my words from Chinese to English. "How's Noah?"

Yeah. Not going there. The kid was hardcore, but I could tell he cared about my niece, and if I give in and tell her that, she might go running back. I've made some parts of my life a mess by running. I can't let Elisabeth do the same thing.

"We didn't have a heart-to-heart," I say. "Elisabeth, this doesn't change any of my rules. I want you to settle here in Groveton and let your old life go. Trust me on this one, okay, kid?"

She starts to nod, but then stops herself like she figured out the movement was traitorous. "I can wear my clothes?"

As much as it kills a portion of my soul because I don't like the idea of some perverted old man looking at my niece… "Skin has to be covered and no rips in indecent places. Push me on this and I'll burn every stitch in that bag." I incline my head toward the kitchen. "Breakfast in thirty."

She cradles the bag like it's a baby, and the gesture causes an ache to flow through my muscles. "Thanks."

The word is stiff, like she's never formed it before on her lips, but it's possibly the best gratitude I've ever received.

BETH ENTERS the kitchen in a pair of faded blue jeans, a black T-shirt, silver hoops in her ears and a fake diamond stud in her nose. She reminds me a lot of her mother in her outfit, but her mother never had the hop to her step that Beth has now. I make a mental note to send Allison roses today. As a reminder that I love her. As a thank-you for understanding a teenage girl better than I do.

I'm standing near the stove making scrambled eggs. They used to be Beth's favorite as a child and even though she says she hates eggs now, I have a hard time believing it. I guess this is a test. For me. For her. If she rejects the eggs, I also made enough toast, sausages and bacon to fill her up and I'll know not to make eggs anymore. If she eats the eggs, then maybe, just maybe, it'll mean Elisabeth is willing to start working to build a relationship with me, too.

Beth takes a seat at the kitchen island, at the place setting I made for her. Next to her plate and glass of orange juice is the stack of buttered toast and sausage patties.

"Is it turkey or tofu or whatever you try to pass off as food?"

I stymie the smile. My wife is a health nut and is hardcore about what she puts in her body. Elisabeth, on the other hand, is more human and enjoys grease—just like me. My niece picks up a piece of toast like it might eat her back. She sniffs it then quickly takes a lick, as if I'm feeding her poison. I laugh. Can't help it. She used to pull crap like that when she was four. And like she was four, she begins to eat as she realizes she likes the taste.

The kid has always been picky as hell.

"No, it's not turkey. It's real. I'm tired of watching you not eat." I place a plate of bacon and eggs between us and I sit beside her. "If you'd try Allison's cooking, you'd see it's not half bad."

She bites into the toast. "That's the point. Food shouldn't be half bad. It should be all good."

Point awarded to Elisabeth. I spoon some scrambled eggs onto my plate. "I like the stud. When did you pierce your nose?"

"When I turned fourteen." She helps herself to the bacon and sausage, but I'm certain it's the eggs she's secretly lusting after. I internally will her to take the eggs, but I try not to seem concerned over it. *Come on, kid. Give me something.*

"Your mom wanted one," I say to keep myself from discussing eggs. "She talked about driving into Louisville to get one several times."

She deflates and her reaction gives me pause. *Note to self—anything involving her mom gives her pain.* Elisabeth draws in her bottom lip as she continues to stare at the eggs. *You know you want the eggs. You know the eggs are good. They're fluffy. I made them just for you.*

A look of determination crosses her face, and she taps her fork against the counter. In less than a heartbeat, she scrapes the remaining eggs onto her plate. I smile, and I shove a piece of bacon in my mouth to hide it. From the evil glare being thrown in my direction, I know she caught it.

"Is that a baseball thing?" she asks.

"What?"

"Ryan has that same I-know-everything smirk when he thinks he's one-upped me."

I sip my orange juice to buy myself time. Ryan Stone is a kid Elisabeth goes to school with. He's a baseball player, but he's better than me. Even before Elisabeth came back into my life, I had heard how talented Ryan was at baseball. He's also smart, has a good head on his shoulders and hangs out with the right people. The type of right people Elisabeth needs to start making friends with. Since he and Elisabeth know each other from school, I've made it my job to know everything about him.

Plus, I'm curious. "Have you and Ryan been hanging out at school?"

She shrugs. "Kind of."

"He's a good kid, Elisabeth. It would do you good to make more friends like him."

Elisabeth has this expression that warns me she'd like to stab me with her fork, but it passes quickly and I take that as a win. "I go by Beth."

I got Elisabeth her clothes. How about she lets me heal from one battle before beginning another? "How's school?"

"I'm gonna fail."

I stop eating as the frank statement catches me off guard. I was expecting a nonanswer and the truth was appreciated but unsettling. Elisabeth stares at her plate as she shoves more food into her mouth. I weigh my words. Each one tips the scale one way or another. This is the first time both of us are trying, and I don't want to set her off. This conversation is like playing with live explosives.

"Are you trying?" I ask.

Elisabeth nibbles on a piece of bacon, and I give her the time to weigh her words as well. Finally, she says, "Yes. But I don't expect you to believe me."

What she doesn't know is that I do believe her, and I understand that ache of not feeling good enough—especially in academics. But Elisabeth is not me—she's better than me, and I have the resources to help. I toss my napkin onto my empty plate. "I'm not smart. I can throw a ball, catch a ball and hit a ball. It made me a rich man, but it's better to be smart."

"Too bad for me. I can't do any of that. Smart included."

"Allison's smart," I say, and I hold up my hand when she rolls her eyes. "She's real smart. Has a masters in English. Let her help you."

"She hates me."

She doesn't. Allison's upset with me, and I'm going to make that better, too. But my problems with Allison, our pain at losing our child, aren't Beth's issue—they're mine. She has enough burdens and doesn't need my baggage crashing down on her. "Let me handle that. You focus on school."

"Whatever." She glances at the clock. "Shouldn't you be heading to work?"

"I'm working from home today. We're going to do this every morning. I want you up at six and out here for breakfast by six-thirty."

"Okay."

I gather the dishes and go to the sink. "About last night...."

"Let's not discuss last night."

"You were shaking." I was mad at her for upsetting Allison, and I lost my temper, but my words, my actions—they weren't bad enough to provoke the reaction Elisabeth gave me. She has her own demons, and I want to know their names, addresses and phone numbers.

She stands, fidgeting from head to toe. "I should get my backpack together."

"Has someone hurt you?" I push. "Physically?" Because the emotional part is obvious.

She picks up her dishes and brings them to me. Her words pour out as if she's in freefall. "I really need help with calculus. I want to drop it."

I take the dishes from her, place them on the counter and cross my arms over my chest. I'm not letting this go. "What happened after I left town? My dad was dead and buried. Did my brother take his place as residing bastard?"

Elisabeth begins to shake, and her fear causes a wave of protectiveness to course through my veins. But her fear quickly turns into red-faced anger. "Fuck you."

Fuck you. Elisabeth is a smart girl with a smart tongue. If that's the best she's got, it means that I just punched through a few layers of those walls she's been fortifying for years. *Fuck you*. What a great comeback. I chuckle. "You're still as stubborn as you were at four. Go get your stuff ready for school. I'll drive you in today."

"I'll take the bus."

I turn my back to her and load the dishwasher. "I'm making pancakes tomorrow."

"I won't eat."

I laugh again. "Yes, you will. Allison's making goat-cheese-and-tofu casserole tonight."

AND THEY ALL LIVED HAPPILY EVER AFTER:

A THUNDER ROAD NOVELLA

CHAPTER 11

PIGPEN

Growing up I didn't believe in true love. I couldn't wrap my head around the bull about a princess trapped in a castle and how some random guy who never met the chick before takes one look at her sad blue eyes and feels compelled to place himself in front of a fire-breathing dragon to save her life. No way that type of love was real.

Don't get me wrong. When I was younger I believed in caring love, protective love. The type you have for your family, your friends, and then for your friends who become your family. That shit was and is real. For my friends and family, I'd take on the dragon without the armor and the sword. I'd slay that bastard with a smile on my face just to piss it off, but no way could there be some woman out there who owned me more than I owned myself.

Fairytales. That's all that kind of nonsense was. Then I met her—a woman who slipped under my skin without even trying, who took possession of my soul with a smile and a blah blah blah, and that makes me grumpy. Like a damned toddler who had to eat peas and doesn't want to take a nap.

In the back of the high school's auditorium, I lean against the wall with my arms crossed over my chest and do what my club has allowed me to do—look from a distance.

Ms. Whitlock.

Let's all take a moment to savor that name. Whitlock. Ms. Whitlock. Ms. Caroline Whitlock. Her name rolls off the tongue like a Spanish "r." Blond hair slicked back in a perfect bun, white silk shirt, gray slim skirt that fits her so perfectly I can't stop staring and blue eyes behind dark-rimmed glasses. She's in her twenties, like me, and I have so much respect for this woman that I can't bring myself to call her by her first name without her permission.

She's gorgeous, she's intelligent, she's cold and she's feisty. I can't name one student who doesn't think she's a tyrant, and she has never looked once in my direction. Worse, I haven't been able to do more than savor her from a distance. Why? Because she has been the English teacher to some of the teens of our motorcycle club. I've been told that throwing her on the back of my motorcycle would cause a conflict of interest.

Translation? If I were to date her and suck at the whole dating thing—which I do—then that might cause Caroline Whitlock to take it out on the Reign of Terror teens. I say they're big kids who can handle failing a class, but when I saw those stupid doe-eyed teens going through all their life-threatening issues, I took a step back.

That's all ending today. In a matter of minutes, all the pictures of Chevy, Violet and Razor's coma-inducing high school graduation ceremony will be taken, and there will be two years before another club teen will grace Caroline Whitlock's gum-coated classroom.

Tonight, I begin my quest to woo the most desirable woman in the world.

"The fact you like my English teacher is creepy." Chevy

stands beside me, graduation cap tilted on his head. He's the spitting image of his uncle and my best friend, Eli. Dark hair, dark eyes and every bone is dedicated to taking care of the people he loves.

It's gonna break a lot of people's hearts when this kid leaves town to go to college in the fall. He lost his dad before he was born, but the club took him on, and now he's everybody's son. Chevy hasn't patched into the club, the club's initiation to officially become a member. Whether he does or not, he's part of this big, messed-up family.

No doubt most of the club will be there when he plays college football. It'll probably scare the hell out of the small college town when the stands are full of Reign of Terror biker cuts, but they'll figure out quick that we're all about supporting our boy and not about causing trouble.

Chevy makes a show of glancing back and forth between me and Ms. Whitlock. "There's something wrong with you."

"No, there's not."

"Yes, there is."

"No, there's not."

"For some reason, women think you're good looking and that you're funny, so when you have women who give you their phone number without you asking, why her?"

Hence my road name, Pigpen. The guys in the club said I was too good looking, with blond hair, blue eyes, and a ripped body, courtesy of my service in the Army. To even the playing field, they gave me a road name designed to offset my appearance. I don't have problems walking into bars and finding a one-night stand, but I don't want a one-night stand. I want a date with Caroline Whitlock.

"That woman revels in people's pain," he says. "Do you know how many football games I almost missed because of her?"

"None."

"That's not the point. She'd shut her door to class thirty seconds before the bell. If you didn't make it in, you were locked out and ran the risk of being reported for cutting. And as I stood outside waiting for her to let me in, she'd give the class a quiz no one could make up. I almost missed games because my grade would be low that week from the missed quiz."

"Yet, you played." Because he learned quickly to get his ass in his seat early.

While all the other teachers are taking photos with students, Ms. Whitlock is gathering papers at the podium and straightening them. Her long fingers slip along the edges to nudge them into line. How is it that she makes that simple gesture seem sexy?

"The point is she's a sadist."

"She's an angel."

"That's messed up."

I flash a grin at him because I'm aware how messed up I am. "No, it's not."

"Yes, it is."

"No, it's not, and I can do this all day."

Chevy laughs and shakes his head. I offer him my hand, he takes it and I pull him in for a hug. One that includes a strong thump on the back. "I'm proud of you."

"Chevy, Mom wants a picture of us," Violet says from my right. I let Chevy go, and my smile grows at the sight of Violet decked out in the purple cap and gown, and with honor cords and sashes around her neck.

I hold out my arms. "I need a hug."

Her eyes go wide because she and I both know I'm not going to give her the polite public hug going on all around us. I'm too crazy for that. Violet sticks out her finger like I'm a rabid dog that can be told to sit.

"Stop. My hair is still curly, my cap is still on my head, my knee is not aching, and I still have pictures to take and you can only approach if you behave."

Arms still out wide. "I'm behaving."

She laughs in spite of herself as she slowly backs up. "*Behave* isn't in your vocabulary."

She's right. I pick up my stride, and in three steps I lift Violet until her feet dangle in the air. She squeals, slaps my shoulders, and demands that I let her go, but I hug her regardless. After enduring a colorful tirade about how she's going to nail me in the balls if I don't put her down, I comply. Violet's just dangerous enough that she'll do it.

God, I love this kid.

Violet's all smiles as she pulls back and looks at me. "You're the craziest person I know."

"Which says a lot since you're part of a motorcycle club."

"I'm not a member."

She can deny it all she wants, but every drop of blood in that girl screams Reign of Terror—like a genetic predisposition. But she needs her space from the club, and I understand why. It's been a tough few years for her, but thankfully, she's made her peace with the club and loves us again.

This fall, she'll be heading to college with Chevy. If forever is possible, then those two will have it. They love each other too much to let go.

I hook an arm around Violet as I lead her to where the club moms have set up their own paparazzi team. On the way, I tease her that I'm going to ruin the curls in her long red hair. In return, she threatens my life multiple times, and I award her bonus points for creativity as to where she plans to hide my body. I smile wider because the club raised her right.

We reach the moms, and as I release Violet, I kiss the side of her head. Despite the crap I just gave her, I'm careful not to disturb her hair, her pinned-in graduation cap or her makeup. Chevy takes her hand, and in seconds, the two of them are fussed over by the moms who are sending me dirty looks for messing with Violet before all the pictures were taken. But Violet looks over her shoulder at me and winks. I wink back.

It's weird: if someone had asked me years ago when I was in the military, knee-deep in the mud of some foreign country with a rifle slung over my shoulder, if I could be so full of pride for some kid I wasn't even related to, I'd tell you that you were out of your mind. Now? I might as well be joining the group and taking two million pictures with my cell.

There's a few disagreements about where to take the pictures, but when Chevy leans down and kisses Violet, so many flashes go off that I'm nearly blinded.

I glance around in search of the other graduation boy, Razor, and then for the other power-couple teen duo, Emily and Oz. If I know the women associated with this club, they're going to want a group photo. Half the time, none of us can do a damn thing without us all posing. If I'm going to woo Ms. Whitlock, I need these pictures to wrap up now.

Emily and Oz are off to the right with Emily's father, Eli. Oz has his arm around Emily, and she's held tight to his side. I was one of the skeptics who wasn't sure they could pull off a long-distance relationship, but they did.

Emily graduated from her high school in Florida last week, and she'll be heading to college here in Kentucky in the fall. A different one than Chevy and Violet, but the schools are close to each other. Oz has been working full time for the security company the club owns, as well as taking a full load of classes, thanks to online courses. This fall, he'll head to college with Emily, then return home on the weekends and breaks to continue his work with the company.

The babies are growing up and leaving the nest. Granted, I only got involved with these kiddos a few years back, but they grew on me.

I do another scan of the room, and Razor's nowhere to be found. Rebecca, Oz's mom, is looking around, too. She catches the eye of Eli and Hook, Razor's dad. We're all on the same page—Razor's not around. After a quick survey of the auditorium, they all look to me to be the man with the plan. With a nod, I'm on the move.

Hook may be Razor's dad, but Razor's mine. Razor and Hook have had a rough few years, though they're patching things up. Razor's even going to be the best man at Hook's wedding next month. While they've found a way of talking to each other without shouting, Razor and I have a connection. I have a way of speaking so that he'll listen, and I have a way of listening to him. Having the ability to listen is a rare talent that's lost on a lot people in Razor's life.

The reason I rolled into Snowflake, Kentucky, after I left the military, the reason I joined the Reign of Terror Motorcycle Club, was because of this kid. He doesn't know it, but years ago things were set into motion that made me his dark arch-guardian-angel.

I step out into the spring evening and do a sweep of the sidewalk, half expecting to see Razor in the shadows kissing his girlfriend, Breanna. I don't spot him, and I'm slow rounding the corner in case I need to allow him some space. Razor's there, but alone. Standing by himself staring off at the sunset.

Razor lowers his gaze to the white rose in his hand, and my heart rips off my arteries and drops to the mud on the ground. Damn, he's missing his mom.

Sometimes, the world is tone deaf. It was a good intention—handing out roses to the graduates so they could give them to their moms. But Razor lost his mother and it's a wound that still stings.

I move for the auditorium as this may be something Hook wants to handle, but then Razor slides his eyes in my direction. I've never been able to walk away from this kid when he's in pain. Don't see a reason to start now.

I hold out my hand to him as I approach, he takes it and we go in for a short and strong hug. I step back and look the kid in the eye. "What's going on, brother?"

Razors shrugs and then goes back to studying the horizon. His graduation cap is off, the gown open and underneath he wears jeans and a black T-shirt.

"Where's Breanna?" I ask.

"In taking pictures with Addison."

Addison is his girlfriend Breanna's best friend. Breanna is home for the weekend from her boarding school. She'll graduate herself in two weeks. "I'm going to ask again, and this time I'd like a real answer. I have a woman I need to hit on before the evening is done, and if it doesn't happen because I'm pestering your sad ass over feelings, I'm going to be seriously pissed."

Razor snorts. "Ms. Whitlock?"

"The woman begs to be wooed."

"You're crazy."

"I hear that a lot. Enough about me. Let's talk more about you."

He twirls the rose. "I thought about giving it to Jill." His father's fiancé. "I thought about giving it to Rebecca, too." Oz's mom, Man O' War's wife. While Oz is her only biological child, she cares for all the teens as if they were her own.

"Either of them would have loved the gesture," I say. Either would have cried their eyes out that he had chosen them.

"Yeah." His eyes glisten, and that kills me from the inside out.

I place my hand on his shoulder and squeeze. If I could take his grief, I would. If I could take whatever weighs down this kid at any time, I would. I'd lay my life down for his in a heartbeat.

"I think—" He pauses as his voice becomes too thick to talk. "I think I'm going to buy other flowers for them. This one needs to go to Mom."

"Want me to go with you?" To the cemetery where she's buried under a flowering apple tree. I've gone with him before. He doesn't know it. Followed him at times when his demons were close to destroying what was left of him. Those times I gave him space, but I was nervous about leaving him alone.

He clears his throat and looks me in the eye, and for the first time in years, I spot peace along with pain. "I'm going to take Breanna with me. It's a nice evening for a ride, and she hasn't been on the back of my bike in a while. It's time she meets my mom."

Next time I see that girl, I'm going to give her a Violet-worthy hug. In months, Breanna found ways to help heal Razor in ways none of us could accomplish in years. "Are you going to bring her by the party later?"

"Yeah."

Good news. It's all good news. "They want you for pictures."

The smooth, cool kid returns. "I'll pass."

"You either come in now or I send Rebecca out. I'm going to warn you, she will kick your ass."

Razor chuckles, but he doesn't disagree. Rebecca is one scary and fantastic woman. Razor's cell pings, and he pulls it out of his jeans pocket. His smile fades, and I don't like that.

"Everything okay?" I ask.

He mashes his lips together. "No."

I hitch my thumbs in my pockets, because now I'm not going anywhere. "Spill."

"I'm not sure you can help with this one."

"Brother, I can launch rockets in space from my cell. Besides finding time to ask your English teacher out, I can do anything." I don't mention how his keeping problems to himself almost caused nuclear fallout for him and Breanna a few months back. I'm not a told-you-so type of guy, but I'm betting the glare I'm giving this kid is saying it all in plain, short sentences.

Razor turns his cell in my direction, and on it is a picture of bruises on someone's arm—a feminine arm. The texts are from Breanna, and that causes a dark rumble in my chest. "Is someone messing with your girl?" Because that's trouble I'll happily take on, any day, any time.

"No, but her friend Addison is having problems with her father, and Breanna's scared because it's getting worse. If you have ideas of how to help someone who doesn't want help, I'm all ears."

Good thing for Razor, Breanna and Addison, I'm all too well-versed in helping people who don't want to be helped. It's all I've done with Razor, Chevy, Violet, and Oz for years. "Give me a few, and I'll see what I can do."

"I'm not looking for you to beat the hell out of him."

I bob my head as that sounds like a great idea, but... "Have some faith, okay?"

The side door opens and the utter look of love and devotion that radiates from him when Breanna walks out would be sickening if it were coming from anyone but him. Razor, though, deserves the world. I love her for handing the world to him.

"Pictures," I say, then turn on my heel to give the two lovebirds time.

I round the corner, pull out my cell, and shoot a text to Dust, a brother of mine in the club. He's closer in age to Razor, Oz, Chevy, and Violet than he is to me, but his soul is old. That happens when you experience hell on earth.

Me: *I'm going to need your help on something.*

Dust: *Anything.*

Good, because what I have in mind might take time.

At this rate, I'm never going to corner Ms. Whitlock and discover my own slice of heaven. When I walk back into the auditorium, Ms. Whitlock is chatting it up with Addison, the one Razor's concerned about, and that causes me to focus. I don't believe in coincidence, and I'm wondering if Ms. Whitlock is zeroing in on the same problems Razor and Breanna are crushed over.

Their conversation is intense. Ms. Whitlock talking more than Addison. Their movements are rigid and clipped. As Ms. Whitlock speaks, Addison shakes her head violently, and then they both fall silent. Addison's shoulders crumple, and Ms. Whitlock, the woman I've been told is colder than an iceberg, wraps her arms around Addison and offers comfort.

Addison rests her head on the teacher's shoulder only briefly, and then she's gone so fast that I wonder if she has superpowers. After taking a second to absorb the loss, Ms. Whitlock pulls keys out of her purse. I don't have much time to make initial contact—for multiple reasons. In case I need some background on Addison—background from someone over the age of twenty-one—and for my own selfish motives.

A girl in a cap and gown surrounded by a mob of family members is all smiles as she holds about two dozen red roses. She won't miss one, right?

While I'm not as smooth at sleight of hand as Chevy, I'm able to swipe one of the roses as I walk in Ms. Whitlock's direction. She's heading for the door, which means I have to make an arc to make it appear I'm randomly walking in the opposite direction. She's looking straight ahead, past me, because that's what most people do when they see someone in a black leather biker cut.

As we start to pass, I inch toward her. Our shoulders brush and her gaze snaps to mine, the first time she's laid her solid blue eyes on me. My heart stops beating. I switch my focus forward, keep walking past then pause, reaching out to lightly touch her wrist.

She jolts with the touch, and I have to admit I shake, too. She whips her head back to look at me. I regretfully drop my hand from her wrist and offer her the rose. "You dropped this."

Ms. Whitlock blinks, confused. "No, I didn't."

I keep my hand outstretched, and my eyes glued on hers. "You must have. Someone as pretty as you deserves a rose."

Her eyes smile first, then a sarcastic smirk slips across her lips. "That's a terrible line."

I crack a crazy grin. "Yeah, but it was worth it."

"Why?"

I shrug one shoulder because I'm out of corny come-ons. "So I could talk to you." I shift to extend the rose further to her. She's hesitant, but she accepts.

Because even I'm aware that if I stick around I'll find a way to screw this moment up, I wink at her and walk away.

It's hard not to look back at her for the first few feet forward. Doing so will kill any credibility and mystery I hope to create. Yet I lose all self-control by the time I hit the folding chairs. I glance back, and I'm rewarded with the sight of her lifting the rose to her nose to inhale.

Takes everything I have not to lift my arms in the air to signal that I just scored. But I can't celebrate. I have yet to ask her out, and she has yet to say yes.

CHAPTER 12

ELI

Watching my daughter laugh is one of my favorite sights. Her head back, smile across her face, her entire body shakes with laughter. It's a gift I never knew I wanted, and now I can't imagine living without.

It still takes my breath away to say those words—my daughter. Emily. She's here, in Kentucky, at my clubhouse, and I'm still in awe that she willingly spends time with me.

Little over a year ago, I never would have guessed she'd be here, much less an actual part of my life. I thought I had screwed up my relationship with her beyond repair years ago, but I didn't, and now I get to watch her laugh. Whatever part of my soul I unknowingly sold for this was worth the cost of admission.

Emily sits on the top of the picnic table in the middle of the grass halfway between Dad's house and the clubhouse. Beside her is Oz. His arm is wrapped around her, and while I can't admit I'm thrilled she's so attached to someone at the age of eighteen, I can admit that if she had to fall for somebody, I'm glad it's Oz.

He's a good man. Works hard. Adores my daughter. Treats her with respect, and gives her enough room to live life without him on her toes. Plus, being that he's part of the club and I have seniority, I can threaten to rip his arms out of their sockets without having to worry about the police being called in for harassment.

"Do you feel old looking at them?"

I can't keep the surprise off my face when Chevy's mom, Nina, walks up the steps of Dad's house and sits on the top step about a foot away from me. When my brother James died before Chevy's birth, Nina did her best to avoid my family and the club. She only associated with us on a have-to basis. With all the shit that went down with Chevy this year, we've talked more, but most of that was fighting over what was best for her son—my nephew.

Chevy found a way to shut us both up, and I respect him for that. I also respect Nina for loving her son and standing by his side, and for coming here tonight for his graduation party. She's not a fan of the club, but she's a fan of her son, and it's nice that both of us are waving the white flag. Giving peace a chance is a good change of pace. God knows I'm tired of complicated.

"Do they make me feel old?" I repeat the question she asked me, feeling it out. I study the group of teenagers ready to take on the world. It feels like yesterday when me, Oz's parents, Emily's mom, Meg, and my brother, James, filled that table. "Not old as much as nostalgic."

"Nostalgic," Nina murmurs as if weighing the word.

Nina's a few years older than me, early forties, and she's a five-four tiny beauty with a personality that's the equivalent to gunpowder. Gasoline flows in my veins, so the two of us have been a deadly combination, especially with our wildly different ideas of how to raise Chevy. She wanted him away from the club, I wanted him in. He needed his family. To be honest, we needed him more.

"Nostalgic is better than saying I feel old," she says.

I've always been able to appreciate why James was involved with Nina. She's brave, independent, strong-willed and gorgeous. Long black hair, dark eyes and an olive complexion that makes her looks as if she's forever been kissed by the sun.

The group by the table break into laughter again as Razor tells them a story, and I watch my daughter as she smiles in complete joy. I remember eighteen, being carefree with friends and being in love.

" 'When to the sessions of sweet silent thought I summon up remembrance of things past, I sigh the lack of many a thing I sought, and with old woes new wail my dear time's waste,' " I say, then drink from my longneck.

Nina offers me a side-eye. "What was that?"

"Nothing." I could blame the beer, but this is my first one and I've been nursing it most of the evening. My daughter's in town, and I want a crystal-clear memory of her every moment in my presence. I missed too many years of her life, and I'm determined not to miss any more.

"That sounded very Shakespearean," she says.

The right side of my mouth tips up. "Do I look like Shakespeare to you?" Faded blue jeans, black T-shirt, hair shaved close to my head, and plugs in both ears. Maybe I could pass for Shakespeare's twin brother who grew up in a motorcycle club and spent several years in prison.

Nina looks straight into my eyes, and I give her credit. There's not many who will meet my stare, much less hold it.

"Play it off all you want, Eli, but that was Shakespeare."

It was, and she's looking at me with more respect than I deserve. "I did a lot of reading in prison."

"Chevy said you earned your bachelor's degree while you were incarcerated."

She makes it sound like that was an act to be proud of. For me, self-forgiveness and prison aren't on the same page. "There wasn't much else to do."

"You taught my son to own his choices, so I expect you to do the same. Earning your degree was admirable, and I respect you for that." Nina returns her heavy gaze back to the open field, and our teens. "I'm thinking about going back to school. I don't regret having Chevy, and I don't regret the choices I made to survive, but I do regret not fighting harder to earn my degree."

I roll the bottle of beer in my hands. "It's not too late."

"No," she says in the most unconvincing tone I've heard from her. "It's not."

For eighteen years, this woman has been in my face and full of confidence in every word she spat at me. It's weird to hear doubt fall from her lips.

"Nina," I say, and wait for her to look at me. She finally does, and I wonder how my brother didn't fall for those deep, dark eyes. She was his best friend, but he wasn't in love with her, and that baffles me. "You've fought with me, my parents and this club to do what you thought was right for your son for years. Going to college after dealing with us will be a walk in the park."

That grants me a sarcastic grin and the fire in her eyes that I'm used to seeing aimed in my direction. "As if you weren't in my face just as much as I was in yours."

"Never said I wasn't. In the end, though, we raised a good kid."

"We raised a *great* kid," she corrects.

I tip my beer in her direction in agreement. I return to watching the teens, and I'm caught off guard when I spot Emily watching me. Her gaze flickers between me and Nina.

I raise my eyebrows at my daughter. She only smiles at me before rejoining the conversation with her friends.

"Thank you," Nina says. "For what you said about college…and for helping to raise my son."

I'm usually a fast responder. Half the time I speak before I think a thing through, but this time, I'm stumped. I'm so used to fighting with Nina that I'm speechless. We drove each other nuts over the years. We didn't realize until recently, though, we were pulling Chevy in two different directions. I apologized to Chevy for that, and from what I understand, Nina did, too.

"You're a great mom. Not one of us ever thought differently."

Nina cocks an eyebrow as if she's skeptical, but I'm telling her the truth.

"Isaiah's coming into town tomorrow, around noon," I say. "It's going to be my and Dad's first time meeting him. Chevy's going to meet with him at the diner first, then he'll bring him to the clubhouse.

"We're going to play most of this by ear, but we plan for the first meeting to be small—me, Dad, Chevy and Emily. Oz and Violet will be around, but they plan on holding back to give Isaiah some space. Considering your relationship with James, would you like to be a part of this meet-up?"

Isaiah Walker was a shock to all of us. It turns out my brother had another child in Louisville. Many issues with all this, the main one being Isaiah's not a child anymore. He grew up in foster care, and that causes the demons that live in me full time to growl. If we had known about Isaiah, he would have lived here in this house surrounded by a club full of people who would have loved him as if he were their own.

Nina rests her arms on her bent knees and clasps her hands together. "James was in love with Isaiah's mother. Do you really think Isaiah is going to want to meet the woman his father sought refuge with when his mother broke his heart?"

"Chevy said Isaiah wants to meet his family, and he wants to understand who his father was. James was my brother, but you were his best friend. Who better than you to paint the real picture of James?"

"James was complicated," she says.

"Of course he was. He was a McKinley."

Nina gives a short laugh, and that causes me to smile. Our group of teens howl in hilarity again, and that grabs both of our attention in the way it does with parents full of pride.

"What do you say?" I ask. "Do you want to help?"

"I'll help."

Good. I expect Nina to leave, but she doesn't, and I find myself oddly okay with that. We sit in a comfortable silence on the steps and watch as the next generation plots and plans their life.

CHAPTER 13

ADDISON

Life should have theme music. On demand, the perfect song should blast in the background to fit the mood. Even better, when everything's about to go to hell, the freaky music should play.

How many of us have yelled at the stupid girl creeping down the stairs to the dark, spider-infested basement because that serial-killer-is-on-the-loose music began? I mean, seriously, we all knew *Jaws* was coming because a cello was playing, right? Otherwise that fin sticking up in the water could have been a cute, snuggly dolphin.

If I had *Jaws* music that played when everything was about to go bad, my complicated life would be a lot easier. I'd know when to run or lock myself in my room. Only problem: lately, it'd be playing all the time.

My fingers tighten around the backpack in my right hand, and my left grips the bus ticket harder. The bus was supposed to leave the station an hour ago, and we keep getting delayed. Ten minutes here, fifteen there. It all adds up to sand sliding through the hourglass.

I roll my neck as the stress of sitting perched on the edge

of the wooden bench seat causes my muscles to lock. This is the furthest I've made it in my three tries to flee.

The first time I attempted to leave, my father caught me as I was sneaking out my bedroom window. The second time, my father found me walking along the side of the county road. Both times he reminded me that I'm only seventeen and that he's still the person that runs my life.

I hate him. I've hated him for years and, because of that, this is attempt number three and I'm counting on it being lucky. I'm not seventeen anymore, and I'm done living at home.

"I like girls with blond curly hair," mumbles a guy sitting behind me, making it perfectly clear to his sidekick that he's talking about me.

My skin prickles, and I'm swamped with the urge to shower. The way his voice deepens when he says something about me, no matter the words, sounds dirty.

He kicks my bench and my body jerks with the impact. I whip my head around. "Cut it out."

His lips turn up, and there's nothing cute about this guy. He's tall, too thin, and when he tries to show teeth, there are two missing. Everything about him screams meth head.

"The cheerleader is feisty."

This cheerleader is about to shove a pompom up his butt, but the goal is to not bring attention to myself, so I turn back around. The goal is to make it to Bowling Green. I need options, and the only way I'll discover them...screw that... the only way I'll believe I have options is when I see the proof for myself. This means Bowling Green and running away.

No point in asking Meth Boy how he knows I'm a cheerleader. I wasn't thinking when I grabbed my Snowflake High Varsity Cheer warm-up jacket. If he caught a glimpse of it from the front, he'd know my name, too. Never realized how stalker-attracting these jackets were until now.

Speaking of creepy, bus stations are scarier than I imagined, though I'm not sure what I was expecting. Not the homeless man with a beard longer than Santa's talking to himself by the trash can about Jesus coming again. Nor was I expecting the two guys behind me who keep switching seats when I do, and totally in the serial-killer way.

Meth Boy kicks my seat again, and I scoot until I'm two spots away from the trash-can, Jesus-returning homeless guy. My odds of survival are better next to him.

"He's coming to save you." Homeless guy slips in front of me to sit cross-legged. I slide all the way until my back hits the seat. His ice blue eyes are too wide and too wild.

"What?"

"He's coming to save you," he repeats.

My heart stutters. *Dad.* If Dad finds me, I'm dead. "No, he's not." He's who I need to be saved from.

"Jesus always comes to save."

Hysterical laughter bubbles up from deep inside me. "No one is coming to save me."

He tilts his head as if he's sorry for me. "You need faith."

Puhlease—faith. What I need is the announcement that it's finally time to board.

Faith. It's a dirty word in my vocabulary. I tried doing all the things the pamphlets and the teachers and the public service announcements told me to do, but here's the truth: faith in anything besides myself is the equivalent of stupidity. The system's broken, the government's broken, the world's broken.

At least it is if you're a female. It works amazingly well if you're a male.

The old man scoots on his bottom down the floor to the woman sitting on the opposite end of the bench from me. I no longer feel special when he says the same words to her that he did to me.

"Hate to tell you"—hot breath from behind me causes me to shudder—"but there's a cop that walked in and the person he's talking to pointed in the direction of where you once were."

My head snaps to the entrance. Damn it. It's Deputy Heinz. He and my dad were high school friends, and his presence here might mean—

"My friend and I can help." Stalker guy invades my space from the seat behind me. "That is, if you're running from the cops."

This is when I need the *Jaws* music. Adrenaline socks me in the stomach. My father checked in on me, he knows I'm gone, and he does the one thing I never thought he would do…he called the police.

"Crap!" I go to stand, but my backpack slips from my hand and drops to the ground with a loud clunk that echoes down the tiled walls. Deputy Heinz whips his gaze in my direction, and our eyes meet.

My heart beats so hard it nearly knocks the wind out of me. I've got to run. I've got to run now.

Deputy Heinz holds up his hand. "Stay there, Addison."

And have my father beat the hell out of me because the good deputy brings me home like a dog fetching a stick? Hell, no.

My feet angle toward the exit opposite of him. Once I get outside, I'll be safe. It's dark out. There's woods to the side, and then there's a busy restaurant on the other. I can lose him. I can hitch a ride into Bowling Green. I can escape.

Fear tastes bitter in my mouth as I suck in a deep breath. The deputy steps toward me, and I grab my backpack and sprint. He's yelling my name now. Shouting at me to stop. The fliers on the wall become a colorful blur as I push myself faster than I've ever gone before.

People are in front of me, but I don't care. My shoulder

slams into theirs, and I mumble apologies as I pass, but I can't stop. Pounding feet are too close behind and my eyes burn. I can't fail this time. I can't.

"Addison!"

I pump my arms as I near the exit. Five more steps, three more steps, two more…

A strong grip on my arm, I'm being pulled—away from the safety of the exit. The deputy—he has me. Down a hallway, then another turn and down another hallway then out a door. I'm outside. My heart thrashes through my chest, and a sob wracks my body. "Let me go!"

"Stop fighting, and come with me now."

The door clicks shut behind us, and I shiver at the cold and indifferent voice. We're in an alley in the back, and a utility light casts a glow over us. I look up and into the deepest brown eyes on the planet. This guy is taller than me, thick with muscle, doesn't appear much older than me, but there's a silent power about him that warns anyone within ten feet to allow a wide berth.

I've seen this guy before, a Reign of Terror member, but I don't know him. I'm vaguely familiar with some of the members since my best friend Breanna has been dating Razor. A chill runs through me as I can't decide if I should be thrilled it's not the deputy or if I should run back into the arms of law enforcement.

"Who are you?" I ask.

"I'm Dust. A friend of Razor's, and I was asked to watch over you. If you're looking to run, I'll help, but we have to leave now."

"Where?" I'm thankful my voice comes out stronger than I feel, as my knees are super weak.

"Wherever you want, but your friend Breanna's at the clubhouse. Do you want to start there?"

Breanna, my best friend. If I'm safe with anyone, it's with her.

"We don't have time for waffling. We go, or you walk back in. Take your pick."

Terrified of heading home, I make the easy choice. "Take me to Breanna."

CHAPTER 14

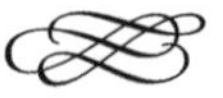

PIGPEN

Rapidly moving pieces don't make me happy. Especially when I haven't had time to study the rules of the game, and I hate it more when all my players aren't even on the field. In fact, most of my players are still listening to music in the locker room. Thank God Dust is in motion; otherwise, I probably would have lost the whole war. Losing the war is still a possibility, but at least now I have a fighting chance.

Even though we have problems, I'm slow maneuvering through the crowd in the clubhouse. Most people pat my back, call out for me to hang, even offer me beers. Though I'm in sloth mode as I slip out, I'm a man on a mission. There's no sense being dramatic and stomping my feet. I've found I get my way by being cool, calm and collected.

If you act like you don't give a damn, most of the time, people will hand you what you want. Must be some reverse psychology crap going on, but who knows.

Eli's in the same place I saw him last, on the steps of the house, soaking in his daughter from a distance. Emily's chatting with her friends. With the way Oz keeps looking at her and running his hand along her back, through her hair, it won't be long until he'll be searching for some time away from Eli's watchful eyes.

I cross the grass, and I gape at the sight of Eli and Chevy's mom sharing a casual conversation that includes some chuckles. This day is full of surprises.

I make a slow approach, go out of my way to step on a stick, slide my feet so that my footsteps are known. I was an Army Ranger and could go stealth at any point, but it's better in this scenario if they hear me coming. It'll break up this conversation faster.

Eli and Nina glance in my direction. Oddly, they're both grinning. I didn't know it was possible for either of them to show the slightest amount of happiness in each other's presence. The four horsemen of the apocalypse must be at my six because this is unreal. "What's up, chief?"

"Nothing much." Eli sets down his beer, and we share a short clasp of hands.

I nod toward Nina, and she nods back. While she's fought with most people in the club, the two of us have never had problems. She's aware my heart has always belonged to these kids.

I need to talk to Eli alone, so I go direct. "I'm grumpy, Eli."

Both of his eyebrows rise because that's the equivalent of me announcing someone has a gun to my head.

I shrug my shoulders in fake annoyance. "I thought we were friends, and I've been waiting at that bar all night for you to buy me a beer, and nothing. You're a terrible friend."

"You men are strange," Nina says in a light tone, and I offer her a wink and a lopsided grin because I don't disagree.

Reading my intent clearly, both Eli and Nina stand. Nina smooths out her jeans, looks at me and then offers Eli a shy glance. "Thank you for keeping me company."

"Are you leaving?" Eli asks, and I need to pinch myself because it almost sounded as if he wants her to stay.

"I didn't take tonight off, just told them I'd be in late." Nina's a bartender in town.

"Do you want someone to ride in with you?" Eli rubs a hand over his head like he's a nervous teenager. That's interesting.

There's a slight roll of her eyes. So slight, it was hard to catch, but it was there. "I've been a big girl capable of taking care of myself for a long time, but thank you for the offer. You gentlemen have a good evening." She doesn't look at either of us like we're gentlemen, and that's what is admittedly sexy.

Nina's not my type—not when I'm stuck on an English teacher who's out of my league—but Eli's still looking. I shove my hands in my pockets and wait. Eli will eventually stop staring at Nina as she walks away, and the build-up to this is worth it.

One second toward busting his balls. Two seconds toward busting his balls. Three...it continues long enough that when Eli slowly swings his attention to me, the smile on my face tastes like a full steak dinner with apple pie for dessert. À la mode because ice cream makes everything better.

Once he meets my eyes, his head drops. I love my life.

"Chevy's mom?" I say with the right amount of *Nina and Eli sitting in a tree* without having to sing the *k-i-s-s-i-n-g*.

"You're annoying," Eli responds.

I didn't know it was possible, but I smile wider. "Yeah, I get that lot. Not to spoil this moment, but we've got problems."

"What size problems?"

He's going to love this. "Mia Ziggler-size problems. The

type that fit on the back of a motorcycle and will be here in about five minutes."

Any trace of humor on his face is gone in a flash, and back is the man who knows how to hide bodies. "Mind filling me in?"

Sad part? "I honestly don't know much other than I've got an eighteen-year-old girl with bruises who just tried to run away from home via bus. The police showed at the station, and now she's on the back of Dust's bike, and she's on her way here. Don't know about you, but here I thought with the rug rats graduating, our life was going to get boring."

He grunts. "Why would you think that?"

I shrug an I-don't-know. "Stupidity, I guess. Real question should be how do we want to play this out?"

"Carefully," he says. "As careful as it gets."

Agreed.

CHAPTER 15

ADDISON

I did not enjoy that motorcycle ride. It was too fast, too cold, too frightening. It was nauseating and absolutely out of control, and I don't like out of control. I like things in their place, I like things in order, I like knowing that I have some sort of ability to save myself if needed, and on the back of that bike, it was chaos.

Dust pulls off the gravel road and turns off his motorcycle. I'm super quick sliding off, and Dust snatches my arm as I stumble and almost faceplant. The moment I'm steady, he lets go and I back away from him, rubbing the spot he touched. I don't like people touching me, especially guys.

In the distance, beyond the woods are lights and the sounds of people laughing and talking. This must be the infamous Reign of Terror clubhouse. "Why are we parked so far away?"

"To give you a chance to regain your land legs without an audience. I figured this was your first time on a bike, and the first ride can leave you shaky."

He's right. My legs tremble beneath me as if I were a newborn foal. Dust swings his leg over his bike then leans against the seat, crosses his arms over his chest and stares at me. I stare back because it's obvious he's waiting on me, and I don't know what he's waiting for.

Breanna has mentioned Dust before. She doesn't know too much about him other than he's one of the youngest members of the Reign of Terror. He has a nice build. Not the overpowering type, and not too lean. Just the right amount of muscle in his arms. He has brown hair that makes me think of the sand down at the lake, and he looks relaxed in his black biker vest, jeans, and brown work boots.

"What do you do for a living?" I ask.

Surprise flickers over his face. "What?"

Okay, sure, that was out of nowhere, but I'm curious because he's in the Reign of Terror motorcycle club, and Breanna keeps going on and on about how they don't do illegal things. I want to know if the guy I just ran from the police with is a felon. "What do you do for a living?"

"I'm a welder."

Wow. That was…unexpected.

"I also fix cars part time. Will that do, or would you like a more formal resume in order for me to walk you to the clubhouse?"

Hardy har-har. "So, you don't work for the security company?"

"No."

"Why?"

"Because I don't like guns."

Yep, that brings me up short.

"Can we go now?"

I start walking along the gravel road, toward the lights and the laughter, and Dust keeps step alongside me. The woods surrounding us are dark, pitch black, an eerie sight that makes me uncomfortable.

When I reach Breanna, she'll have questions, plenty of

questions, and I won't know how to answer a single one. My lips purse as I realize none of what's happening is making sense. "Do you know why I was at the bus terminal?"

"Do you?" he counters.

"Yes." I graduated today and decided I couldn't take living in my house with my abusive father one more second. I wait for Dust to level me with the millions of questions people typically ask, but there's only stark silence and I don't know if I like it. "You aren't going to ask for specifics?"

"I figure if people want you to know something, they'll tell you. Otherwise, leave them alone."

"Why were you at the bus terminal?"

"Because Pigpen told me to follow you."

That's creepy and causes me to go slower. Breanna has mentioned that Pigpen is this hot, twenty-something guy in the club who is super close with Razor, and it's weird that this Pigpen guy knows me. "Why?"

He shrugs. "Ask him."

"Do you always do what you're told to do?"

"No."

"So why did you follow me?"

"You ask a lot of questions."

"Because I have a lot of questions," I press. "I'm someplace I don't know with a complete stranger. Questions will happen. At least they should. Why did you follow me?"

Dust halts and stares down at me. "Do you want me to take you back to the bus station? Is that where you want to be?"

I don't know where I want to be. I just know that I don't want to be home. His question makes me feel small, and when it's clear I'm not going to say anything, he starts walking again. I follow and speed up until I'm by his side again. "Are you sure Breanna's here?"

"She was earlier, but if she's not we'll have Razor hook

you up with her somehow," he says. "And in case you're curious, I don't think you should go home with her. I realize that familiar would seem safe, but it won't be. If you're trying to stay under the radar, you can't do what's expected of you. Running to your best friend's house? Expected. My advice is to crash here for the night. Eli's daughter Emily is in town, and Violet's staying the night with her. I bet you could stay in the cabin with them."

"Why are you helping me?"

He stops walking again, stares up at the stars in the sky then down at the ground. "Eli and Pigpen once picked me up from a bus station. Doing so saved my life."

"How?" I whisper, desperate to know if he understands the line of crazy I walk on a daily basis. Because that would be a comfort—to know I'm not alone.

"Ask me again some other time," he says. "Maybe I'll tell you then. Maybe I won't."

"Tell me now," I push.

"Do you want to know why I followed you when Pigpen asked me to?"

I want the answer to the other question more, but knowing he won't give it to me, I nod. Any information is better than none.

"I followed you because evidently you have people in your life who are worried about you, and those people are connected to the club. I offered you a ride on my bike because from the moment I saw you interact with you dad at graduation, well...."

He shuts his mouth and somehow his not finishing the sentence makes me edgy. I try to trace through every interaction I had with my father and think of what he might have seen. I wince at the memory and absently rub my arm where Dad had grabbed me.

"I've been through anger," Dust continues in a soft voice.

Softer than I would have thought possible for a rough guy like him. "I'm helping you because no one else should be pushed to the point that I was, and I'm trying to help you figure out your problems without it having to go as south as it did for me."

There's a weird buzzing sensation in my head as I look into the eyes of a stranger, and see for the first time someone who understands the madness in my mind. "What's going to happen to me?"

"That's up to you, but first you need to know your options. So, let's walk to the clubhouse, find your friend, and take this one step at a time. Until you decide your next move, I'll stick around the clubhouse in case you decide you want to bail. I always feel better knowing I have an out."

Relief shoots through me and I could hug him for his offer, for this gift. He's not the only one who feels more secure knowing there's a way to leave. That's the only way I know how to survive.

CHAPTER 16

ELI

Pigpen and I sit on the picnic table Emily had been on earlier, and the two of us watch as Razor listens to his girlfriend, Breanna. They're on the front porch, and her head and hands move as she speaks. Razor's one hundred percent locked onto her every word, nodding occasionally, and his shoulders are squared like he's ready to jump off the porch and throw the punch that will start a gang war. The kid's quiet by nature, so the silence on his end isn't unusual, but what hits my stomach is the intensity of his eyes. Evidently nothing she's saying is good.

Breanna just spent thirty minutes inside Cyrus's cabin with her friend Addison, and from the hopelessness on Breanna's face, Addison didn't leave because her father asked her to clean her room.

"If this is as bad as I think, Addison needs to leave her home." There's no joke to Pigpen now, and when he's serious, my skin crawls with the sensation that death's not too far behind.

"I know," I say.

"We can call the county extension for domestic abuse," he continues. "They'll come get her and take her to a shelter, but I think us taking her out of town will be the better option."

I know that, too. "She doesn't trust us."

"Mia didn't know me, and she got on the back of my bike."

"But Dust trusted us, and she only left town with you because he told her that you'd lay down your life to protect her." Truer words have never been and will never be spoken. When Pigpen's sworn to protect someone, no one could ask for a better guardian.

Breanna stops talking, and Razor pulls her in for a comforting hug, the type that offers strength and security. The type that hopes to hide how bad the situation really is.

Pigpen readjusts beside me. "I keep waiting for that kid to catch a break."

"Razor's only hurting because he cares. That's not a bad thing."

"No, but I want something to be easy for the kid. Maybe he could have two months without his heart being torn out."

Pigpen watches Razor, and the guilt and the pain Pigpen keeps buried deep slips out into his expression. I can't help but wonder if, in all these years, Pigpen's had two hours without having *his* heart ripped out. "Razor's pain isn't your fault."

Not at all interested in what I have to say, Pigpen leans forward, rest his arms on his thighs and rubs his hands together.

"Do you ever think of telling Razor the truth about why you came to Snowflake? The reason you joined the Reign of Terror?"

The glare he sends me would make lesser men piss their pants, but I don't flinch.

"Why would I do that?" he demands.

Because I love Pigpen like a brother, and while I respect what brought him here, I had hoped that through the years, he'd find a way to forgive himself for a sin he never committed. "Razor can handle the truth."

"Maybe I can't."

Razor draws back from Breanna, mumbles something to her then leaves her there as he jogs down the stairs. His path is straight to us, and when he stops in front of the picnic table, he appears as grim as the reaper himself.

"How bad?" I ask.

"Addison's father is Satan, and she wants to run away."

That much I already knew. "Does she have a plan?"

Razor shakes his head. "Not one that Breanna could get out of her. Breanna told her what you said, Eli, about the club wanting to help, but Addison's scared. She's not sure if she should listen to what we have to say, much less take our advice."

I don't blame her distrust. Most people aren't trained to look at bikers as people who want to help or people you should accept help from.

"I have to get Breanna home soon," Razor says. "Her parents asked for her to be back by one, and I'd like to show them respect. Plus, if she doesn't go home and Addison's parents contact Breanna's parents, it won't take long for Addison's father to connect the dots."

That gives Addison an hour with someone she trusts. For a girl going through huge problems, that's not a lot of time. "Is there somebody else we could bring by? Another friend? A family member?"

Razor shrugs. "Besides Breanna? She has lunch with Violet at school, but they keep each other at a distance. There's no one else she keeps close."

Pigpen stands and digs his keys out of his pocket. “I can help with this.”

A thousand questions form on the tip of my tongue, but I stay silent. If Pigpen says he has a solution, he does. My brother, if anything, is loyal and solid.

CHAPTER 17

PIGPEN

A few hacks into the right website and it took me less than ten minutes to find out where Caroline Whitlock lives. Public schools don't have the best internet security. Security costs money, and considering they can't afford text books, I'm guessing secure online databases weren't in the cards. It's a shame, and I make an entry in my mental to-do list to volunteer my services next week.

I park my bike in front of the small Cape Cod and cut the engine. It's a tiny brick place at the end of a cul-de-sac. Manicured, well maintained, and close to every inch of the yard is filled with bushes and flowers. It's Eden in a neighborhood where there isn't much individuality. If this is what the front looks like, I'm curious about what's inside.

Rosebushes line the stone path to the front door. Red, white, pink and orange. The red rose at the graduation was the right call as it's evident Ms. Whitlock likes flowers.

Too bad what I'm about to do will ruin any chance I had with her. I'm guessing she's not going to be a fan of a near-stranger knocking on her door close to midnight and even less a fan of that stranger begging her to hop on the back of his bike, but I don't have much of a choice. An eighteen-year-old girl is in pain, and she's more important than me.

On Ms. Whitlock's front stoop, I take a moment to grieve the loss of my dreams for the past four years. As I'm all too aware, some things aren't meant to be.

I swipe at the number I was able to find through a few clicks online, and there's a ring. Another. Then another. On the fourth, a groggy voice fills the line. "Hello?"

I briefly close my eyes. She sounds so damn sexy, and this is probably the only time I'll ever hear that perfect voice at midnight.

"Caroline Whitlock?" I ask.

"This is she."

"This is..." Road name isn't going to help, but there's also no point in lying. "Abel Campbell. This evening, a student of yours, Addison, tried running away from home. We haven't returned her to her parents because we believe she's not safe at home. We have some resources in place that can possibly help, but she needs someone she can trust to help her make decisions. I'm hoping you're that person."

There's shifting on her end, and light streams from the window upstairs. "Is Addison okay?"

"Yes, and we'd like to make sure she stays that way, but as I said, she needs someone she can trust, and I think that might be you."

"Who is this *we* you keep referring to? And how do you know Addison, and how did you get this number and—"

I inwardly groan because there's a part of me that really thought I had a shot with her. A slim hope, but it was a stupid, pathetic, road-worn hope. "I'm Pigpen with the Reign of Terror Motorcycle Club. Addison's best friend, Breanna, dates a member of our club. You know him. Thomas Turner. We helped Addison out of a bad situation tonight. Now she's at our clubhouse and she's scared to return home, but she's also scared because, besides Breanna, she doesn't know any of us. We want to help Addison, but before we can do that, we need to make her feel safe. Can you help us with that?"

There's a long pause on her end. Long enough, I glance at my cell to see if she hung up. She hasn't, but that doesn't mean she's going to agree.

"Where's your clubhouse?" she asks.

"Out of town off the state road. It's tricky to find at night by yourself when you don't know where you're going."

"Just give me directions, and I'll—"

"Addison doesn't have time for that. I'm already here, at your house. Why don't you get ready and then you can follow me to the clubhouse?"

Another long pause, and I wait for her to disconnect and call the police.

"Why are you at my house?"

Simple. "Because if you didn't answer your cell, I was going to knock. Addison needs help, and I need you to help her."

"Can I say no?" she asks.

"Yes, but good luck looking at yourself in the mirror in the morning. From experience, not doing anything to stop a car from going over a bridge ruins the rest of your life."

CHAPTER 18

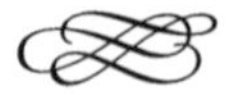

ADDISON

Even though the evening is warm, I'm cold to the bone, and no amount of clothing or blankets can thaw my frozen marrow. I perch on the window seat of the bedroom Breanna brought me into and watch as she rides away on the back of Razor's bike.

In theory, I'm not alone. Violet sits on the bed. We're friends...I guess. With Breanna attending private school this year, Violet and I bonded the way girls do when trapped in high school and surrounded by people who judge. Violet doesn't judge. I don't either. We aren't soul sisters, but at least I had someone to partner with in math.

I'm quiet. Violet is, too, and I appreciate that she's giving me the time to reflect on the Reign of Terror's offer, my life, my future and my fears.

A knock on the door, and adrenaline courses through my veins as my mouth dries out. The logical part of my brain screams that my reaction is exaggerated. That there's no way that's my father on the opposite side of the door. The four-year-old in me is cowering in fear because no matter where I hid in the house he found me. He always found me.

The door opens, and I breathe out when Dust appears. In his hands is a steaming mug of something. "Breanna mentioned that you like hot chocolate."

It's clear from how his eyes are locked on me that I'm the one he's speaking to, yet I glance over at Violet. She's watching me with curiosity. I glance back at him and shrug. "I do."

"I made some, if you want it. It's not the good stuff. Just the powdered mix kind."

Another glance at Violet and this time she's watching Dust with her eyebrows raised in disbelief. Maybe people around here don't make hot chocolate. While my stomach is so upset that I can't fathom eating or drinking a thing, I do like the idea of holding something hot. And I also like the idea of Dust walking in.

It doesn't make sense. I don't know him. He doesn't know me, but my gut tells me I can trust him. That if I asked him to take me from this place, he would. Unfortunately, there's a familiarity about the pain in his beautiful blue eyes. It's the same ache I see whenever I look in the mirror. I wish nobody understood my pain and my fear, but I think he does, and that helps me feel less alone.

"That would be great," I say. "Thank you."

He's slow crossing the room, watching the mug as if he's terrified he'll spill a drop. When he reaches me, he meets my eyes again, and the concern there touches my heart. It's weird that a stranger cares. So many people through the years have seen the signs, yet still turned their heads in the opposite direction. Scared they read between the lines wrong, scared to get involved, scared to know the truth.

Dust hands me the mug, his fingers brush mine and electricity rushes through my veins. I lower my head as my cheeks fill with warmth, and I cradle the mug in my hands. "Thank you."

"You're welcome," he replies.

I'd like him to stay. I'd like him to sit on the other end of the window seat. I'd like to pretend I was a normal girl on the night of her high school graduation. What is it that normal girls would be doing on a night like tonight? Staying out until sunrise? Skinny-dipping with friends? Kissing a boy a little too long and a little too much? Pushing delicious boundaries?

I sigh heavily. I am pushing boundaries. My boundaries. There's just not anything delicious about it.

A motorcycle engine revs, and then the sound of a car engine catches my attention. I watch as the motorcycle flies past where all the other bikes are parked and stops in front of the house. My forehead furrows as the car follows and parks close by.

I start to shake as panic sets in. They lied. They called my father. They've doomed me to hell. They've....

The mug in my hands becomes weighted, and I glance down to find Dust's hands steadying it. My hands had been shaking, I'm still shaking, and I allow him to take the mug from me.

"It's just Pigpen," Dust says. "He's brought someone he thinks can help, but if whoever it is makes you uncomfortable, I'll make them leave."

I believe him, and there's a comfort in knowing that he's on my side.

The screen door to the house squeaks open, there's multiple footsteps and I freeze at the sight of the woman standing in the doorway. It's one of the few adults in my life who have questioned my bruises, my hesitancy, my fear. She's the lone adult, until now, who hasn't accepted my answers. It's my English teacher. It's Ms. Whitlock.

One look at me and the crumpled expression on her face as if she's ready to cry causes an ache in my chest. I'm breaking, she sees it, and I wonder how long it will be until the pieces that are me tumble and shatter on the floor.

Ms. Whitlock enters, everyone else leaves, and as she sits on the window seat next to me. I have a choice to make, and in reality, I've already made it. It's just time for me to accept my unknown fate. I take a deep breath, and I do something I've never done before—I tell someone the truth.

CHAPTER 19

ELI

Edgy.

Those of us who understand the ticking time bomb of a situation currently hanging out in the bedroom of the cabin are teetering on that tense line. We can't make the decision for Addison. It's one she has to make on her own. But if she doesn't accept the options we've offered her, we have no choice but to send her home, and the odds of her surviving that either emotionally or physically intact are small.

That's the problem with free will—there's always the possibility people will choose wrong.

The picnic table shifts as Emily sits next to me on top of it. Her feet rest like mine on the bench. She hesitantly smiles at me, and I offer a sad smile back. When I was eighteen, I was desperately in love with her mother. I never imagined I could love anyone as much as I loved Meg. I was wrong. I had yet to have a child. Now, I can't imagine loving anyone more than I love my daughter.

"What's going on?" she asks. "And don't say nothing, because it's something."

"It's something, but it's not my something to tell."

She nods like she understands, and I hope she does. I made a lot of mistakes with Emily. Some of it due to my keeping secrets from her. I thought I was helping her, saving her, but all my lying hurt her in the end. Emily's given me a second chance, and I don't have plans to screw that up. That means being honest with her when I can, and hoping she understands that while I have no intention of keeping my secrets from her, I can't spill the secrets entrusted to me from other people.

"Are you having a good time?" I ask.

"Yeah. Due to whatever is going on in there with Addison," she motions toward the cottage, "Oz offered to let me stay the night at his house. Rebecca said she's fine with it. Breanna said Addison's hanging out in my room, and I don't want to disturb her."

"That would be a good idea." I make a mental note to threaten Oz's life before they leave to make him think twice about going too far with my daughter.

"Did you love Mom?" Emily asks, and that question was like being hit with an electric cattle prod.

"What?"

Emily's dark eyes bore into mine, and there's so much sincerity there that I'm screwed. "Did you love my mom?"

I nod before I have the ability to speak. "Yes." Deeply and always.

"Are you still in love with her?"

I lower my head because that question physically hurt. Like a bullet through my chest. No point in lying because it's written all over my face. "Yes."

Emily goes to say something else, but I stop her because I don't want to be sucker-punched in the jaw again. "It doesn't matter. Your mom is happy with your dad." He adopted Emily when I was in prison, and he deserves the privilege of being called her dad. He earned that and my respect by taking care of Emily when I couldn't. "And that's all I've ever wanted for you and your mom—for you two to be happy."

"Are you happy?" she counters.

"Yes." Without a doubt. "You're in my life, Emily. I couldn't ask for anything more."

Her expression softens at this, and she leans in and places her head on my shoulder. My soul that's forever troubled settles. There's something I can't explain that comes with the love a daughter gives a father. It makes all the parts of me that are sharp smooth.

"Can I ask you something else?" The uncertainty in her voice makes me want to drop the f-bomb over what's to come, but because I'm determined to keep my relationship with Emily growing, I move my fingers in a "bring it" motion.

She lifts her head and nibbles on her bottom lip as if she's thinking, and that's not good for me. My daughter is smart, determined and resourceful. Somehow my happiness being on her radar feels a lot like walking the green mile of death row.

"Have you thought about dating?" she asks.

I have to work hard to keep from smiling. "I date."

She rolls her eyes. "So I've heard, but I'm not talking about that type of dating. I'm talking about dating someone to maybe fall in love. I guess I'm asking if you allow yourself the possibility of liking someone."

I pull on my earlobe because while I should be able to easily answer that question, I can't. "So you know, dating and love don't mean happy. You can live a happy and fulfilled life without being married or in a relationship."

"I know," she says. "But I'm asking if you're not in a relationship because that's what makes you happy or because you haven't given yourself an opportunity to try."

And I've hit my limit. "Can we stop talking about my love life?"

Emily laughs, and I can't help the lift of my lips. She hops off the table, and I stand. I then kiss the top of her head and bring my daughter into a hug. She hugs me in return and when she pulls back, she says, "I saw you talking with Chevy's mom."

My smile falls. "What's that have to do with anything?"

"Emily," Oz calls from his bike. "You ready?"

"I'll text you when I reach Oz's," Emily says.

No, I want to know. "What does that have to do with anything?" I call out as Emily walks away.

She glances over her shoulder at me then walks backwards so she can see me. "You were smiling when you talked to her."

I shrug. "I smile at people."

She snort-laughs. "No, you don't."

"I smile," I push, and she only laughs again.

"Bye, Dad." And she turns to head toward the man she loves—Oz.

I'm dumbfounded and mute for several reasons. One, she's right—except with a chosen few, I don't smile. Two, Emily called me Dad. While I wasn't prepared to have a daughter up in my business, I wouldn't trade a moment with her for the world. Then my thoughts wrap back around to the fact I can't deny: I smiled.

CHAPTER 20

PIGPEN

Dust and I sit at the kitchen table in silence. I'm straining to hear any indication of which way this situation's heading. Dust stares at the nothingness of air. Guilt festers between my tendons. I should have thought harder before dragging him into this. By asking him to play along, I tossed him into a replay of some of the worst moments of his life.

"Eli and I have this if you want to bail," I say.

Dust doesn't move a single muscle other than to grant me a side-eye.

"I'm serious," I say.

"I told Addison I'd stick around until she makes her decision. Plus, if you offer her what I think you're going to offer her, you'd have no choice but to involve me."

He's right. The solution we intend to give Addison, if she chooses to talk to us about her problems, involves something very personal to him, and we would never disrespect him by leaving him out. "But if you need a few hours off—"

"I'm not going anywhere."

I've got nothing to say to that. I roll my neck and cross

my arms over my chest. "Ms. Whitlock still looks great even when she rolls out of bed. I swear to God she's part mermaid or something."

"Mermaid?" He looks at me like I'm insane. I'm used to the expression.

"Didn't mermaids tempt men? Lured them in with their beauty?"

"They're part fish."

I shrug. "And I said *or something.*"

Dust grants me another side-eye, and I wonder what it would have been like to kiss her at least once. Now, I'll never know.

The door to the bedroom opens, and both Dust and I stand. Ms. Whitlock in all her supernatural beauty sweeps in with Addison under the shelter of her arm. "Addison and I talked, and we have questions. A lot of questions."

"And we'll answer them," I say. "Each and every one."

CHAPTER 21

ADDISON

If I leave, I'm heading to Louisville. There I'll be staying at a house supported by a woman's shelter that's only for teenagers like me. No longer a minor, but not old enough to be truly independent. In theory, the people there will help me navigate breaking free from my father. They'll mentor me, counsel me and help me figure out how to earn my degree while working to support myself.

I'm shaking like a leaf stuck on a tree during a hurricane. Occasionally, my teeth chatter. Judging by the sweat on the men in the cramped kitchen, it must be warm, but I'm frozen.

Ms. Whitlock rubs her hand along my back, but removes it when I flinch. "You're in shock," she whispers, but everyone hears.

I guess I am. This decision to leave frightens me to the core. "I don't know if I can do this. My father will find me."

"He won't," Dust says. My eyes flash to him as these are the first words he's said since I walked into the kitchen forty minutes ago.

"You don't know that," I respond.

"You're right." Eli leans forward on the table across from me. "We can't predict the future, but we can tell you that we believe in this program and they are committed to keeping you safe. If you aren't comfortable with this particular program in Louisville, we'll take you to wherever you are comfortable. There are women's shelters all over the state. If you don't want us to take you, we'll call them, and they'll come get you. The point of all this is for you to know you have options that don't include returning home."

Dust is shaking his head as if he's annoyed. "Your father won't find you."

"Dust," Eli snaps in a tone that would frighten me if I was the one in trouble, but Dust doesn't flinch.

"He won't," Dust repeats, and his insistence annoys me.

"You don't know that," I spit out. "And it's my life on the line."

"I do know it." Dust stares straight at me. "Because my dad didn't find my sister. He didn't find Mia, and he never will."

I blink so hard I swear it made a sound. "Mia? As in Mia Ziggler?"

Mia Ziggler is an urban legend in this town. A girl a few years older than me who was there one day and then the next she was on the back of a Reign of Terror bike and never seen again. Rumors were that the Reign of Terror had killed her and buried her body where it would never be found.

"Yes," Dust says. "And she's happy. She'll help you if you let her. I'll introduce you myself."

I blink several more times as the cold starts to subside and pieces click into place. Mia Ziggler is Dust's sister. Mia Ziggler left town on the back of a Reign of Terror motorcycle. The Reign of Terror stopped Mia and Dust from running away.

"Mia and I would be living on the streets if the club hadn't stepped in," Dust says. "You can trust us."

I return my attention to Eli. "Did you offer Mia the same deal that you're offering me?"

Eli glances over at Dust, as if searching for approval. Dust nods. "She'd be okay with you telling her."

"Yes and no," Eli says. "The program for girls under the age of twenty-one wasn't available yet, so we took her to a women's shelter where she got the help and support she needed."

"She graduated from college," Dust says, with a hint of pride that causes dangerous hope to flutter inside me. "And she just got married. She's happy now. She's healed."

Healed. The word is like a hug that I've never been given, but so desperately want.

Dust's words are pretty, but I have a hard time believing them. "Will you take us? Can I meet her?" Because if I make this leap, I need solid proof that someone else survived.

"Us?" Eli asks.

That brings me up short because I made an assumption, and before I can address Ms. Whitlock directly she places her hand over mine. "I'll go with you. You don't even have to ask. In fact, I insist you don't go alone."

I exhale in relief then look over at Dust, because it's not Eli who I want to take me, but him. He gives me a subtle nod. He just agreed, and I dare to let that spark of hope within me multiply.

CHAPTER 22

PIGPEN

Ms. Whitlock owns a Honda Civic. It's shiny black on the outside, and even though it's a few years old, it still has the fresh-out-of-the-showroom smell on the inside. I'm in the passenger side soaking in the glorious fact I'm in a confined space with the most beautiful woman in the world.

She's driving, and she likes driving fast. We're not in a hurry. In fact, if she keeps going at this rate, we'll be there early. But getting there in time isn't the reason her foot is pressed down on the gas. She likes the feel of going past the speed limit. Likes the challenge of weaving through traffic and controlling her own destiny. I know because the same fire lives inside me. Maybe if I'd had the time to play my cards right, we would have had a chance.

I glance at the backseat again and wonder if what's going on there is a picture of what could have happened or the start of something bigger. One barely eighteen-year-old and the other not even twenty. Addison had fallen asleep against the window ten minutes into the drive. Doubt she meant it to happen, but it did. Through the ride, she's shifted until her head came to rest on Dust's shoulder.

At first, he looked as scared as a rabbit facing a freeway, but then he relaxed, placed his head back against the seat, and he's also down for the count. Since falling asleep, Dust's head has angled toward Addison, as if in sleep, he subconsciously wants to be closer.

I've known Dust since before he became a member of the club, and he's not the type to let girls hang all over him. While he says Mia has healed from their past, I'm not sure he has. Maybe, just maybe, helping Addison can push him into the land of the living.

I return my attention to the road, and I'm surprised to catch Ms. Whitlock sneaking a peak at me.

"You okay?" I ask. "Do you need to stop off somewhere for coffee? It'll be my treat."

"I'm fine," she says. "Are you okay? Do you need caffeine?"

"Naw. Sleep's overrated." And I'm not ready for conversation with her to be over. "Thanks for driving."

"You're welcome." She tucks her silky hair behind her ear. "I'm going to be honest. I didn't think you'd agree to my driving."

"Dust's been up for too long. I wouldn't have trusted Addison on the back of his bike, and it's not like Dust, Eli or I had a four-door available."

She smirks, and I try to memorize how beautiful she looks with that snarky expression.

"What?" I push to figure out her mind.

"I didn't mean it that way. I thought you would demand that a man drive the car."

"It's your car."

"Yes, but that never stopped any man I was dating from telling me he should be the driver."

"Sounds like you were dating the wrong people."

Her head jerks in my direction, but she recovers quickly and watches the road. We ride long enough in silence again that I start to rack my brain for possible subjects to discuss.

She clears her throat once, then again. "I never knew Mia was being abused."

My spine straightens because I'm not into gossip, but I understand her sad undertone. Guilt is a mean beast. "Not many people did."

"If I had known, I would have helped."

"I believe you." Because I do. "We just got to her first."

"The Reign of Terror aren't as bad as everyone says, are they?"

I don't know how to answer that because we aren't Boy Scouts. "We help where we can, and never mean harm where we can't."

She drums her fingers against the steering wheel. "You introduced me as Ms. Whitlock to your associates. I'm comfortable with your calling me Caroline."

"Caroline." I say the name as if it's a gift, which it is. "It's nice to officially meet you. My friends call me Pigpen, but if you want, you can call me Abel."

She turns her head in my direction again, and I stop breathing when her gorgeous blue eyes sparkle at me. "It's nice to meet you, Abel. And thank you not only for helping Addison, but for involving me. I'm afraid I've held some misguided notions about your club, and for that I apologize."

A smile slides across my face, and I feel like I was just reborn. "That's okay. Maybe one day when we aren't trying to save the world we can meet up, and I can tell you more about the club." Then I realize how forward that sounded, and what bad form it was for the situation we're in. "For educational purposes, of course."

She has a cute laugh. One I wouldn't have expected, but like all the same.

"For educational purposes, I'll accept."

Cloud nine. That's what I'm on, and I have no intention of ever touching the ground again.

CHAPTER 23

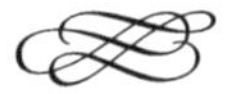

ELI

Sitting in the Adirondack chair on the front porch of Dad's cabin, I drink from the mug full of coffee. It's ten-thirty in the morning, and not one of us in the house got enough sleep. After Pigpen left with Addison, Dust and Ms. Whitlock, I stole a couple of hours in one of the beds at the clubhouse. I had considered heading back to my apartment in town, but it wasn't worth the drive in to turn around and drive back.

I'm at the clubhouse and Dad's cottage so much that Dad's told me to move in. I think about it at times. With Mom now gone, I know he's lonely, but there's been something holding me back. Something I've never looked too hard at, and after that conversation with Emily, I'm starting to take a peek. Maybe I hold onto my own place in the hopes I'll someday have someone special to bring there, someplace to make a home.

On the arm of the chair is my cell, and I glance down at it for the hundredth time. I'm waiting on a message from Pigpen telling me that Addison has decided to save her life and accept the offer being presented to her. I'm also waiting on a text from Chevy informing me that he and Isaiah are on their way.

Uneasiness swirls through me. Isaiah—my brother's son. I want to meet him. More than want, I need to meet him, but nothing about this is going to be easy for any of us or for him. He's a man now—young, but a man all the same. Working a job as a mechanic, and from what I understand, not just any mechanic. He's some sort of genius with custom cars. Isaiah has made a life for himself, and Dad and I—this entire club—we want in.

There's no reason for him to give us a shot, but I'm going to ask for one all the same.

A car engine rumbles in the distance, and Nina's two-door rounds the bend. She parks near the house and has my immediate attention as she slips out of the car. I'm used to Nina in her jeans and shirts, but it's one of the first times I've seen her in a dress. A cotton sundress at that. Red, form-fitting, and possibly the most mesmerizing outfit I've ever seen.

Nina shrugs a white sweater over her shoulders, and then she catches me staring. She slow blinks, but then there's a smile—one that's just as slow as her blink. I nod my head at her, and she waves at me then returns to gathering her purse from her front seat.

I rub my chin. Holy hell. How did this happen? Emily was right, I am smiling.

I stand as she starts up the stairs, and I meet her at the top. "Morning."

"Good morning. Chevy received a text from Isaiah a half hour ago telling him he was nearing town, so Chevy left to wait for him at the diner. I hope you don't mind, but I wanted to be here when Chevy and Isaiah showed."

"That's no problem. You look great by the way," I say, and

Nina, who had been slipping her car keys into her purse, snaps her head up. Our eyes meet, and though I know I should look away, I can't.

Nina flushes then tucks a stray strand of hair away from her face. "Thank you. I thought I should wear something nice but casual. It's not like there's wardrobe guidelines for a meeting like this. As in, 'Hi, I'm Nina. Chevy's mom and the other woman your father was sleeping with.'"

No, don't guess there is. "I appreciate your being here. Isaiah's going to have questions, and I want him to have answers." Even though it punches me in the gut to admit it.... "You knew my brother better than I did."

Nina's face softens, and I stop breathing when she reaches out and wraps her fingers around my wrist. "He loved you, Eli. James loved you all. Never doubt that."

Problem is, over the years since his death, I have doubted my relationship with him. But that doubt has slowly been receding as I've learned more of what my brother had done to protect me, my dad and this club during the last year of his life. Meeting Isaiah though, knowing he's going to demand answers to tough questions, that doubt has resurfaced. But having Nina here helps. She's an ally I never would have imagined having a year ago.

The rumble of a motorcycle engine approaches, and Chevy appears. Behind him is a black nineteen ninety-something Mustang that looks as if it just rolled off the assembly line. The motor has a loud growl, a pissed-off one, and I wonder if that's an omen.

Chevy parks, and the Mustang slides up beside him. Its door opens, and Isaiah, my nephew, slides out. My heart freezes in my chest, and when Nina's soft fingers slip from my wrist and link with mine, I immediately grip them in return. We hold onto each other in shared shock, in shared awe, in need of support. She's one of the few people who can understand the avalanche of emotions overwhelming me.

Standing in front of us is a mirror of my brother, of Nina's best friend, and it hurts like hell that this is the first time we've ever met.

CHAPTER 24

ADDISON

I have the third-wheel feeling as Dust hugs his older sister and Snowflake's own urban legend, Mia Ziggler. The third-wheelish feeling is because I'm not sure there's anyone in my life who family-loves me like Dust and Mia family-love each other. As in blood does mean something. It's obvious with just a few interactions, they would move heaven and earth for the other's happiness.

They step back from each other, and Mia smiles up at her brother with so much admiration that my chest aches with longing. I want to know what it's like to look at someone like that, and for someone to gaze at me with so much love in return.

Mia has short black hair that's cut in a razor sharp blunt edge angled toward her face. Sort of like a manic-pixie. She playfully shoves Dust's shoulder. "You don't text me back."

He shoves his hands in his pockets like the reprimand equal parts bothers him and was deserved. "I text back."

"A day later. That's so uncivilized."

Dust's only response is an adorable lift of the ends of his lips.

She turns to me, and gives a smile I wouldn't have thought possible from her if all that she went through in her childhood was true. "You must be Addison. Dust and Eli called and gave me a very brief rundown of your situation. I'm Mia."

"Nice to meet you," I say, and glance around the living room. It's an old house. A massive house. One with hardwood floors, huge windows and a winding staircase. There's laughter in the kitchen, the sound of girls my age, and upstairs I hear multiple feet and voices.

I shove my hands in my pockets, unsure where I fit into all of this.

Mia tilts her head, and the sympathy that seeps into her expression is hard to watch, because I know it's for me. "Did Dust tell you what this place is?"

I nod. It's a place for girls like me. Girls who are too old to be placed into state custody, but too young to make a fresh start without some help. It's a place that works with a woman's shelter. A place that Mia runs to help girls like me—girls who were like her.

"I have an opening," Mia says. "One of my girls, Neveah, just moved out, and that means Charity will need a roommate. Neveah's down the street in an apartment with friends from college. She's a junior and a nursing major. Watch out, she likes to talk gross, bloody things at dinner, and she plans on being here for dinner a lot."

Mia is friendly. Everyone so far has been friendly, but I'm so freaked out that I sort of want to run. Is new better? Am I going to be okay here?

"Do you want a tour of the place?" Dust says, and his deep voice gains my attention. "I helped with a lot of the renovations. I can show you what I've done."

He looks straight into my eyes, and the reassurance in his gaze is like a hug. I nod again. When he tilts his head toward the dining room, I follow and listen as he starts to tell me about drywall and flooring.

~

SITTING at the end of a long dining room table, I push my half-eaten plate of spaghetti and meatballs to the side and accept the packet of papers Mia's been going over for the past hour. The lunch was good, very good. A petite girl named Charity made it, and she was very nice and very welcoming and will be my roommate if I agree to all the terms and conditions being laid out for me now.

After a grace period of finding a job and getting on my feet, I'll be required to pay rent. The price is very reasonable, and helps with the upkeep of the house. In exchange for staying here, I will have chores, will be responsible for cooking dinner on rotation, and will have to follow all the rules listed on one of the papers—including a requirement that I participate in emotional counseling, financial counseling and career counseling.

Mia runs this house and the program, but lives next door with her husband. Despite sleeping under a different roof, she said, she remains our guide, our mentor, our house mother, a stern voice of reason and a friend—all available to us twenty-four hours a day, seven days a week.

"So, what do you think?" Mia says, and I stare down at the pieces of paper that are filled with printed words I'm too overwhelmed to comprehend.

Eli and Dust ate lunch with us, but disappeared outside after Mia started discussing details of the program. Ms. Whitlock has remained by my side. She's been wonderful. Asking questions that had been in my head, but I'm too paralyzed to ask. She has encouraged me with eye contact, or a gentle touch. Like now, as she places her hand over mine and squeezes.

Mia asked me a question, and I need to answer. Problem is, I don't know what to say. "Do you mind if I have a few minutes to myself?"

"Of course," she answers. "Take all the time you need."

"I'll be right here if you need me," Ms. Whitlock says.

I try to smile at her, but it must fall short because I don't feel movement on my face. I stand, leave the dining room and do my best to wave at the girls in the living room who say hi to me. The heavy front door squeaks as I open it, and I step out into the warm, spring day. It's weird for the sky to be so blue, so full of light, when my brain feels swamped by fog.

"Are you okay?" Dust asks. He leans against the railing of the porch, and he's so incredibly handsome that he takes my breath away.

Yes, no… "I don't know. All of this is…a lot."

"When Mia and I left home, we were scared to death. We felt that way for a while afterwards, too. There were times I never thought I'd feel safe again. I never imagined I would find a normal. But eventually I did find a normal, and I found safe."

Exhausted and heavy, I drop onto the top step of the porch and think of home. I think of my room, I think of my mom and I think of all the things I love, and I'm overwhelmed by grief.

But then I think of my father's anger if I were to return, of his harsh voice, of the way he'd raise his hand at me and…I shiver. My head falls into my hands, and I wish it were six months from now. I don't know what will be solved in six months, but six months wouldn't be today. And six months from now has to be better, right?

"What happened to you?" I mumble through my fingers

then lift my head. "Mia said the woman's shelter helped her. What happened to you?"

Dust closes the distance between us then sits on the step next to me. Not right next to me. He leaves about three inches in between us, but he's just the right amount of close. As if he's practiced in finding the perfect comfortable space for someone like me.

"Eli talked a family in the club into taking me in," Dust says. "They fostered me until I turned eighteen then let me live with them until I could support myself."

It makes more sense now. "And then you joined the club?"

"And then I joined the club," he confirms.

We're in a quiet neighborhood. The type where even the squirrels are mute. A car ambles by, doing the speed limit, and I wonder if Dad hit me so hard that I died.

I swallow and tell Dust the truth, because I think he'll understand. "I'm scared."

"I was, too, but I'm not anymore. I understand that relying on strangers is terrifying, but the people Mia is going to introduce you to are the real deal. They want to help. You just have to decide to let them in."

I breathe in deeply, then let out an even longer breath. When will life be easy?

"The unknown is scary," Dust says. "It'll help if you have some 'known' to pull you through. I'll drag Razor and Breanna up once a week to visit you, and I've heard you and Violet have become closer. I can bring her up, too."

I nibble on my bottom lip. Razor and Breanna will be in Snowflake for a few weeks, but they plan on leaving soon for the northeast. Breanna wants to be settled in before she starts her fancy Ivy League university, and Razor is supposed to be opening a new MC chapter and expanding the security company. Violet will visit, but she and Chevy are planning on a road trip before they begin college in the fall.

"I'd like that," I say. "But if they aren't available, or can't come, will...you?"

"Yes," he says. "As long as you want me, I'll visit."

I close my eyes, as this is the first time in months that I feel like I've heard something I can truly trust. "Thank you."

"Anytime."

I reopen my eyes, and Dust and I fall into a comfortable silence as we stare out at the world. It's weird how things change, how plans fall apart then new ones come together. Twenty-four hours ago, I had plans to leave town and leave behind everything in my life. I had plans to be forever alone. Now? I might be able to keep some parts of my life, like my friends, and not be alone. And I have a new friend, and his name is Dust.

"It's going to be okay now, isn't it?" I ask.

"Yeah," he says, and he glances over at me as if I'm someone worth looking at. "It is."

CHAPTER 25

ELI

Isaiah likes Nina. Every time she talks, he pays attention, and he often cracks a grin. I don't blame him. The woman is a born storyteller. Better than any bar-hugging brother in the club can spin a tale. The way she talks about my brother James brings him to life so vividly that part of me expects to turn and find him walking from the clubhouse to join us.

His body might not be here, but with each story Nina tells, I can feel his spirit. For that, I will forever be grateful.

We sit in a circle of lawn chairs in the yard, near the clubhouse and under the shade of the trees. It's evening, the sun has started to set in the sky, and the white Christmas lights hanging from the limbs above us twinkle.

Beside me, Nina leans forward in her chair and is explaining how James used to beg her to cut class in high school, and how one time, when things went bad on their way out of school, they spent an entire class period hidden in the boys' locker room to keep from getting caught. Isaiah laughs at parts of the story, and he reaches over and takes his girlfriend Rachel's hand.

It was an unconscious movement. One he makes often. Touches her when he has a burst of emotion. He gravitates toward her and she's always there. An ever-present rock. Rachel's shorter than Isaiah, and at first glance, she appears as if she could be fragile. But it didn't take us long to realize that if we looked at Isaiah the wrong way, she'd take us out faster than a sniper in a war zone.

Good thing for us, she likes Nina's stories as well. Rachel also took to Cyrus. She was gracious enough to flip through my mom's photo albums full of baby pictures of my brother and me, and Rachel was a willing ear for Cyrus's long-winded stories of our misspent youth.

It's been a good day, but it's gone by too fast. I was grateful when Isaiah agreed to stay for lunch, and even more grateful he's agreed to stay for dinner. Oz's parents, Rebecca and Man O' War, and Razor's dad and soon-to-be stepmom are manning the grill. The scent of barbecue lingers in the air and causes my mouth to water.

Oz, Razor, Violet and Breanna have been beelining it back and forth between the kitchen and the long row of picnic tables they put together with dishes, cups and large trays of sides. Everyone has stayed back to give me, Dad, Nina, Emily, and Chevy the opportunity to talk with Isaiah and Rachel.

The teens laugh hysterically at the ending of Nina's story. With a dazzling smile on her face, Nina glances over in my direction, and I nod back in gratitude. She's the reason this day has been a success.

"Dinner will be ready soon!" Rebecca calls from the picnic tables, and that's our cue to start moving in the direction of the food.

Most everyone stands, and Rachel attaches herself to Emily's side, asking her to explain again the events of last summer when I was shot. Emily recounts the story for the second time, telling the truth at every turn, while reassuring Rachel that she feels safe being around the club and that she and Isaiah should feel safe, too.

We've been honest with Isaiah and Rachel. Emily has taught me to do that. There are ugly things in my past, ugly parts of the club's history, but we're trying to do better going forward. Isn't that all any of us can do?

Chevy wraps an arm around Violet's shoulder as the two of them and Cyrus head for the picnic tables. I glance over, and I'm surprised to find Isaiah still in his seat. I imagine the world finds him terrifying. Tall, tattoos, broad-shouldered, earrings, black shirt, ripped blue jeans and boots built to kick.

Isaiah intimidates me, not because of his appearance, but because he's my nephew— close to a grown man—and I want so badly for him to like this family. He may not need us, but we need him. Badly. So much has happened over the past eighteen years; so much has happened in the past year alone. It's time for the bruises and cuts to mend, and I'd like him to be a part of that healing.

"Thank you for coming out," I say. "It's meant a lot to this family." To me.

Isaiah shifts forward, the pose indicating a man on a hunt for real knowledge. "Is it true? None of you had any idea about me?"

Cyrus and Nina have both told him the truth already, but if I were him, I'd be doing the same thing—digging deeper.

"The way I see it," Isaiah continues, "everyone around here looks at you as their leader. It's nothing they said, nothing they overtly did, but it's the subtle stuff that matters. A leader is who people look at when someone cracks a joke or when a moment gets serious. The glance is quick. Most people don't notice they do it or when someone else does it, but it's there, and they all look at you."

I'm not sure what to say to that, so I'm grateful he keeps going. "I need to know, man to man, did any of you know about me?"

He's asking if we ignored his existence when his father died. That death left him and his mom alone. He's asking if we denied him a home after his mother went to prison and he was dumped into foster care.

I pull on my earlobe then mirror his position. "Isaiah, blood means everything to this family. If we had known about you, we would have brought you and your mother here and we would have taken care of both of you. If we had found out about you later, after your mother went to prison, there's no doubt Cyrus would have taken you in. But because we didn't know about you, we're on the losing end of this. You're too old for us to swoop in and take you in, but we want you here all the same. But the choice is yours. We want you to be a part of this family. I want you to be a part of this family, and I hope you'll allow us to be part of yours."

Isaiah stares at me for a few beats, longer than most people can stand, then nods like he's come to some type of conclusion. I only hope it's in my favor. He stands, so do I and he extends his hand to me.

The warmth overtaking my body is as good as it felt the first time the doctors placed Emily in my arms. I take Isaiah's hand, we shake and when I pull him in for a quick hug, he leans in and gives me a pat on the shoulder. I draw back and cup the side of his head. "You're family now, and there's nothing we won't do for you. Anything, anytime."

A softening in his gray eyes as he does another nod in understanding.

"Ready for some food?" I say.

Isaiah chuckles. "Do you people always eat so much around here?"

On the picnic table is enough to feed an army, and I grin.

Rebecca must have given the signal for the club to arrive. "Hopefully you'll visit enough to figure out if it's too much food or not enough."

His eyebrows rise. "Not enough?"

Motorcycle engines rumble in the distance and I angle my head to the road. "You're about to find out. Isaiah, your world is about to get a lot bigger."

He smiles, just like my brother used to, and I start to make plans. Plans I hadn't thought I'd ever make—plans to build Isaiah his first motorcycle. He's a McKinley, and being around us, he's going to need it.

"What type of Harley do you like?" I ask him, and his forehead furrows.

"I'm more of a Mustang Man."

I shake my head at him. "That's because you've never been on a bike. We're going to have to change that."

"Fine, but if I do that, then you're taking out a fully loaded Cobra on a drag strip. Twenty bucks you'll be changing your mind on your mode of transportation."

Doubt that, but I like how easy the conversation's flowing, so I take that bet and listen as he fills me in on the car he's currently working on at his shop.

CHAPTER 26

PIGPEN

Caroline pulls her car into the grass next to the line of bikes, and I'm surprised when she cuts the engine.

"Thank you for helping Addison," Dust says from the backseat. Addison decided to stay with Mia. She gave Caroline a hug goodbye and gave Dust an even longer one.

"Thank you for involving me," Caroline responds, but she looks at me instead of Dust. Then she switches her gaze to the backseat. "Addison said you're going to visit her."

Once a week was the rumor I heard, but I keep that to myself. I'm happy that Dust is breaking out of his shell, and I'm happier it's for Addison.

Dust cracks open his door. "Yeah."

"Would you mind if I came along sometime?"

I glance over my shoulder for his response. He looks at me for approval, and I nod.

"Sure," he says, and he's out the door before she has the opportunity to ask anything else.

"When you want to see her," I say, "I can go with you. Dust isn't much of a conversationalist."

Her lips quirk up. "He's a good man."

"Agreed."

"And so are you."

That catches me off guard, and I do a double-take. Her gorgeous blue eyes meet mine, and for one of the few times in my life, I'm at a loss for words.

I'd love to lean forward, brush my lips against hers and lose myself in her forever. But tonight's not the night. I'm hoping she'll give me another chance. "It looks like the club is hosting a family dinner tonight. I don't know about you, but I'm starved. Do you want to stay?"

"I don't want to impose."

I flash her a grin that causes her to smile in return. "One, that's too formal. Two, they make enough food to feed an army. Three, you helped us out today. Whether you like it or not you're a friend of the club now."

Her eyebrows rise at this, and I'm impressed when she's bold enough to open her door and slip out. I immediately join her as we cross the field for the crowd near the food.

"What exactly does being a friend of the club entail?" she asks.

I shove my hands into my pockets and silently berate myself. Usually with women I'm as smooth as silk, but Caroline twists me all up inside to the point I feel like a middle school boy working up the courage to ask a girl to slow dance. "It means you get first dibs on Rebecca's potato salad."

She laughs, and I love the sound.

"It also means that if you have a problem, we'll be there for you like you were there for us today."

She pauses, and the serious set of her eyes freezes me in place. "I did all of that for Addison."

"I know, and that makes me respect you more. There's not many people who care like you do. That's rare, and that makes you a friend of mine."

She tilts her head, and there's a soft curiosity there that

fires up every cell in my body with the need to touch her. "A friend of the club or yours?"

"Both."

"Why do you do it?" she asks in bewilderment. "Why do you give so much to these teens? They aren't your children, yet at every turn I've seen you there for them. Tonight with Addison, for Chevy and Violet after the kidnapping, for Oz after Olivia's death, for Violet's younger brother Brandon when he's been picked on relentlessly at school, and then for Razor. Three quarters of the school forgot Razor had a father because they believed you had taken on custody of him. Why do you fight for them so hard?"

I shrug, off balance at the realization that she's noticed me before. "Why do you?"

She shakes her head like she doesn't believe she's as much a fighter as I am.

"You're hard on them because you demand the best out of them. You see their potential, and you push until they see it themselves."

"It's my job."

"You could pop in a movie for your English class, sit back and do Sudoku all year, but you don't."

"There's more to you," she counters, evading my comment. "It takes a huge heart to love when that person doesn't love you back. Teens can be tough that way."

Adults, too, but I love these teens because they *do* love. I didn't understand that type of love at their age, but I've been learning how to love like that in the years since. "I guess you're going to have to hang out with me to get a handle on this 'more' you say that I possess."

She brightens like a supernova, and I will never be the same again. "I feel like there was a challenge somewhere in that."

"Depends. Do you like a challenge?" I ask.

"I love one."

So do I. "Then consider yourself challenged. Let's get some food. You're going to need the energy."

"Why is that?"

"Because I plan on asking you to take a ride with me later on the back of my bike."

"And you're assuming I'll accept?"

I want her to accept. "Your choice."

"That was the correct answer."

I like that I'm a fast learner. Because I'm just as bold as she is, I take her hand. Nothing in my world has felt right until this moment—the one where her fingers lace through mine and she holds onto me just as tightly as I'm holding on to her.

CHAPTER 27

ELI

Once again, I'm on the front steps of Dad's cottage, watching my family as they gather around a bonfire under the spring night sky. Oz finishes a story, and there are a few chuckles, but then Razor adds something to the conversation, and the group breaks out into full blown laughter—Emily holding her stomach as she leans forward in a fit of giggles. Even Isaiah and Rachel, the newest to our clan, join in as if they have always belonged. Oz smiles as he flips Razor off, and Razor smiles back as he returns the gesture.

After I was sentenced to prison, I never thought I'd experience joy again. I'm glad I was wrong.

"Is this your favorite spot?" Nina asks as she climbs the steps to join me.

"I like the view."

She follows my gaze to the bonfire, and the softness of her expression is beautiful. "I agree. It's a good view."

"Thank you for being here today. You made a huge impact on Isaiah."

"He reminds me a lot of James. If I didn't know better, I would have thought he had been raised by him."

I'd thought the same several times throughout the day. I also had a lot of other thoughts—most of them about Nina. After tonight, there's no reason for us to interact again. Chevy will be heading to college, and she can visit Isaiah through her son.

For years, we wanted to be rid of each other, but I don't feel that way, not anymore. "How would you like to have dinner with me this week?"

Nina's head whips in my direction as though I'd announced there is a shark on dry land. "What?"

Not a hopeful initial reaction. "Dinner. With me."

She blinks repeatedly. "Is the club having another family dinner?"

I shake my head. "I was thinking we could go out someplace. We could stay in town if you'd like, but there are better restaurants near the army base."

A faint smile, a hesitant smile, slowly spreads across her lips. "Are you asking me out?"

I am. "I've enjoyed talking with you over the past few days, and I'm not ready for that to end."

Nina laughs lightly and relaxes beside me. "I'm going on a date with Eli McKinley. My, how my world has changed."

I chuckle along with her, knowing mine has, too.

CHAPTER 28

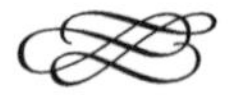

PIGPEN

Leaning against the bar in the clubhouse, I watch in awe as Caroline and Rebecca swap potato salad recipes and discuss what it's like to have overbearing bosses. There's a part of me that wonders if I was in an accident on my bike earlier today. Or maybe before graduation I was blindsided by a semi, and I'm now in a coma dreaming happy dreams.

If so, I'm fine with never waking up.

Razor walks to the bar and orders a water for him and a diet for Breanna. Doesn't take long for the order to be filled. I glance over and give him a nod. I expect him to nod back and return to his girl, but instead he stays where he is.

"You okay, brother?" I ask.

"Yeah."

"How's Breanna?" She has to be torn up about her best friend leaving town.

"Concerned for Addison, but relieved she's getting help."

"I'll keep an eye on Addison," I say.

"Thanks," he responds, and I once again expect him to leave, but he stays still. My spider sense is screaming so loudly I'm surprised other brothers in the club haven't drawn their guns in response.

Razor places the water and the diet back on the bar. "I need to talk to you."

Aw, hell. Is it too much to ask for this kid to go through one night without having his heart ripped out? "Talk away, brother. I've got nothing but ears and time."

Razor takes a deep breath, and I hide the fear of what falling off this cliff is going to be like. This kid has never been easy.

"I know," Razor says.

My forehead furrows. "Know what?"

"I've known for a while. I didn't know how I should talk to you about it or if I should avoid it all together."

It's like he's speaking Latin. "You lost me."

"After everything that went down with the detective that was investigating my mom's death, and Chevy and Violet being kidnapped, I ended up reading more of the files that the police released."

"Yeah?" We all did.

"I saw that there was someone from the Riot Motorcycle Club who had been funneling information to the cops."

My stomach drops as I figure out the road he's going down. My younger brother started working with the police after everything that happened with Oz and Emily last summer. His goal was to take down the Riot—the MC our father belonged to.

A muscle in Razor's jaw twitches and then the truth comes tumbling out. "I met with your brother. I know that your father is the one who ran my mom off the road and killed her during the war between the Riot and the Terror, and I know that you know. I also know that the reason you're here is because of me."

A hand over my face as all the blood drains from my

brain. "I'm sorry, brother. I swear to you, I am. If I had any idea what my father was capable of, I would have taken a gun to him myself."

Razor places a hand in the air. "It's not your fault."

"I knew he was following your mom. I overhead him talking about it with another member of the club. I should have done something. I should have stopped him from going out that day."

"You couldn't," Razor says.

"I should have."

"You were a teen," Razor pushes as if that's a good enough defense.

"And you were a kid," I shout, and the guys surrounding us go quiet. "My flesh and blood took away your mom, and I'm to blame!"

Razor stares at me in that slow, calm way of his. "It's not your fault."

His words are like a hook to the head. For years, I've blamed myself, felt the guilt, felt the blood streaming through my fingers. I couldn't look at my dad, and I couldn't look at myself. How could I be related to someone so horrible?

So, I left, joined the Army and when I was honorably discharged due to my wounds, I came here to Snowflake and begged this club for forgiveness. Forgiveness they said I didn't need because her death wasn't on me. They took me in and gave me the chance to make it up to the son of my father's victim. To watch over Razor because his mom was no longer on this earth to do so.

"I appreciate your looking out for me," Razor says. "Being there for me at every turn, but I think it's time you take a step back and focus on you."

"You're my brother." I close my eyes to try to contain the emotion raging within me. "I'll always have your back."

"And I'll always have yours, but I'm leaving next month, and you need to stay here." His eyes flicker to Caroline, who thankfully is on the other side of the room and has no idea of the drama taking place near the bar.

I never thought twice about the prospect of packing up and leaving town with Razor. It's what I've done: watch over this kid. A guardian angel he never knew he had—until now. "Are you telling me you're too good for me now?"

He chuckles. "I've always been too good for you."

I can't help the short, bitter laugh.

"I'm living my life for me now," Razor says, "and you need to live your life for you. I buried my mom's ghost, and it's time you do, too."

"When did you get so wise?"

"I guess from the years of you talking at me."

Smartass. Yet I bring the kid in for a hug that includes hard pats on the back. We let go and he shoves my shoulder. "It sucks that every time I come home I'm going to have to talk to my English teacher."

I can only hope. "Go be young and not stupid, brother."

He gives me one of his rare smiles and leaves.

A soft and gentle touch on my bicep and I turn my head to see Caroline gazing up at me. "Is that offer for a ride on your bike still available?"

For her? "Anytime."

I take her hand, and we weave through the crowd so I can take the most beautiful woman on the planet on the ride of her life.

AND THEY ALL LIVED HAPPILY EVER AFTER:

A PUSHING THE LIMITS NOVELLA

CHAPTER 29

NOAH

My eyes snap open and my body jerks so abruptly that the bed shakes. After all that I've been through in life, I've acquired the ability to sleep through fistfights in school, screaming foster fathers, and even gunshots in the crazy neighborhood of the first apartment I shared with Isaiah. But where the harsh world couldn't break my sleep patterns, the shadow of a three-year-old doing nothing more than staring at me can wake me from a deep sleep with the same dread I'd feel at a clown hovering over the bed with a machete.

"What's wrong, buddy?" I sit up on my elbows and squint in the darkness to try to make out my son. All I see is his outline and the glint of light reflecting off the plastic eye of the stuffed rabbit held close to his chest.

"I used the bathroom."

My foggy brain tries to weigh whether or not that means he needs a pull-up change.

"I didn't pee in bed."

And there's the answer. He made it to the bathroom in

the middle of the night. "That's awesome." And I mean it. Took forever to night train his sister Macie.

"There's a monster in my room."

I'm too tired for this. "No, there's not."

"Yes, there is."

Here's the thing about three-year-olds: they can continue this type of conversation for hours. A doggedness I swear my children inherited from their mother—my wife.

Exhausted from a few late nights due to finishing a project—designing a high-end house, one of many on my growing list of clients—and then from helping Echo clean up after the vomiting hurricane that was kiddo number one this evening, I fall back onto the bed. Damn that pillow feels good, and I'd give a kidney to keep my eyes closed.

"Echo?" I say. She rolls onto her side, away from me, while simultaneously kicking my leg. Hard enough that it should sting, but I'm immune to the action. "It's your turn."

"No, it's not," comes that sexy groggy voice that still has a way of making me want to wrap my arms around her and kiss her until she's breathless.

"Yes, it is."

"No, it's not."

As I said, doggedness that can go on for hours.

"I put Macie to bed tonight," I say. That meant four books, two sips of water, three trips to the bathroom, six laps around the dining room table and me falling asleep in her bed as she read book number five to me.

"And after two grueling twelve-hour labors, you sweet-talked in my ear how much you wanted another baby." She drops her voice to mimic me. "A third baby will be a piece of cake. The labor will be shorter. We have this baby thing down." She returns to her sexy drowsy tone. "Do I need to remind you of the twenty-four hours of labor followed up by an emergency C-section and then two months of a colicky baby while you travelled three of those weeks for work? And I'm the one Macie threw up on tonight because you were determined to play that stupid jelly bean game with her. I call not my turn for the next four years."

For people so small, my children can expel horrifying amounts of puke in the span of thirty seconds. Plus, they spew like a lawn sprinkler, that is until you actually deposit them in front of a toilet. That's when they're empty.

While I'm exhausted, I can't argue with Echo's well-thought-out, two-in-the-morning argument. Makes me wonder how long she's been forming this speech, and whether I need to step up my game for a planned counterattack.

Tonight, or rather this morning, she wins. Echo has clients tomorrow. After a few years of doing freelance artwork, which she still does on the side, she eventually earned her master's degree in art therapy. Helping traumatized children is a tough job, but Echo has a gift, and at the end of the day feels she's making a difference. I believe that, too.

I roll out of bed and swoop Seth into my arms. He lays his red-haired head on my shoulder, and any annoyance that I had from my two a.m. wake-up dissolves.

Our oldest, five-year-old Macie, is headstrong, determined and exudes confidence. So much, it may be possible to bottle it and sell it in bulk at Costco. Her only downfall is she can't stomach dead-fish-flavored jelly beans. Our baby, Oliver, is only eight months, but he's as chill as they come. A constant smile on his face, and not counting his first three months, rarely cries.

Seth, though, is the one that yanks out your heart and hands it to you. His soul aches for every lost cat and every puppy without a home, and he's terrified caterpillars are lonely when they go into their cocoons. If he needs monsters scared away, I'm the man for the job. After all, I'm his dad.

I head down the hallway and take the first door on the right. His nightlight is on and it gives his room a soft glow. I lay him down in his toddler bed, a gift from my best friend: a red racecar made out of thick plastic that holds his tiny mattress. Even though it's a shrunken version of a twin bed, my son looks small as I pull the blanket over his pajama-clad body.

I then do the dad thing—check under the bed, open and close the closet doors and mock a ninja chop when sneaking a peek behind the door, which earns me a fit of giggles from the bed.

Content that his room is safe, Seth rolls onto his back and stares at the colorful glow-in-the dark stars hand-painted by Echo. Then his eyes roam over the walls and across the mural of trees, grass, butterflies and bunnies. Once again, painted by Echo with some help from Seth and Macie and a handprint from Oliver.

There are rabbits on the wall, stuffed rabbits surrounding his bed, and his pajamas even have bunnies. Seth has a love of rabbits—an influence of his godmother.

"I'm in the wedding?" Seth asks.

"Yes. They specifically asked for you."

Seth smiles, and I tuck the blanket around him. I never knew it was possible to love anyone as much as I love Echo and my children. I never knew it was possible to be loved so much in return.

"But they aren't going to want a cranky boy," I say. "I need you to go to sleep. Tomorrow is going to be a big day."

With his stuffed bunny cuddled tight, Seth rolls to his side and closes his eyes. "I love you."

Hearing those words never gets old. "Love you back."

I stand and watch him longer than needed. It doesn't take

long for him to fall back asleep and hopefully he'll be out for the rest of the night.

There's no way to wake up at two a.m. and not check in on the rest of my kids. It's a gravitational pull I don't try to ignore.

Macie has her covers kicked off and is sprawled out in her bed with arms and legs in every direction. She has Echo's features, but she has my dark hair and brown eyes and too much of my mischievous side. If she's going to continue to be a little too much like me, I dread high school.

In the room next to hers is a white crib that once held both Macie and Seth. It now holds Oliver, our other redhead. I'm quiet as I approach the bed. If I wake Oliver, Echo will castrate me. Luckily, he's sound asleep in his terrycloth sleeper, and his little mouth squishes as if he's sucking on a pacifier.

I search around the crib, and sure enough, the pacifier has fallen to the floor. I pick it up and stick it back within arm's reach. Maybe he'll find it in the morning and give Echo and me a few extra minutes of sleep.

Oliver takes a breath in and a breath out. After Echo had the emergency C-section because the cord had wrapped around Oliver's neck, I spent a lot of nights watching his chest move up and then down. Somehow, I had never appreciated the simple act of my child's breathing until then.

During the C-section, Echo experienced a blood loss. So many things had gone wrong in a short period of time, and it was awful to do nothing more than stand back and be helpless. My child in a nurse's arms not crying, my wife's hand going limp in my mine, and me watching her eyes close against her will. The anesthesiologist asking her to open her eyes and her not responding. The way my heart stopped beating and I grew cold.

My mind cracked with the quietness that had overtaken

the doctors as they worked quickly and in desperate determination to save both my wife and my son. Those brief few moments were the longest of my life.

I couldn't lose him. I couldn't lose her. Without them, I would be lost.

Then my baby cried, Echo opened her eyes and my knees went weak. I almost fell to them, but instead held my wife's hand, crouched down to her eye level and told her that our child was alive.

I'll never forget the wetness that filled her eyes, the tears that fell down my cheeks and how good it felt when I pressed my lips to her forehead.

The gravitational pull is now in another direction—toward my siren. She calls to me, always. I keep our bedroom door open only a crack and climb back into bed. Echo's still on her side. I wrap my arms tight around her and mold my body to hers. Spooning her close, relishing her soft skin, my hands moving along her curves, my nose nuzzling the spot behind her ear. She stirs as I place a kiss on her neck.

Echo leans back into me, her hands gliding along my arms, and as I continue to kiss her neck, she turns to face me and places her hand on my cheek.

"I need you," I say.

"You have me," she whispers against my lips.

She doesn't understand. "I need you."

"I'm here." She gently kisses me, and I start to lose myself in her.

"I need you," I say again, and Echo weaves her fingers into my hair and encourages me to rest my weight on her.

"I'm yours."

And I'm hers. Forever and always.

CHAPTER 30

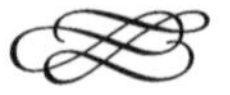

ECHO

Noah's youngest brother, Tyler, will make an amazing father someday. He's in his early twenties, has recently graduated from college, and is courageous enough to have started his own company, making video games. He's quiet, single, resourceful, looks just like Noah, and my children adore him.

Tyler's on the floor, playing a very intense game of dolls with Macie, Seth scales Tyler's back as if he's climbing a mountain, and Oliver kicks and blows bubbles on Tyler's lap while trying to grab for the doll in Macie's hand. There aren't many people I'd trust all three of my children at the same time with, but Tyler has made the top of the list.

I'm arranging flowers in the tent where the wedding reception will take place. Noah and I agreed to be in charge of setting up in here. The couple could have afforded to have people set up for them, but they really wanted something small and intimate without a lot of strangers around, so we volunteered to help. Knowing how much work it would be, we enlisted the help of Noah's two brothers, Jacob and Tyler, and my younger brother, Alexander.

While Tyler is the best babysitter on the planet, our other volunteers have been lacking in the helpfulness department. Noah and Jacob are engaged in a showdown of wills on the other side of the room when they should be setting up chairs around the tables. My brother, Alexander, stands beside me with scissors in one hand and the same bouquet of flowers I handed him ten minutes ago in the other.

I keep an eye on the confrontation between my strong-willed husband and even stronger willed brother-in-law, while also keeping my attention on my sibling. He's seven-teen, in all of its glory. Quite aware that my teen years were complicated for different reasons, and that Dad had a hand in why those years were complicated, I have the urge to call my father and apologize to him for any of the times I might have been a bit overly dramatic.

"Dad's so unfair," Alexander says.

He can be, but Alexander doesn't exactly make his life easier by turning everything into an argument, even when the argument doesn't need to be had. It's times like these that I wish for the millionth time that my older brother, Aires was still alive. Maybe he would have known how to handle the war that is my father and brother.

There are times that Alexander looks so much like Aires that it hurts, but most times, I love seeing a bit of my lost brother within my brother who is very much alive.

"I'm going to be honest," I cut the end of a rose and stick it in the vase, "Noah and I will give Macie, Seth, and Oliver curfews when they are in high school."

"My friends get to stay out until midnight. Dad and Mom treat me like a baby with a curfew of eleven."

"Dad was stricter with me than he is with you."

"You always choose his side, and that's not fair. Mom said you and Dad argued when you were my age. You should be on my side."

I sigh, because Dad says the same thing to me about Alexander when I try to talk to Dad about his relationship with my brother. "I choose both of your sides. The problem is that neither of you ever tries looking at it from the other's point of view."

Alexander glares at me, and I can tell by the set of his jaw he's upset. I cut more flowers, give him a few seconds to stew, and wish I could hand him a piece of paper and some crayons to try to figure out what's really going on with him.

"Then give me something to help you," I say. "If you want to have a later curfew, then you have to give a good reason to have one and why you're responsible enough to handle it."

"Are you saying I'm not responsible?" he shoots back.

Did I twist every sentence around when I was his age? "I didn't say that. I'm saying that if you want a different curfew then you need to build a case as to why Dad should give it to you. He responds better to well-thought-out conversations than to overly emotional arguments."

"You won't understand."

"Try me."

Alexander drops the scissors on the table and fiddles with the leaves of the roses. "There's a girl."

And there it is—the real issue. A million questions form in my mind, most of them belonging to the protective and giddy older sister who wants to know *everything* about this girl, but I need to help Alexander and Dad first. "What does this girl have to do with curfew?"

He shrugs his shoulders like he doesn't know, yet he answers. "She works, almost every day, and she doesn't get off until ten. I'm able to give her a ride home, but when she asks me to hang out with her, I have to tell her no. I don't want to seem like a baby by telling her I have a curfew, and I can tell that even though I'm saying no nicely, she feels like I'm blowing her off."

All the puzzle pieces start to click together. "Have you tried explaining this to Dad?"

He mashes his lips together. "Dad won't understand. He's ancient."

True there aren't many people Dad's age with seventeen-year-olds, but ancient is a bit of a stretch. "I think you should try telling him. He might surprise you."

"No, he won't. I've heard how much he hated Noah for years."

True again, but…. "Noah and I were different, and Dad's changed a lot since then. He's admitted to me he was wrong on a lot of things with Noah, and Noah and I didn't exactly make it easy on Dad. I told you the story of how I once had to call Dad for bail money for Noah. If Macie ever called Noah for bail money for her boyfriend, Noah would probably lose his mind."

Lose his mind would be an understatement. After being the bad boy, Noah is already on the lookout for any boy in Macie's class who could be a potential leather-jacket-wearing kind of trouble he was. With Macie's tendency to enjoy being a bit wild, even for six, I'm not sure any of us will survive her teen years.

Alexander finally glances up at me, and his open body language informs me that for the first time since we started this conversation that he's listening, so I continue, "Dad isn't a stranger to love. He fell in love with my mom, and he tried for years to help her, even when she didn't want to help herself." They're even friendly with each other now when we have combined family functions. Mom has been doing very well for years and even has someone special in her life.

"And he fell in love with your mom. When I say fell in love, I mean fell hard. I was in middle and high school and had to watch their disgusting teenage lovey-dovey behavior. Each time I had dinner with them I wanted to vomit."

Alexander chuckles and his posture finally relaxes. "Will you be there when I talk to him?"

"If you want me there."

"I do."

On the inside I'm smiling like Seth with a cookie, but I keep the sister joy off my face.

Alexander's cell chimes with a text, and by the way he lights up, it must be this mystery girl. He jacks his thumb over his shoulder. "Do you mind if I take a few minutes off?"

That would have required him to have worked to begin with, but instead of mentioning that, I shoo my brother away to go woo a girl. The moment he's out of the tent, I look over in time to spot Noah giving his brother Jacob a hug. Good. The last thing I wanted was for them to get into another argument.

Noah and Jacob share the same type of relationship Alexander and my father do. Lots of love and lots of arguments. Noah has always been more of a father figure to Jacob than a brother. Jacob and Tyler were adopted and have a mom and a dad, but Noah and Jacob fell into those roles with each other while Noah is able to just be Tyler's older brother.

Jacob pulls away, offers Noah a crooked grin and then sets off to start the task of putting up table and chairs. Better late than never. Noah glances over at me, and even though he has thrown me that heart-stopping glance a million times since we were seventeen, those mutant pterodactyls take flight in my chest.

A blush hits my cheeks as I remember the way Noah loved me last night, and I return my attention back to the flowers, while catching a peek at Noah walking in my direction. It's moments like this that I see glimpses of the rebellious teen who I first fell for all those years ago. That sexy swagger, those dark eyes set on me, and finally his touch as he puts a hand on my waist.

"S'up, Echo," he says in a deep, sensual voice that causes my blood to tingle.

I giggle with the reminder from our past. "Hello, Noah."

Noah leans down and kisses me. It's brief, but it's a promise of events to come later this evening when the kids are tucked away into bed. He pulls away and watches as our children use Tyler as a jungle gym. "How's Alexander?"

"Seventeen, falling in love and thinks he's the first one to have ever experienced it."

Noah snorts. "Sounds about right."

Because we felt the same way at his age. While all of those moments we shared as teens were new, fresh and exciting, I wouldn't trade what I have now to experience any of that again. There's something comforting and peaceful in the love and life we have now. A comfortableness in every simple touch, word and action.

Do we argue? Yes, definitely, yes. But even in the arguments, there's a deep understanding and love that keeps us from going too far. As the years go by, the apologizing comes faster, the need to see the other's side more apparent. Adulting is hard, but growing in a relationship with the man I've married is one of the greatest joys of my life.

"What's going on with Jacob?" I ask.

"Do you really want to know?"

Flipping fantastic. Where Tyler is driven and focused, Jacob has been using his twenties to find himself, hopping from job to job and girl to girl. Not that he has to have everything figured out right now, but Jacob has a tendency to create drama with his choices.

"When you put it that way, not really, but tell me anyhow."

Noah rubs the back of his neck then drops the bomb. "You're going to be an aunt."

I blink repeatedly and try to process the words. "Jacob's having a baby?"

"Technically the girl he slept with is having a baby, but yeah, that's the gist. She's four months along, and she's keeping the baby regardless of what Jacob decides to do. Jacob doesn't want me to tell you who it is yet, but I'll give you three good guesses and the first two don't count."

Crap. Just crap. "It's Sylvia, isn't it?"

"Give the woman a prize."

My stomach sinks. Sylvia is in the middle of law school. She and Jacob have been best friends since high school. I've suspected she's always been in love with him, but Jacob has been too free of a spirit to notice.

Just... "Wow."

"Yeah. Wow."

"What's he going to do?"

"Be involved. Help in any way possible. He said he intends on being a full-time dad. He asked if he could move in with us, so he can save money and focus on getting his life on track. I told him I would have to talk to you."

My mind swirls. Jacob moving in with us, probably in the basement. I nibble on my bottom lip, not very thrilled with the idea of someone else in our house and less thrilled with the idea that if he moves in, he might never leave. But being that this is Noah's brother, there's no way I can turn him away.

"Has he told his parents?" I ask.

"Not yet. He wants me to go with him tomorrow night when he tells them. He thinks they'll be mad, but I think once they get over the shock, they'll be okay. Jacob's pride is keeping him from asking them for help, just like it kept him from telling me for the past month, but I'm hoping he'll come to his senses soon. There's no room for pride as a parent."

Noah and I learned that lesson quickly. "If Jacob needs to

move in with us, then he moves in with us, but I think we all need to sit down and discuss his objectives for the future before making any big decisions."

"Agreed." Noah places an arm around me, and I wrap my arms around him in need of his comforting hug. "Have I told you how much I love you?"

"Yes, but you can tell me again."

"I love you more than you can imagine."

I can imagine pretty big, but I believe him. "I love you, too."

We stand there, hugging each other then turn our heads to watch as our children play and laugh. This is life, real life. There's always going to be an issue, but it's how we love each other through it that counts. That's how Noah and I have our happily ever after.

CHAPTER 31

BETH

I glance at the clock—seven a.m. It's time for me to leave, yet instead of heading to the locker room to change, I watch as they wheel the bed away. The teen on it is heading for surgery. I hope he makes it. He's got too much life in front of him not to.

A squeeze of my shoulder, and Dr. Clark smiles as she passes. "Good job, Beth."

My response is a chin lift, and then I lean back against the wall. I am utterly and completely exhausted. A teenager walked in—*walked in*—to the ER after a car accident, and collapsed at the front desk. That was one of those "work fast, be thankful for years of trauma experience" moments. The kid crashed, but we were able to stabilize him. It was a long night, and as nausea sloshes around in my stomach, I have doubts I'll cover anyone's overnight shift ever again.

"Don't you have an appointment this morning?" Renee asks in a sugary tone. She's escorting a worn-out mother and her child to a room. The kid is holding a tray to his mouth in case he vomits. I hate flu season.

Seventeen-year-old me wants to flip Renee off. Instead, I glare.

She laughs at my expression, and I shake my head. We went through nursing school together, have navigated the ups and downs of being in a profession where we're underpaid, underappreciated and overworked. More important, we've lived through having to act confident when we were really scared to death.

And today, she knows I'm terrified. I'm a far cry from the girl who left a rough neighborhood and an even rougher home life. But days like today, I don't feel years removed from the frightened seventeen-year-old who had an exterior of stone. Right now, I feel like I could reach out and she would be so real I could take her hand—that is if she let anyone near.

An unwanted hot flash rolls through my body, and I duck into an empty room and breathe out to keep from dry-heaving. "Not now." Though I'm not sure I want to go through this later either.

"And I was just crazy enough to think I'd find you in bed at home."

My heart beats so hard that it almost flies out of my chest, and the sight of those kind dark eyes causes every sore muscle in my body to relax. Ryan closes the door behind him, walks toward me and, for once, I'm speechless. Could be due to the exhaustion. Could be because he isn't supposed to be here. Could be that after all these years he still takes my breath away.

Ryan was built when we were teens, but the man in front of me now makes the seventeen-year-old I initially fell in love with look like a beanpole. He's broad-shouldered, defined muscle and all man.

Wearing jeans, a T-shirt and a baseball cap, he stops in front of me, and I smirk as I reach up and touch the scruff on his jaw. It's not a long beard, but if things go as planned for his team, it probably will be in a few weeks.

I'm not a fan of the facial hair, and he knows it, but there are concessions when you're married to a major league pitcher. Not just any major league pitcher, but a fan favorite, leader in league strikes, and the man on the cover of every sports magazine in the country.

Daily, there's a part of me that's amazed that I'm his wife.

Ryan gives me a heart-squeezing grin. "It's playoffs. Facial hair is part of the territory."

Oh, October, how I alternately love and loathe you. I roll my eyes to make him chuckle then lean into him. With my head on his chest, I close my eyes. He wraps his arms around me, reminding me of a thick, safe blanket, and I swear to God I could fall asleep on my feet.

"I'd like to kiss you," he says. "But should I?"

"Flu season is starting early this year, so nope. You probably shouldn't be hugging me either. At least not until I take a decontamination bath."

"I'll take my chances."

"I missed you," I whisper into his chest, and he hugs me tighter.

"I missed you more." Even though I warned him, he kisses the top of my head.

My lips squish to the side as I realize how badly I suck as a baseball player's wife. "Wow. That game last night…." I intentionally trail off, and his shoulders shake with his laughter.

"We won."

I squeeze him with joy. "Congratulations. And I'm sorry I didn't know. I checked between patients and you were up one in the bottom of the fourth, but then we got slammed."

"Busy night in the ER?"

"Yeah." I barely had time to breathe.

"Bad night?" he asks.

I sigh heavily, and he holds me as if he would take on the emotional burden of my bad night. It wasn't just a bad night, it was a terrible one. We lost a patient—a man with a family. Two GSWs, both too young, so young they can't even vote. Multiple drug overdoses, and one premature baby with RSV that had to be put on the ventilator. I hope that the teen they just wheeled away makes it, because I need some good news.

He kisses the top of my head again. "I'm sorry."

I draw back, and he keeps his arms around me. He's been gone several days, and all I want to do is touch him and keep touching him and then sleep for a week. "What are you doing here? I thought your plane wasn't going to land until later this morning."

He had booked his flight so he could be back in time for the wedding.

"You honestly think I could stay away from this appointment?" Ryan had a late game last night—on the west coast.

"Have you slept?" I ask.

"On the plane. Have you?" he counters.

I don't answer because I haven't, and I promised him yesterday, via video chat before he went to the stadium, that I was going to take it easy. But worried about today, I couldn't stay still, so when I received a call asking if I could fill in, I said yes. "I told you it's not serious."

He silences me with the tenderness in his eyes and the tuck of a stray piece of my blond hair behind my ear. There's still a few streaks of black in my hair and a few streaks of red. Even though I'm a charge nurse for the ER, I've never fully embraced conventional.

"You need to sleep," I say. "You're the best man."

Ryan has the most incredulous expression. "Who gets married during playoffs?"

I raise an eyebrow as I still don't know how to explain

that the sun doesn't rise and set around baseball for the rest of the world as it does for him. "Did you hire a private plane?"

He shrugs.

I point at him. "You promised me normal. You became a big boy major league pitcher and you promised me normal. Private planes aren't normal."

"We can afford a few private flights, and if doing so gets me here in time to be with you when you need me, then that's what I'm going to do."

"I'm okay. The doctor said my bloodwork looked good. She said she just wants to take a look. This is what happens when I make friends. They do random things like being overly concerned."

Ryan tucks my hair behind my ear again, not because anything is out of place, but because he's out of place, because I'm out of place. We're out of our element—off track. Leaning a little too left when we should be more right. There's concern in his eyes, and that causes the anxiety in me to twist further.

"I don't want you to feel scared or alone," Ryan says.

"I don't." I do feel scared, but I love that I'm no longer alone.

I wrap my arms around myself because I am terrified. It took me a long time to get my head around jumping into this scenario, and one of the reasons I did agree to it is that since Ryan entered my life, he has always been by my side.

All through the up and downs of college, when Ryan and I lived in an old apartment and were two struggling students with crappy jobs. Yeah, my Uncle Scott was and is loaded, but to teach me responsibility, he paid for my college education while I paid for my rent and associated bills.

Ryan stayed by me when he was drafted into the minors by a team across the country after college, and I was about to begin my masters in nursing. Before he left, he got down on one knee, asked me to marry him and in one week we threw together a backyard wedding at Scott's. The reception held near the old barn where we first kissed.

He moved, I stayed, we video chatted, we texted, we talked. We cried, we fought, we froze each other out. We cried some more, we talked, we visited, we loved. He entered the majors, I graduated from school, he bought a house and I moved to be with him. His career, my career, a balance and imbalance, a constant push and pull, and we daily fall deeper in love.

In the end, our love has done more than survived, it's flourished.

Ryan places his fingers under my chin, and I meet his eyes. "You, Beth, are my number one. We're in this together, and if I have to fly halfway across the world to be here, I will."

"What if I'm not any good at being a mom?" I ask, because my mom was terrible. We haven't had contact since I was seventeen, and I don't have plans to speak to her again.

Ryan places his hands over mine, and that's when I realize that my fingers are over my abdomen, over our child.

The love radiating from Ryan's face fills me with so much joy that I could cry. It's crazy, I hardly ever cried before my pregnancy, and now I'm a sobbing moron over a Facebook video of a child receiving a puppy for his birthday.

"You cover our child when you're scared," Ryan says. "You protect our baby because that's who you are. You protect the ones you love. That is going to make you a great mom."

And our child is going to have an excellent father. "I love you."

"I love you, too." Ignoring my flu warning, he lightly kisses me, yet it's enough to get my heart moving.

"What time is the appointment?" Ryan asks against my lips.

"Eight."

Another kiss, and he releases me just in time for us to overhear someone in the hallway say, "I think I saw Ryan Stone. I swear it was him."

It is, but Ryan doesn't belong to his fans this morning. He belongs to me. "I'm going to shower and change, and I have a favor to ask."

"Ask away."

"There's a kid who's had a rough night, and he may or may not have come in wearing a Ryan Stone baseball jersey. I can't tell you why he's here, and I can't tell you what room he's in, but you may want to wander very slowly past room two and poke your head in."

"Did you tell him I'm your husband?"

I gasp and dramatically place a hand over my heart. "And divulge my alter ego status as Ryan Stone's wife?" I waggle my eyebrows. "Never. Anyhow, around here, I'm more popular than you."

"Yes, you are." Ryan pulls me in close for another hug, and my favorite thing in the world is being in his arms. "You save lives, Beth. You inspire me."

His words make me smile, and I playfully push him away. I head right for the locker room, and Ryan heads left for room two. I have the absolute best husband in the world.

I WASN'T PREPARED for the home crowd in the waiting room. Scott and his wife Allison, along with Ryan's mom, made the two-hour drive from Groveton to Cincinnati. Scott and I are very close, Allison now feels like my sister, and Ryan's mom has become a mom to me. The death of Ryan's father last year devastated his family, yet has weirdly brought them closer together.

After a round of hugs for all, Ryan and I enter the examination room and share nervous small talk about how I didn't tell anyone else besides blood family what was happening because I didn't want to ruin the mood of the wedding if the news was bad.

Soon the door opens, and Dr. Julia Greenwood walks in. She greets me then Ryan, and even though she already knows the problem from our text conversations, I tell her officially how I'm cramping and that the cramps are so painful that I've doubled over. Then I tell her the worse, how there was blood when I used the bathroom. Not a lot, just some, but it scared me.

With a practiced comforting smile on her face, she asks me to lie back in the chair and squirts cold gel on my stomach. Ryan holds my hand as I hold my breath.

We stare at the screen. Waiting. Hoping. Praying.

Julia presses down on my stomach, moving the transducer this way then that way. Images fill the screen as she continues to search. Even with my experience in the medical field I can't make sense of anything, because I'm desperate to see and hear a heartbeat.

I grip Ryan's hand harder, and he holds on with his solid strength.

"I believe I've discovered the reason for your cramping," Julia says. Terror seizes me at the idea of what she'll say next. She turns the screen fully toward me and Ryan, pushes a button and over the speakers comes the most beautiful sound—a quick, swishing heartbeat. A mixture between a sob and a laugh leaves my throat, and Ryan leans down and kisses my cheek.

"The baby's okay?" I finally say.

Julia smiles. "Yes. And so are the other two."

I blink repeatedly as my mind trips over itself. "I'm sorry. What did you say?"

"I think the reason you've had cramping isn't because you're losing the baby, it's because your babies are growing, and your tendons are stretching quickly. That happens when you're pregnant with triplets."

My mouth goes dry, and I lose the ability to form sentences. "Triplets?"

"Are you sure?" asks Ryan, and as my hand goes limp in his, he leans into me, as if he can sense how I'm falling into an emotional abyss.

Julia points out three individual heartbeats and three individual sacs, which she says is a good thing.

Within seconds Ryan's expression changes from shock to wonder to pure joy. He kisses the top of my head, kisses my lips and then places his forehead to mine. "Triplets."

My response is a squeak.

"Our babies are okay, Beth, and you're going to be a great mom."

Babies. Not just baby. My brain hurts. I swallow as I stare imploringly up at him. "Are you sure?"

"That there are triplets and that they look okay, I'm sure," Julia says. "And I also agree that you're going to make a great mom. Would you like pictures?"

Ryan tells her yes, she hands me tissues to clean my stomach, prints out the pictures and I think I've gone into shock. Ryan asks questions, lots of questions I should have the presence of mind to ask, but don't. He's so happy, so energetic, so positive, so Ryan. She says things. Things I'm sure I should be listening to, but I only hear buzzing in my ears.

Three. We are having three babies.

Julia hands Ryan the pictures, congratulates us, and tells me to make another appointment with the receptionist before we leave.

We are having three babies. At once.

The door shuts and my eyes automatically shoot up to Ryan. "Three? I'm not even sure I can be a good mom to one, but three? How is three possible? That's like impossible? What if she's wrong? What if there are more in there and she didn't see them? Good God, am I having a litter?"

I swing my legs off the bed, but Ryan stops me before I stand by sitting beside me. He cups my face in his hands and looks straight into my eyes. His rough hands are warm against my face. A physical reminder that he loves me. "You can do this."

"Ryan," I start, but he cuts me off.

"I believe in you, you can do this, and you are not alone. You have me, you have Scott, you have Allison, you have my mom, Mark and his husband, and once we tell our friends you know they'll be there the moment you say the word."

"But they're in Louisville, and I'm here."

"Then we'll buy a place in Louisville, and we stay there when I'm not needed here or in Arizona for spring training."

"But my job."

"We'll work it out, Beth," he says. "We have some time before they're born, and I'm telling you, we'll work it out."

My lower lip trembles, and Ryan repeats. "You're not alone."

I nod, and I whisper, "I'm not alone."

"You aren't alone."

I'm not alone. "I want them."

"So do I."

And I hate that I didn't do a very good job of listening to Julia. "They're healthy?"

"Yes. Strong heartbeats, every single one. She said some spotting can be normal, and that because of the multiple pregnancy, she'll want to see you more often and that you may deliver early, but she said you're healthy, the babies are healthy and there's no reason to worry."

Three. I blow out a slow breath. We are having three babies at once. My heart soars and aches because I want them all, and there's so much that can happen between now and when they're born. So much I can't control.

A hand over my stomach and I close my eyes, promising them I'll do my best to care for them all, to love them all and try not to screw it all up. I open my eyes, gaze up at Ryan, and blink back tears. I wipe at them while half laughing at myself. "I hate this whole emotion thing."

He gives me an endearing half-smile. "I sort of like it."

I smack his arm. "You would."

Ryan envelops me in a hug, and I willingly fall into him. My rock, my love, my best friend.

"Three babies," I say.

"Three babies," he repeats. "I love you, Beth."

I love him more. I lift my head, weave my fingers through his hair and kiss him. It's slow, it's warm and it causes a floating warmth in my veins. His hands begin to wander, and I break away before we go any further. "You know, this is how we ended up in this situation."

Ryan blushes, even after all this time, and it still brings me joy. He wraps an arm around my shoulder and guides me toward the door. "Six more and we can have a baseball team."

I elbow him, and he mock grunts. We enter the waiting room, see the hesitant and concerned expressions of the people we love then see their happy grins as we show them pictures of the three babies who I can't wait to hold in my arms.

CHAPTER 32

ISAIAH

Ariel is on a high of fluffy dresses, rose petals and chocolate doughnuts, and because Noah hates me, he gave her a Coke. Caffeine to my daughter is like acid to a nineteen-sixties hippie.

Rachel and I sit on a bench near where the wedding is going to take place and watch as our daughter chases a group of geese. The male one is a mean bastard. He's spent most of the morning honking and snapping at kids who get too near, but he's terrified of Ariel. She's a big ball of energy in her huge flower girl dress, screaming a *Moana* song at the top of her lungs as she charges down the hill. My daughter does not possess a single ounce of fear.

"We should stop her," Rachel says. "She's going to fall into the pond and ruin her dress."

"Abby won't care. In fact, she'd think it's funny."

"True, but we should stop her because that goose is going to drop dead of a heart attack."

"Ariel," I call, and she spins on her toes to look at me. Her gray eyes are full of light and her face flushed with life. Her blond hair is falling out of the complicated braid Rachel has already re-done twice, and the daisies at the crown of her head are no longer in a neat row. "No ducks."

"But they *need* me." She pulls two clenched tiny fists to her chest.

"They aren't coming home with us."

"Just one."

"No."

"But Dad...." Ariel brings out the big guns: wide, innocent eyes and a practiced lower lip tremble. "They'll be sad without me."

"They'll live."

Rachel stifles a giggle at the nice side of shade my daughter just threw me. Ariel's not happy, but she does move on. She skips toward Noah's son Seth, takes his hand, and tells him the ducks are more scared of him than he is of them. The way Seth's eyes are about to pop out of his head, I'm betting she's wrong.

At least Ariel walks Seth away from the geese, but I am concerned with her trajectory toward the horses grazing in a nearby field. Ariel talks to Seth the entire time. There aren't many people who can keep up with her, as she has something to say about everything at any time.

The wedding is at a winery in the middle of nowhere, and it's about an hour until the start. It's a beautiful fall afternoon, blue skies and all that, and we're here early since Rachel has had a big hand in the planning.

Rachel and I own a custom car shop, and my cell is on vibrate in case a problem arises. So far—nothing. We don't have a huge staff, but those we employ are trustworthy and know how to do their job.

My wife leans her head against my shoulder, and I take her hand. I never knew there could be so much happiness in just sitting with my wife and watching a six-year-old walk. A daisy falls to the ground by my booted feet. I lean down and pick it up, forcing Rachel to straighten.

I take a long look at my wife, snapping a mental picture of how gorgeous she is with her long blond hair curled and hanging around her bare shoulders. Rachel is in the wedding and is wearing a fitted purple dress. I'm not a stylist, but I do my best to tuck the daisy back into my wife's hair, and the smile I receive in return takes my breath away.

Maybe that's the next tattoo I should get—a daisy to remember this moment.

Her near violet eyes shift to something over my shoulder, and the spark in them gains my attention. Rachel grabs my hand, squeezes, then motions for me to look. Her silence tells me that if we make a noise, we'll break the magic.

I glance over my shoulder and watch as Echo stands next to Dalton as he gingerly holds Oliver. Oliver kicks his feet the way eight-month-olds do, and Dalton looks as comfortable as that goose with Ariel.

Dalton is new to our family. Fifteen, gangly, all arms and legs with no muscle, thick glasses and a slight stutter when he's nervous—which for the first two months that he lived with me, Rachel, and Ariel was all the time. But in the past month, he's seemed to have relaxed some into our world. I'd love to take credit for that, but I think most of it is due to Rachel's kindness, Ariel's insistence that he's her older brother for life, and Dalton's twice-a-week appointments with my old high school guidance counselor, Mrs. Collins.

Mrs. Collins no longer works in the school system, but has a private practice. She has three kids of her own now, and most people in the wedding party owe their life to her. When Dalton entered our home, she was the first person we contacted.

Dalton has been in and out of foster care his entire life. His dad is out of the picture, and his mom is serving out her third court-ordered detox. He's quiet, which I understand and respect. He often reminds me of a turtle with his head tucked into his body, and he's slowly peeking out of his shell.

Echo has Dalton sit with Oliver, and Dalton holds the baby by the armpits as Oliver jumps on Dalton's thighs. The baby makes a loud raspberry noise, and Dalton's face twists as if he doesn't understand the conversation. Oliver does it again, and this time, Dalton does it back. The way Oliver cackles causes Dalton to crack a grin and Echo to giggle.

I squeeze Rachel's hand, and she squeezes back. It's good to see the kid smile. He deserves more carefree moments in his life.

"Maybe, hopefully," Rachel whispers in my ear, and I kiss her lips in response because I can't find words to express how this hope of keeping Dalton is killing me. But I don't regret opening our home to him. I never will.

We want to adopt him and make him a permanent part of our family, but the system is complicated, and so is Dalton's situation. Regardless, we're going to be here for him, even if they take him away and place him back with his mom when she's released.

"Isaiah!" Noah calls. "We need help setting up the chairs."

I kiss Rachel again and head off to help my best friend set up for the wedding.

CHAPTER 33

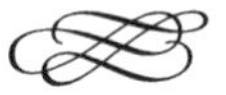

WEST

It's weird how the world works. One day you're speeding down a road until bam—there's a sign that the bridge is out. You take a left, not really thinking where the left is going to lead, and you keep going. Then it dawns on you that maybe the person you were with may not have taken the left with you and has instead turned right. By then, you've both gone so far down your own roads that there's no turning back.

That's what happened with me and Haley. We graduated from high school in love, went to different colleges, thought we could make it work, thought we were making it work, until, one day, we realized it wasn't working.

Through college, I fought my fair share of MMA fights, but I had never been as gutted open and ripped apart as the day Haley and I walked away from each other. There was no yelling, no fight, just a ton of regret and hurt.

I haven't seen her in years, but I think about her all the time. I've been reduced to hearing about her through my sisters Rachel and Abby, who remained friends with Haley after we broke things off. Haley's a physical therapist now.

She has her own practice, and she's associated with the gym, her brother and cousin, Jax and Kaden, own.

Rachel and Abby say Haley's happy, and she looks happy. Through the window, I watch as Haley releases a beautiful smile as she hugs Noah and then Isaiah.

Her hair is long, like I remember, but the brown has more of a chestnut hue. I remember the way her dark eyes flashed with fire the first time we met. She's just as beautiful as she was back then. Today she wears blue. Blue always looked good on her, and that dress she wears fits her in every perfect way.

A snap of fingers in front of my face, and I'm drawn back to the reason I'm here: Abby.

"Young," Abby says. "Where's my something blue?"

I raise an eyebrow at her, and I'm tempted to point at Haley, but I don't. Instead I pull a jewelry box from the pocket of my tuxedo and hand it to her. In a slim-fitting white wedding gown, Abby tilts her head at me. "What's that?"

"Your something new and blue. I don't do borrowed, so you're going to have to live with the disappointment." That's what happens when she asks me to be her best man. She could have done the whole maid or matron of honor thing, but she didn't go that route. It's Abby so I roll with it.

Her expression softens. "I was kidding. I wasn't expecting you to get me anything. The whole present thing isn't why I'm getting married."

Why she would think I wouldn't buy her anything, I don't know. She's not just like a sister to me, she is my sister. My entire family is here because years ago, during her senior year, my parents adopted her. Abby, the former drug dealer, officially became a Young before her eighteenth birthday and also became a member of one of the richest families in Kentucky.

Since then, she took on the role of a Young better than any of us born into the title. She is even one of my father's top salespeople.

Is the top salesperson, or was—not sure of that yet. Medically, it's been a rough two years for her. She's better now, and her spot at Dad's company will be there if and when she ever wants to return. For now, she's doing what Abby does best—living life her way.

No rules, no regrets.

Abby accepts the box from me, and the soft smile on her face is the reaction I had been hoping for. It's a bracelet. Tiffany, of course, because my mom would be appalled if I bought anything else for her daughter. There's four colored stones in silver settings. Three of the stones have names engraved in the silver—Abby's name, the Youngs' and Logan's. The blue stone doesn't have a name because the person who gave me the stone didn't want the name on it. He told me Abby would know who it was from, and from the tears she's batting away, she does.

"When did you see him?" she asks.

"A month ago," I say. "He told me to tell you he loved you, and congratulations."

Abby's father—the man who raised her for the first portion of her life—is serving life in prison. He only allows her to visit him once a year, and she does, faithfully. I took a chance to see if he wanted me to do anything on his behalf for his daughter's wedding day. He gave me explicit instructions, and I followed them to the letter.

"He told me that you'd know what it is."

She nods as she holds the bracelet out for me to put it on her. I do and then she touches the blue stone. "This belonged to my gran."

That's what I thought.

Abby clears her throat, smooths back her short chestnut

hair and gives me her best Abby-rules-the-world stare. "Haley's single."

That causes both of my eyebrows to raise, but I turn and check my bowtie in the mirror. "I thought she was dating some guy who thought he was as smart as a brain surgeon."

"He is a brain surgeon, and she broke up with him—about two months ago."

I'm dying to know why, but Abby's baiting me, and I'm not going to give. Not even on her wedding day. If I do, they'll be no reining her in. Abby, if anything, is incorrigible.

"She asks about you," Abby continues as she slips off the socks she had been wearing.

Sure she does. "Probably wondering what's wrong with the world that they allow me to be a high school guidance counselor."

"What if I told you she broke up with him because you are a high school guidance counselor?"

I need to be done with this conversation. My phone buzzes. It's a text from Rachel, the actual brains of this wedding, telling me that everything is ready to go. I show Abby the text. "Are we doing this wedding thing or not?"

"Whatever, Young. Play it off as much as you want, but you still love Haley."

I do. "We grew apart." It's the truth, yet not. Haley grew, and I didn't—at least not until it was too late.

"Maybe you can grow back. Logan and I did."

Abby and Logan broke up after graduation. She went to college on the West Coast. He went to college on the East Coast, and they decided not to torture each other with a long-distance relationship but swore to remain friends. They did.

She graduated and started working for our father. Logan graduated, went to medical school and ended up spending half his time in some practice and the other half in some laboratory looking through a microscope. That is until Abby was diagnosed with an autoimmune disorder. It hit her hard, hit her fast, and there were a few days at the beginning when the doctors prepared us for the worse. She defied death, but it was touch and go for two years, especially during the several rounds of chemo and the bone marrow transplant.

Her disorder is something she'll always have to deal with, but right now, she's healthy.

The moment Logan heard Abby was sick, he took the first flight from New York City to Louisville, and he's never looked back. After the wedding, they're taking a year and traveling the world. After all she's been through, she deserves the break.

Abby checks herself out in the mirror beside me and then takes a deep breath. "I'm ready now."

My eyes flicker to her bare feet. "Forgetting something?"

"Nope. Now, lead me to my wedding."

I learned in high school never to argue with Abby. It's safer for everyone that way. I offer Abby my arm, she accepts, and we head for the rest of her life.

THE VOWS HAVE BEEN SAID, most of the fanfare over and now the gathering only made up of close friends and family has entered a relaxed and celebratory mood. Logan and Abby are in the middle of the makeshift dance floor under the tent put up at the winery. He holds her close as they dance. They whisper and laugh with one another in a way that's so intimate it feels like I should look away.

Today has been one of the best in a long time. While we all stay in touch, our lives are busy. To have everyone in one place is a rare occurrence. Today feels good and right.

Rachel and Echo are gathered around Beth, carrying on

about triplets. Congrats are deserved, but I can't figure out how you feed three at once.

Isaiah, Noah, Ryan, Logan and Ryan's high school friends Chris and Lacey and I are catching up while we watch their children have a dance-off on the corner of the dance floor. Everyone's deep in conversation they believe I'm listening to, but Haley has my attention. She's across the tent chatting with my mother and father. Both of them adored her, and I'm not surprised that they cornered her. My entire family grieved when we ended.

Haley politely laughs with my mom, and I don't miss how Haley's gaze flickers toward me. It makes me think of my birthday in high school when my mother hijacked Haley to show her baby pictures of me. Back then, Haley was equal parts fascinated by Mom and ready for an escape. She wears the same expression now. I guess some things never change.

Tonight, I'm still bad boy enough to have a few smooth moves remaining. I stand, button my tux coat and take the long walk toward the girl I loved more than my own life.

Mom's telling Haley about the tedious preparations leading to the wedding, and I go old school rude and don't even bother to wait for Mom to take a breath. I slip in between them and offer my open palm to Haley. "Would you like to dance?"

Haley and I haven't said hi, haven't spoken a word tonight or in years. Short of each us catching the other looking from afar during the wedding, we've had no contact. Asking her to dance is bold, but if she remembers, bold is who I am.

Mom falls silent, and Haley studies me. My hand remains still, unwavering, and she finally places her fingers in mine. I breathe out without meaning to. It's been too long since I've experienced her touch.

I lead Haley to the dance floor, and the sensation of her in my arms again is a heady one. Her scent sweet, her skin soft, her body warm. I wonder if she thinks of those nights where we'd spend hours in bed kissing, laughing, and talking, because I do. Almost every day. "Hello, Haley."

"Hello, West," she says with a soft smile, but one that edges toward polite.

"Run into the path of any cars lately?"

She laughs, and this time the smile is real. "That was all you, Young."

It was, yet I fake insult and disappointment. "All these years and you're still trying to blame me for your poor crossing-the-street choices. I'm shocked. Heads up, I'm spinning you now."

I turn Haley with the music, then half enact a dip that brings on applause from the peanut gallery of our friends near the mosh pit of toddlers.

The spark in Haley's eyes appears, and I wish I could go back and throat punch the stupid guy who was more concerned with being free in his twenties than loving this beautiful creature who is currently in my arms.

"I hear you're a high school guidance counselor," she says.

"Yeah, I woke up one morning and thought, 'how can I roll around in the big bucks?' You should see the bonus I get for coaching girls' lacrosse. Five hundred dollars. I'm thinking I have enough to retire next year and live in the Caiman Islands."

Even though she's aware I have a trust fund that could feed a small country for the next fifty years, my words have the effect I'm looking for—she laughs. I haven't touched my trust fund, and don't have plans to in the near future. I want to make it on my own, even on a guidance counselor's pay.

"Abby said you were a guidance counselor in Japan for a few years."

I taught English there as well. "I couldn't resist the perks — free flight to another country."

Haley doesn't laugh this time, but instead scans my face. "The boy I knew all those years ago was so determined to be a fighter."

Being a fighter didn't bother Haley. It was my attitude that pushed her away. The boy she knew all those years ago was determined to never settle down. "I changed."

"Why?"

Because I woke up and realized the worst mistake I ever made was letting her walk away. "I figured the best person to help a kid making all the wrong choices is an adult who made all the wrong choices when he was a kid. I think my Masters courses called this empathy."

I spin us, and there are a few more claps.

"I forgot how good a dancer you are," she says.

"Did you?"

I expect her to tease me, but she doesn't. Instead, she says in a soft way as if recalling a good dream, "I remember."

I meet her eyes, and I try to say everything I should have said to her years ago, "So do I."

A flash of hurt in her eyes, and instinct causes me to pull her closer. Haley doesn't resist; in fact, she places both of her arms around my shoulders like we're eighteen and at prom all over again.

"I was wrong," I whisper in her ear. "All those years ago, I was wrong."

Haley grips me tighter, and I'd give anything if she would never let go. The two of us rock back and forth, and when she places her head on my shoulder, I silently wish that the song would never end, but it does. We stop moving, and we stand on the dance floor just holding one another. Haley eventually pulls back. "Thank you for the dance."

"Does it have to end?" I ask.

The music has switched to a faster song, so she knows I'm not referring to the dance. I want another chance at fixing us.

She glances around, and I follow her gaze. We have an entire group of friends watching our every movement. Won't lie, most of them with smiles on their faces.

That's not helping.

"Are you hungry?" I ask. "I can pull some strings and find us some of those crab cakes from earlier, as I happen to know the people putting on this gig."

Haley smiles again, and when I offer my hand for the second time tonight, she accepts once more.

CHAPTER 34

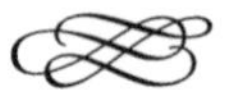

ABBY

My godson is the most amazing child in the world, and the world's best dancer. Seth's dress shoes are perched on my bare feet, and the two of us are rocking back and forth. In our combined hands is the white stuffed bunny he just gave to me for my wedding. Besides my bracelet and Logan saying *I do*, there isn't a better gift anyone could have given me.

Our own personal paparazzi are taking a million pictures of the two of us. The music ends, and everyone claps, causing Seth to let go of me and clap, too. I crouch down, and he gives me the most enthusiastic hug before running into Echo's open arms.

When my immune system had some fight to it, Echo would bring over her children to help bring some joy into my home. While Macie was fun, it was Seth who would cuddle with me and watch cartoons for hours on end. His warm and baby fat-padded hugs got me through many dark times.

Arms circle my waist from behind, and I incline back into Logan. He kisses the side of my neck, and pleasing tingles run along my skin. This day has been amazing, like a dream made into reality, and I'm sleepy. My muscles melt at his touch, and I relax further into him, leaning on his strength as mine is starting to fade.

"Come sit with me," he whispers in my ear. Logan takes my hand, and we weave through our guests. We smile at them, accept congratulations, but no one stops us. Maybe it's because Logan is determined to get me alone, and wears the face of a man who does what he wants when he wants to. I have a feeling, though, it's because I have yet to sit since dinner, and my exhaustion shows.

One of the awful parts of the past year? There were times I was so physically weak that there was no way to hide it. I lived a good portion of my life believing that showing any type of weakness was the equivalent of a death sentence.

The past two years were one tough lesson after another on how pride doesn't win me as many battles as I thought it would.

I'm better now, though I'm not one hundred percent. This battle is one I'll be fighting on some level for the rest of my life, but lucky for me, I'm a fighter, and the man I'm married is a warrior. Between the two of us, we can beat the impossible.

A few feet away from the tent is a fire pit and a couch. The temperature of the fall evening has dropped as stars twinkle in the sky. I sit, and Logan slips off his tux coat and drapes it over my arms before joining me. I draw my feet up and recline into Logan as he wraps an arm around me.

One of the many things I love about Logan: he doesn't ask if I'm okay or if I'm tired or how I'm doing. He doesn't make me feel weak, even when I am. He makes me feel as if it's winning a battle when I take the moment to regain my strength.

Logan lifts my wrist and rubs his finger over the blue stone. "West told me about it. Do you like it?"

"I love it," I say. "Thank you for today, and for my wedding present."

Logan has bought ten acres next to Isaiah and Rachel's place, and on that land will be a house we will design together—with Noah's help. It will also contain a play yard for my bunny army. Along with the deed for the land was a copy of an email I had sent to Logan when I was in juvenile detention as a teen. The email laid out my plan to take over the world with nothing but rabbits.

"I had to talk Seth out of giving you a real rabbit," Logan says. "He doesn't understand why we can't take it on a plane with us."

I tilt my head. "He does have a good argument. I mean bunnies are small, and—"

"No," Logan rejects any part of my statement. "No bunnies on the trip. Nonnegotiable."

"You're no fun."

"I'm plenty of fun."

He is. Since I've known Logan, he has been a free spirit. Living life on his terms, never anyone else's. Logan went to college, went to medical school, and then became a scientist determined to find a cure for diabetes. He works in a practice, he works in a lab, but mostly Logan lives life by traveling to places no one else will go. Doctors without Borders, personal voyages to places where he could help, trips to places where he could be alone.

No rules, just Logan redefining the world.

Living a life without rules cost me dearly as a teen. So, I did what any other young person who was determined to change would do—I ran in the opposite direction.

College, a sales job in a reputable firm, black dress-suits with designer shoes, dinners, lunches, racing up the corporate ladder at a sprint. Responsible, determined, successful, resourceful, independent…and oddly enough I still felt as empty as I did selling drugs on the street.

Then Logan reentered my life….

In the tent, on a table, is a board of pictures taken over the past two years. Pictures of Logan and me as we took a journey. A journey where, when I had enough strength, he took me on every adventure possible. Often against doctors' wishes. Often in the face of brutal arguments with our well-meaning friends. But he understood what I needed to defeat this attack on my body—he knew I needed to live.

To live.

I've seen eagles fly over snowcapped mountains. I've watched the sun rise and set in Key West. I've stood at the edge of the Grand Canyon and realized how small I am in the world. Logan has taken me all around this country, and now we are ready to spread our wings and fly.

"We can bring a small bunny. One that fits in my purse. No one will notice."

"TSA will love that."

"Maybe I can bring two bunnies. I don't want the one to get lonely."

"We're going to spend our honeymoon in lock-up, aren't we?"

"I'll sweet-talk TSA into letting me bring a bunny onto the plane. I'll dazzle the security agents. They won't know what hit them."

"I've created a monster with you, haven't I?"

I shrug innocently. "Well, you did buy me a bunny farm."

Logan places his fingers under my chin and whispers against my lips, "I did."

"Hurry up and kiss me, Logan. You know I don't like being kept waiting."

"No, you don't," he agrees and finally presses his lips to

mine. The kiss is strong, powerful and causes tingles in my blood. It's the type of kiss that makes me want to run my fingers through his hair, unbutton his shirt and…

"Say cheese."

I open my eyes only to be blinded by a flash of light as Noah takes a picture of me and Logan.

"I hate you, Hutchins."

"Consider it payback for that damn toy you bought Oliver that makes all that noise."

I smile because that toy was fun.

Rachel comes up beside him, and I gesture for her to sit next to me.

"We need a group photo," Rachel says. "My parents are watching all the kids so after the photo I vote we all take off before they notice. Ariel is trying to talk my parents into hosting a sleepover for all the kids, and she is going to be mad when Mom says no."

"So will Macie. I vote we go to a pool hall," Noah says as the rest of our friends walk up. "Isaiah needs to be beat at a game."

Isaiah pats Noah's shoulder. "Like you can beat me at pool."

Beth and Ryan enter the firelight hand-in-hand, and she rolls her eyes. "Anyone can beat Isaiah at pool."

He laughs because it's true.

It takes a few minutes to get everyone settled, and a few more minutes for the guys to swap insults about how they look in suits and tuxes. The photographer positions herself across from us, and we're silent for a moment, waiting for the picture to be taken, lost in the joy of being together again.

Logan beside me, West beside Haley, Isaiah beside Rachel, Ryan beside Beth and Noah beside Echo. Exactly how the world should be.

And they all lived happily ever after.

RETURNING HOME

A PUSHING THE LIMITS AND THUNDER ROAD NOVELLA

CHAPTER 35

OZ

I'm kicking ass in college while working close to full time for the security company. I'm studying to be a special education teacher, have been student teaching at Snowflake Elementary School, and I'm an upstanding member of the Reign of Terror Motorcycle Club. What's more, I've dated Eli McKinley's daughter since I was eighteen and have somehow not been shot by him yet.

Today, though, the last part could very well come to an end.

From the infant seat in the bathtub, Pigpen and Caroline's daughter, Adelaide, looks up at me with bright blue eyes and giggles.

Giggles.

I'm going to get shot in the head and the eight-month-old giggles.

"Oz, what the hell happened to Eli's motorcycle? It's—" Chevy stops short as he enters the bathroom. He studies me, studies the baby and does the math quick. "Oh, sh—"

"There's a baby," I cut him off, and I gently scrub Adelaide's hands again with the washcloth to make sure I got all the paint off. Getting her into the bathtub before she could put her fingers in her mouth was a momentous feat. Last thing I need is to leave any paint on her skin for her to eat, and then have Pigpen gunning for me because his kid's been poisoned. "Watch the language or Caroline will rip our hearts from our chests."

"Yeah. I got the lecture, too. Tell me that's finger paint."

"I wish."

"Is she the reason why Eli's motorcycle has purple spots and streaks?"

"I left her alone for less than a minute."

Chevy chuckles deeply then leans a shoulder against the doorframe. "How did she get into paint? Even better, how did she get into paint near Eli's bike?"

Because I was born under an unlucky star. "Mom was putting finishing touches on the going-away gift she's making Emily. She asked me to help take some stuff into the clubhouse. I placed Adelaide on her blanket in the grass, next to her two million toys, and I was in the clubhouse for a second and…then…."

Eli's black Harley-Davidson is now decorated with purple Adelaide fingerprints and her creative streaks. Eli's going to torture me for weeks and then, if he's feeling merciful, he'll kill me.

"You realize the kid can crawl, right?" Chevy shakes his head in amusement. "Even if she couldn't when you left her, that's Pigpen and our high school English teacher's daughter.

Genetically, she's got enough brain power to launch rockets to Mars. If she wanted to decide to learn how to crawl in thirty seconds, that kid could do it. I'm scared to let Adelaide have my cell to gnaw on because not only could she hack into my phone and change my password, she'd probably use the cell to break into CIA databases and then I'd be the one arrested."

"I was gone for thirty seconds."

"You suck at babysitting."

Understatement.

"That paint's drying out there. Once it's dried..."

"I'm screwed." I'm aware, but I chose to clean up Adelaide first because paint is poison and she likes to eat her thumbs. "Can you wipe down Eli's motorcycle while I wash her up?"

Chevy laughs to let me know he's no fool. He's aware how bad this is, and, as a criminal justice major, he's not stupid enough to be caught at the scene of the crime. Instead, he steps past me in the cramped bathroom and crouches down beside me. "I'll finish washing the tyke. You can handle Eli's motorcycle. Or you can run. I suggest running and looking into witness protection, because you're a dead man."

"You're not scared Caroline's going to catch you with Adelaide while she has paint under her fingernails? She and Pigpen will be home soon."

"That's easy. I'll remind Caroline you were the one babysitting."

"Some friend you are," I mumble, and Chevy laughs again as he takes the washcloth from me.

"Who's taking a bath?" Chevy coos at Adelaide as if he's not over six feet tall and close to two hundred pounds of muscle—one hundred percent McKinley, dark brown eyes and hair included. "Does Adelaide like her bath?" A master magician, he waves his fingers in the air and then produces a miniature rubber duck out of thin air. Adelaide cackles. "See, she wants me."

"Because you bribed her with a duck."

Chevy grins from ear to ear as he hands the little paint monster the toy. "You should get moving and clean Eli's bike. Or are you going to use this horrific event as an excuse to coward out and not ask Emily again?"

The glare I throw him should leave him shaking in his black boots. "You're a—"

He mock covers Adelaide's ears. "There's a baby." Then uncovers them and coos at her again, "Uncle Oz is a coward." Chevy glances at me and motions near his cheek. "You've got paint on you."

Because when I snatched Adelaide off the ground and away from Eli's bike, she decided to start painting me. The words I really want to say definitely aren't baby appropriate, so as I walk out of the bathroom, I flip him a bird that's not a duck.

I grab towels, head out of Cyrus's house, and cross the yard to the front of the clubhouse, to where Eli's motorcycle is parked. I groan at the damage. "Damn," I say, running a hand through my hair. It's a hot day and the smeared paint's dried.

As I contemplate the ways Eli's going to peel the skin off my body, my cell vibrates in my back pocket. I take it out and find a text from Emily: *Just finished my last final, my car is packed and I'm on my way to you!!!*

Me: *Congrats and I love you. Be safe on the drive.* Maybe you can convince your dad to leave me alive long enough to propose to you.

Emily: *I will and I love you back!*

Suddenly, my front pocket becomes heavy. In it is a small box. In that box is an even smaller diamond ring. Paying for college—even by going part-time—plus paying for rent and just meeting everyday needs, I don't have a lot to offer Emily.

Emily, my Emily. Long chestnut hair, dark eyes like a doe, and the most beautiful girl in the world. She's intelligent, kind, vivacious, and she's going to become a doctor.

When I first met Emily, she was bold, but she had so many fears. Fear of change, fear of leaving home, fear that loving Eli, her biological dad, would affect her relationship with her adoptive father, and a fear of dead bodies. Now Emily fears close to nothing and will be attending medical after she graduates from college. She wants to be a pediatrician—just like her adoptive father.

She's heading here tonight, dropping off the boxes from her dorm, and then flying home to her mom and dad on Monday. After that she'll go to Europe for a year—to travel with her folks and then to study abroad. I've had this ring for a month, and I've planned several different ways to get down on one knee, but life keeps getting in the way.

My first idea was to propose during our weekend trip to the Smoky Mountains with Chevy, Violet, Breanna, and Razor, but then Emily came down with bronchitis. Instead, I held her in bed while she alternated between watching TV and sleeping. Idea number two was to propose at her favorite restaurant. I made plans to put the ring in her favorite dessert, chocolate cake, but then Eli announced that he and Nina, Chevy's mom, were going to elope in Nashville that weekend, and he wanted us all there to watch them tie the knot. Proposing to Emily during her father's wedding felt rude, so I held off.

Then life got busy. Emily goes to school an hour away. I go to the same school two days a week, then do the rest of my classes online. She works, I work. I student teach, she's had internships. We see each other, but for fleeting moments.

The new plan is to take Emily to the overlook to pop the question. The problem is that while I've asked Emily to go with me there tonight, she hasn't agreed yet, telling me that we will if we have enough time. That's the problem. Time is the enemy.

Yeah, I understand why she's hesitant to go away with me. Violet and Chevy are coming in for the summer from college, Isaiah and Rachel are coming in from Louisville, and Razor and Breanna are driving in from the northeast. It's going to be the first time in months we've all been together, but I need this time with her. I want to ask her to be my wife.

The question is, will there be time, and if there is, will Eli kill me for what I've done to his bike? Even better question—will Emily say yes?

CHAPTER 36

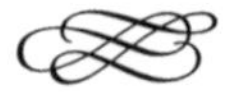

ISAIAH

I love working on any car, but I prefer the classics. There's something genius about the simplicity of an older car. It never fails to amaze me that something made over fifty years ago, with a few tweaks along the way, can still roar with the power of a lion when I hit the gas.

One of the best parts of having family in the Reign of Terror Motorcycle Club is that these men love machines nearly as much as I do. They share a love affair with two wheels, while my desires lie mainly with the four-wheeled version, but most of the guys own, along with a motorcycle or two, a beautiful four-wheeled machine.

My favorite is this one—a 1964 Chevelle. It packs a 300-horsepower, 327-cubic-inch V8. She's gorgeous, and she belongs to Violet, my half-brother Chevy's girlfriend. Afraid, with good reason, that it's going to be scratched or stolen at her college, Violet only drives the car when she's home, and the last time she was home, she heard a rattling under the hood. I changed a few belts and now the Chevelle's running almost as good as when she was driven off the line over fifty years ago.

Eli, my uncle, leans back against the wall of Hook's garage with his arms crossed over his chest. Hook—Razor's dad—and Cyrus—my grandfather—are standing near the hood of the car, inspecting, with awe, my work. Cyrus constantly tells me I have a gift. There isn't much about me I'll brag about, but when it comes to my knowledge of cars, I don't disagree.

Sitting in the driver's seat, I rev the engine one more time just to hear that beautiful purr, then twist the key to turn the engine off. I ease out of the car, shut the door, and toss the key to Eli. "She's as good as new."

"Thanks." Eli snatches the key out of the air. The muscles in his arms ripple with the motion, causing the stars tattooed there to wave. The man might be one of the few in the world who can match me in skin ink. "What do we owe you?"

"Something to drink?" I ask.

"I got it," Cyrus says, and Hook follows him in to the house.

"Besides water," Eli says. "What do I owe you?"

"Same as last time." Chevy's my brother. Violet is the women he loves. That's family, and I don't charge family.

"We'd feed you and Rachel without you working on a car," Eli says. "The least we can do is give you something for your time."

"Naw, I'm good."

"I'm serious."

"I said I'm good." I pick up my tools, drop them back into my toolbox and wish Eli would let it go.

He doesn't understand. Years ago, before Chevy and Violet walked into the garage I was working at, I was an orphan. My mom had spent most of my life in prison, and her getting out during my senior year didn't make me any less alone in the world.

Yeah, I had Noah, Beth, and Abby, fell in love with Rachel, and had met our other friends I consider family, but I never had a family. Those people who are bound to you by blood and have to love you—or at least tolerate you during holidays.

I'm grateful for the family I've chosen and wouldn't trade them for anything, but to find out that I have a blood family who wants me, loves me, well, that still chokes me up. And to be honest, I still don't know what to do with this newfound family.

Everyone has been nice. Friendly. Overly welcoming. They each have a hunger in their eyes for me to accept whatever it is they're offering whether it's a plate of food, a chance to join the conversation or a simple handshake.

The problem lies with me. When I get around my blood family, I close up. Way deep down on the inside, I want to be here, but there's something that clams up, keeps me quiet—observing. Except when I work on cars. Then it feels natural, like being at home.

For the past few hours, I've been chatting with Eli, Cyrus, Hook, Man O' War, and whatever members of the club have dropped by. The conversation is easy, like I'm back in the garage in my old neighborhood talking with Noah, Echo, Abby, Logan, and any other of our friends. We've not really talked about anything serious—just useless chit-chat while my hands are covered in grease—but now that the car is done, I'm brain dead on conversation.

I close the toolbox and straighten. "Is there anything else you'd like me to take a look at?"

"You know you could come down here to visit us, never touch a car and we'd be happy."

I know. It's what I want to say, but I can't. It's stuck somewhere deep in places where only Rachel's been allowed to break through and enter.

Eli stares at me with his steady glare. He's sizing me up for a fight. Not for a physical fight. Nothing in his body language suggests that. I've never felt threatened around any McKinley or anyone in the club, but I can tell his mind is working overtime. Searching for a way to win this battle to give me something in return for work I don't mind doing.

"You're my family," Eli continues. "If you were raised here, you would basically be my son. Cyrus and my mom would have loved and cared for you. The moment I had gotten out of prison, I would have been involved in every second of your life. You have to know—"

"But I wasn't raised here," I cut him off. I was raised by the foster care system. Bounced from house to house. Some of them good, some of them bad. A few were awful. "I'm giving you the best I've got."

"Isaiah," he tries again.

"Let it go, Eli," I say with quiet exhaustion. Enough for him to hear, but low enough for him to know I can't. I turn away, give him a second to be pissed then move on with the day.

There's shifting behind me as he readjusts his footing then he does what I need: moves on to small talk. "How's work?"

My work, his work, Rachel's work. I don't do small talk with many people, but I allow it with the McKinleys. They're trying, and though they might not know it, I am, too.

"Good. Pro-Performance's been busy. The overtime money's been good. Work's been steady over at..." I stumble over Tom's name, but continue, "the shop."

Tom's shop. Tom gave me a steady paying job when I was thirteen. It was he and Mack, the lead mechanic, who taught me everything I know about cars. Tom died a few months ago and left the shop to Mack. Mack's health isn't the best. His joints and bones plague him, and he's looking to sell the shop and retire to Florida.

I make good money at Pro-Performance, the custom car

shop, and don't need to work at Tom's to make ends meet. But I do work there on nights and weekends. I've told myself it's to make extra money so Rachel and I can purchase a garage of our own. But it's also because there are few things I have allowed myself to become attached to, and the garage is one of them.

"You okay?" Eli catches my slip.

"Yeah." No. Tom dying, Mack selling the garage...it's a lot of change I don't care for, and it ends one of the streams of income that helps me reach my and Rachel's dream. I pick up a few more tools off the bench near Eli, drop them into the toolbox and then place the box into the trunk of my car, which is parked next to Violet's. Now it's my turn to try.

"How's the security business?"

Eli's part owner of the security company that he and other members of the Reign of Terror run. "Great. Business is booming. Razor's done a great job expanding our club and our customer base in the northeast."

I nod because it's all good to hear. Then there's a moment of awkward silence as I close the trunk to my Mustang.

"How's The Plan going?" Eli tries again.

The Plan—capital letters always included, when I think of the words. Rachel and I concocted The Plan when we were teenagers making out in the backseat of our cars. My part of The Plan: I work at Pro-Performance, grow my reputation in the custom car community, sack away as much money as I can, work at Tom's garage to make additional money, and cultivate more relationships with future clients.

Rachel's part of The Plan was to go to college and earn her degrees in business and electrical engineering—knowledge that will be helpful with newer-model cars. Rachel earned her degrees last year. Since then, she's been working a desk job at her father's company, soaking in as much business knowledge while she can, as we save the money we need to build our own shop. The timeline—we've got five more years of our ten-year plan.

After we buy the land and start building the shop, we'll get married. For now, I live in a rat-infested apartment I barely let Rachel visit. The place is in a high-crime neighborhood and not worthy of her, but it costs next to nothing. To help save more money, she lives at home.

We're on track for our dreams to come true, but sometimes, when I'm kissing her goodbye at night, our timeline feels too far away. "The Plan's going well."

"I think Oz is going to propose to Emily this weekend," Eli says, and my eyes snap to his when I don't hear happiness.

"You know?" I test the waters.

"Yeah. Oz asked me and her Dad's permission last spring."

"I thought you'd be good with them getting married." Emily is his daughter, and Oz is like a son to him. As long as I've been around, Eli's been in favor of the relationship.

"I am," Eli says. "But Oz keeps trying to create the perfect moment, and I have a feeling with everyone coming home this weekend, he's not going to find the scenario he wants. She leaves for Europe next week."

I stare at him blankly. "If he doesn't, he doesn't. Oz and Emily are solid. Distance and time won't shake that."

"Agreed, but this is something he's been trying to do since he asked my permission. If he doesn't do it before she goes, he'll regret it and beat himself up for it. With Emily being an ocean away, that's a tough regret to have. Oz is waiting for perfection and that doesn't exist."

Yeah, I'll give him that. "Regret's a bitch."

Eli inclines his head in agreement. "That it is. Life changes fast, Isaiah. Sometimes too fast. I wish I had understood that when I was younger." He forces a smile on his face. "You ready to head back to Cyrus's?"

I nod, but can't help but wonder why there's a pit in my stomach and why my brain won't let go of the word regret.

CHAPTER 37

RACHEL

Nina and Eli built a small house in the woods of Cyrus's property. It's quaint and adorable, like stepping into a fairytale cottage, and comes equipped with modern conveniences. It's far enough away that they have privacy, but when cold weather comes and the leaves fall away, they'll probably be able to see the clubhouse from their front porch.

We enter the kitchen, and Nina sets the cup of coffee she had in her hand during the tour of the house on the counter. I glance out the back window and marvel at the beauty of the thick green woods. "Have you seen any deer?"

"Every morning." Nina wears a huge smile, like someone who's in love and happy. Every word that comes out of her mouth is complete with a flourish of her left hand—as if she subconsciously has to show the world not only her engagement ring, but the wedding band Eli gave her when they eloped in Nashville. "Eli and I watch them graze as the sun comes up."

I have a hard time seeing the tattooed, hardcore motorcycle man being a softie for morning deer, but then again, the tattooed, hardcore man I love has a thing for stray puppies. Isaiah owns a German Shepherd mix he found as a puppy outside of Pro-Performance and a small white Shih Tzu he discovered shivering in the rain outside Taco Bell. He named the German Shepherd Mustang and he named the Shih Tzu Ford.

"How's The Plan going?" Nina asks.

The ends of my lips turn up. That is possibly the most-asked question Isaiah and I receive when we visit the Reign of Terror. They are utterly and completely fascinated by our ten-year strategy. Most people thought we would crumble once I graduated from college last year, but we're staying true to our dreams. "It's going well. We have a ton of money saved up, and we're on track to build a garage in five years. Everything will be new and shiny, and it's going to be perfect."

"I often wish I had your and Isaiah's persistence and perseverance at your age. I would have graduated from college in my twenties instead of going part-time in my forties." Nina is studying to become a therapist. She said that after years of listening to people talk about their problems while she worked as a bartender, she might as well do it for a living.

"I couldn't wait to get out of my parents' house when I turned eighteen," she continues. "I wanted my independence so bad I did anything to get it. I am absolutely in awe of you."

"Thank you." Nina is being genuine with me. Unfortunately, I've heard backhanded comments about my choices for years—you're still in college and live at home? You're graduated and working a full-time job and still live at home?

Most times, it's exhausting to explain. The first year of college, I lived at home and not in the dorms because I was still recovering from an accident that happened my junior year of high school. Yes, the accident and my injuries were that bad. My parents would have paid for me to live in the dorms my sophomore year, but I knew if I did that, I'd spend my money on day-to-day things, whereas if I lived at home, Mom and Dad would cover those items.

I don't want to spend money. I want to save as much as I can, especially since Isaiah works almost twenty-four/seven to help with our dream. It only seems fair for me to make sacrifices, as well. Not that living in a mansion with maids and a kitchen staff is a sacrifice, but I am hungry for independence. My mom and dad, even though I love them and we have come to awesome understandings with each other, often forget I'm in my twenties and not twelve. At least once a month I feel so smothered that I scream into my pillow at night.

My parents are financially well-off and have offered to buy the land and build the shop for us, even telling us to consider it a loan if the idea of taking the money from them bothers us. But Isaiah and I both know that if Dad is involved, even though he means well, he'll feel entitled to have a say in our business—and that's not what we want. This road is a lot longer and harder than I thought it would be, but I keep reminding myself it will be worth it in the end.

Nina rearranges flowers in a vase at the counter and the sunlight catches her diamond ring again. Isaiah and I are practically engaged, but there's no ring on my finger, nor has he dropped down on one knee. Getting married is part of The Plan, once we have enough money to build the garage, but I often consider asking for a renegotiation on.

Isaiah and I see each other often, but I'd love to see him more. I'd love to wake up in his arms every morning, instead of a couple of times a week. Instead of having a routine for me and a routine for him, we would have a routine for us. I'm ready for more, but how do I tell Isaiah?

Nina keeps fidgeting with the flowers, even ones she's

messed with several times before. I'm not best friends with Nina, but we've spent enough time together since Isaiah discovered the McKinleys are his blood family that I know when she's nervous.

"Are you okay?" I ask.

She sighs heavily as she quits her assault on the poor plants. "Eli won't be happy, but I think we need your advice on something."

I frown. None of that sounds good. "What could I help with?"

"Follow me."

Nina crosses the kitchen and opens the door to the garage. I follow her into it and pause in awe at the motorcycle in front of me. It's not one I've seen around the club before, and I have an idea of where this is headed. "Whose is it?"

"You have three good guesses and the first two don't count."

Isaiah—the motorcycle is for Isaiah. Wow.

"Do you think Isaiah will like it?" Nina asks me. She's a mixture of worry, excitement and hesitation. "We know he's into cars, but he's a McKinley so bikes have to be in his blood somewhere. Plus, Eli and Cyrus really want Isaiah to have his father's bike."

"I thought Chevy had their father's motorcycle," I say.

"He does. James had two motorcycles. Chevy has the one his father rode, and Eli had the other. James found this one in a junk yard and was fixing it up before he died. Eli finished the job, and now Eli wants Isaiah to have it."

Chevy and Isaiah are half-brothers, though neither knew the other existed until relatively recently. Since then, Isaiah has been slowly—slowly as in snails move faster than him—allowing them to be a part of his life.

On the other hand, whenever Isaiah's in town, the

McKinleys and the Reign of Terror Motorcycle Club follow him around like cats waiting on their food bowl. If they had their way, even though he was nineteen when they met, they would have packed him up and moved him into one of the rooms at the clubhouse or Cyrus's house in a heartbeat.

But besides a relationship with me, Isaiah doesn't jump headfirst into things. Especially with people who say they're family. Because of Isaiah's past, he doesn't love or trust easily. His weariness, though, hasn't shut out the McKinleys. They're patient—admirably so.

I round the Harley-Davidson while playing with the ends of my blond hair. Having been around the Reign of Terror, I've learned some about bikes. "This is a FLSTF Fat Boy. V2 engine, 5-speed gearbox." It's silver, with a shine like it has been well loved, and I have no idea how Isaiah is going to react.

"Spoken like a true member of the club."

I smile at the compliment. The club would love for Isaiah to become a member, but he's not interested. It's nothing against them, it's just that he prefers the family connection he has with the McKinleys over the idea of membership. But that doesn't stop the wives of the club members from trying to talk to me about it, as if I could or would want to change Isaiah's mind.

Isaiah's over at Hook's, working on Violet's Chevelle. The car has sentimental value to her, and she only allows Isaiah to work on it when there are problems. After that, there's a long list of men at the clubhouse who have asked Isaiah to look at their cars, even offering to pay.

Isaiah always agrees because he loves cars, but I often wonder if he sees the real intent—that the only time he loosens up with Eli, Cyrus, Pigpen, Oz, Razor, Chevy, or anyone from the club is when he has a tool in his hand and an open car hood. To keep him talking, to keep him relaxed, to hopefully keep him a part of their world, they will possibly break their cars on purpose.

"So, what do you think?" Nina pushes. "About the motorcycle?"

I think she's smart to show me the bike first. "I think he'll like it." I let my fingers slip along the chrome handlebars.

"I hear a *but* in there." Nina twists strands of her long dark hair.

How do I explain? Isaiah isn't the type to get outwardly excited about much. He feels joy and happiness, but he tempers his reactions. And sometimes when he feels overwhelmed with joy he retreats, just a little, enough for him to quietly reflect upon and explore the emotions that he never allowed himself to feel growing up. "When is Eli going to give it to him?"

"That's why I'm talking to you. When any of the other boys received their motorcycles, even if they were just the frames for them to restore, it was given during one of the club parties, so everyone could take part. Eli respects how private Isaiah can be and he's not sure giving him this at the party is the best way. At the same time, Eli wants Isaiah to feel part of the family, so he doesn't want him to feel excluded by doing something different."

I marvel at the way the McKinleys love Isaiah. "He wouldn't want any of you walking on eggshells for him. I know he's not always talkative, but he does care."

"This gift means a lot to Eli and..."

"He wants it to mean something to Isaiah," I finish for her.

"They all do. I've tried explaining to them that Isaiah doesn't have the same connection to James that they do. Isaiah doesn't remember James. He didn't even know who his father was until he was practically a man himself. It's a miracle Isaiah has let us into his life, but that doesn't mean he should have any sentimentality when it comes to his father and this bike."

Nina's talking to me because she's in love with Eli and doesn't want to see him crushed—which might happen if Isaiah doesn't love this bike the same way he does. Eli, in essence, is handing Isaiah his heart—I guess the way men do with each other. "It'll mean something to Isaiah." Maybe not the way they think, but it will.

I nibble on my bottom lip and consider the multiple feelings at risk and the multiple ways this could possibly play out. "Eli really wants Isaiah to receive the bike in front of everyone, doesn't he?"

"Yes."

"I'll prepare Isaiah, and I promise Eli won't know that I did."

She sags with relief. "Thank you, Rachel."

I'm glad to help Nina, and I'm honored that she feels comfortable with me to talk about something so emotional. But while a small sliver of me is helping because I care for her and Eli, I'm really doing this to help the man I love.

CHAPTER 38

ISAIAH

Sitting on a stool at the bar in the clubhouse of the Reign of Terror MC, I watch Rachel as she plays with Pigpen and Caroline's daughter Adelaide. She looks comfortable with the eight-month-old, as if sitting on the floor on a blanket playing with a rubber duck is a happy place she never knew existed. Adelaide appears just as happy. She cackles as Rachel causes the duck to skip over Adelaide's arm.

Most days I still marvel that a blonde, blue-eyed angel wants to be with a tattooed, earring-wearing punk like me. As if she can hear my thoughts, Rachel glances at me and winks.

She loves me, and I love her. Miracles do happen.

"What's happening?" my brother Chevy asks as he slips up beside me. We share a strong hug that includes pats on the back.

"Nothing," I reply. "You?"

"Same as always."

We release each other, and he nods at Rachel. "She's a natural with kids."

"Rachel's great," I say. At everything. I never thought much about Rachel with babies, but she is good with them. Better than good—she's great. Rachel's just naturally good with people. There's no reason babies wouldn't be included in the mix.

Rachel and babies. Rachel as a mom. Rachel the mom to my children. My heart warms at the idea, and I take a drink from the bottle I'm holding to keep any reaction off my face.

We have a plan though.

The Plan.

Five more years until we own our company and can start our life together.

Five years.

That sounds forever away.

Rachel glances my way, and seeing the smile that brightens her face is like watching the sun rise in a clear blue sky. I smile back, not caring that anyone can see how ridiculously happy I am when she looks at me.

"Can we talk?" Chevy asks, his voice pitched low.

This ought to be interesting. "What's going on?"

Chevy scans the room. Besides us, the clubhouse is relatively empty. Razor had just pulled in, and most everyone followed him and Breanna into Cyrus's cabin. I'm looking forward to catching up with them, but I figure that will happen later, like it always does at these parties. A few hours in, Rachel, Oz, Emily, Razor, Breanna, Chevy, Violet, Stone and I end up at the picnic table outside shooting the breeze.

"Oz wants to propose to Emily tonight."

Seems like everyone is on this—everyone but Emily. "Sounds good."

"Yeah, but Oz got himself into some trouble. I don't think Emily wants to remember the night they got engaged as the night Eli killed Oz."

"What kind of trouble?"

"Eli's motorcycle, paint and Adelaide—that type of trouble."

Any situation with the combination of those three is damn funny—at least from the safe

side of the situation. "And?"

"Do you know how to paint a motorcycle?"

I chuckle. There's never a dull moment in this place —never.

CHAPTER 39

EMILY

Razor and Chevy kidnapped me from the driver's seat of my car and won't stop hugging me. It's not really hugging as much as it's a game of them passing me back and forth between them without my feet ever touching the ground, as if I weigh nothing. I'm laughing so hard that there are tears in my eyes and my sides hurt, and each time I try to slip from their grasp, it seems there's another Reign of Terror member waiting to capture me in a bear hug, then pass me back to the duo of doom.

"Put me down!" I say between breaths.

"Nope," Pigpen says, as he's the next one to lift me from my feet and shake me from side to side. "This is what happens when you stay away too long."

"I..." I'm laughing so hard I can't breathe. "I had papers and finals. And this is no fair, Razor's been gone longer than me."

"Yeah," Pigpen says. "But he's not as fun to hug."

Pigpen shifts me to the right, and when I'm about to scream because I'm not sure I can handle being handed off to someone else, I find myself wrapped tight in strong arms along with a delicious kiss to my neck. My heart skips several beats as I inhale Oz's scent and I melt into him.

"Hey, beautiful," Oz whispers into my ear.

I raise up on my toes as he leans down to kiss me. My hands glide up his back and into his black hair. Around us, people "oooh" and "aaah" in a mocking-fun way as if we've been caught making out in high school. I'm twenty-one now and have been to my fair share of Reign of Terror parties. Some of these men have done way more embarrassing things than what I'm doing right now, so they can shut up.

We eventually stop kissing, and he pulls me close for another hug. It's been three weeks since we've seen each other, and as much as I'm happy to see him, I'm a bit sad—it's just a reminder of how much I'll miss him when I go to Europe for the year.

I considered not going to Europe to study for my last year of college, but then Oz pushed me for the real reason why I was passing up the opportunity since it was clear I wanted to go. When I told him it was because I was going to miss him, he told me that wasn't acceptable.

"I love you," he had said to me, while using his thumb to remove a tear from my cheek. "And I'm not okay with you turning down such a great opportunity because of me."

So, I'm going—with Mom and Dad for a month vacation, and then to settle in and study. Eli, Oz, and Cyrus have plans to visit me while I'm there, then Breanna and Violet are planning a girls' trip, but none of their visits will be for long enough. As much as I'm excited to live in Paris, I'm equally sad. I love this entire group of people, and it's hard to think I can't see them anytime I want for the next year.

"Come away with me," Oz whispers in my ear.

I want to, so much. It's been too long since we've had any intimate time alone. I pull back from our hug, glance around and I'm surprised to find everyone gone. Oz and I are standing alone in the grass near my car. Over Oz's shoulder, I watch as the group of guys who had been welcoming me home head to the clubhouse, so Oz and I can spend time together.

"I haven't said hi to Eli or Cyrus yet." But the words are empty as my blood warms with Oz's gentle caress up and down my arms.

"I'll bring you back. Just an hour, Emily."

With another brush of his lips against mine, the decision is made—I'll say hi to them later, and I'm saying yes to Oz now. I lock my fingers with Oz's and smile up at him. A sexy smile touches his mouth, and he tugs on my hand to guide me forward.

We walk side-by-side, our shoulders and arms touching with our strides, as we head to Oz's motorcycle. There are few places that I love as much as being on the back of Oz's bike. I love my arms wrapped around him, the heat created by our bodies being pressed so close, the wind in my hair and the feeling of flying.

Right as Oz digs his keys out of his jeans' front pocket, Razor calls out to us, "Oz!"

Oz groans, and I completely understand the feeling. I don't want to get sucked into the clubhouse, because then we'll never be alone. I squeeze Oz's hand. "Let's run."

He grins down at me. "You sure?"

"Definitely."

"Oz," Razor calls out again. "I know you want time alone, but Chevy's talking to Isaiah to see if he can fix Eli's motorcycle before he figures out what happened to it."

My head tilts to the side as I take in Razor's words and the look of dread on Oz's face. "What does he mean about Eli's motorcycle? Has something happened to it?"

Oz rolls his neck. “Have I ever told you I suck at babysitting?”

“No.” There’s no way any of this is good.

CHAPTER 40

RACHEL

Behind the clubhouse, Isaiah and I stare in shock at Eli's motorcycle. Adelaide struggles in my arms as if there's a gravitational field calling her towards the bike, but I don't think her going near it is a good idea. From what I've gathered, she's the one who caused the damage.

"What do you think?" Oz asks. "Can you fix it?"

Isaiah glances at me from the corner of his eye and I give him the same knowing glance back. Yes, it can be fixed, but it will require a complete repaint. Something we can do at Tom's garage, but nothing we can do here. And nothing we can do before Eli wants his motorcycle this evening.

As Isaiah starts to shake his head, I place a hand on his arm. Another glance at me and he knows I have something I need to say to him. With a tilt of my head, he knows it's something I want to say in private.

The Reign of Terror family has learned how Isaiah and I conduct subtle conversations in body language. Razor takes Adelaide from me, and they quietly fall back—giving us space.

"I know that look," Isaiah says. "You think we can take

this on, but we can't fix it here. Even if we had the tools, a paint job like this takes time."

"I've done a few paint jobs," I remind him then scan the area to make sure that Emily stayed in the clubhouse. She's not around so I continue, "So I know all this. The whole point is that Eli will be mad, right? Even if he doesn't show it, Oz and Emily are going to know he's upset, and that's not the memory they want with their engagement, right?"

"Yeah, but I can't help. Not in enough time."

"I know, but what if you offer Eli a trade?"

Isaiah is adorably confused. "A trade?"

"A bike for a bike. And trust me, it's a trade he'll like."

"I don't understand."

I know he doesn't, and I take a deep breath as I take the jump. "Eli's going to give you your father's motorcycle tonight in front of the entire club."

I reach out and grab Isaiah's hand as I watch the shock and vulnerability flicker over his face. The muscles in his hand are stiff as he locks up with emotion.

"I..." Isaiah glances around wildly. "I can't accept that."

I nod because I knew that's how he would feel. The gift is too expensive, and the gift is too big emotionally. "Eli wants you to have it."

He shakes his head. "That bike belongs with James's family."

"You are his family."

"I'm not."

"You are James's son."

"But I didn't know him," Isaiah explodes, and his loud voice doesn't shake me. It's not me he's upset with, but a past he can't change. "I'll never know him. These people—" his hands wave toward the front of the clubhouse, "—they loved him, and that bike means something. The same way Echo loves Aires' Mustang, the same way Violet loves her dad's Chevelle."

I place my hand over his heart. "The same way you love the old Mustang you crashed when you were trying to get me out of debt with Eric. I understand that love."

"Then you know I can't take that bike."

I sigh heavily. "Eli's not giving you the bike because he thinks you miss James."

"Then why is he doing it?"

"Because Eli loves you."

That shuts Isaiah up. He stares at me, tongue-tied, and then there's hurt in his eyes—hurt from the fear that's so ingrained in him that he has a tough time ridding himself of the ache. I step forward into Isaiah, and I hug him tight. Hug him so strongly that it seems as if all the pain from his childhood should be forced out. But it's not my hugs that can cure him, it's each and every day that Isaiah accepts that there are people who love and care for him. Not because they need something from him, but because he's enough.

"He loves you," I say into his chest. "They all do. They're your family, Isaiah. Just let them in."

Isaiah finally wraps his arms around me and holds me so tight I can barely breathe. "It scares me."

"I know, but they're in this for the long haul."

With the way he runs his hands along my back, he's aware. We stand there, holding onto each other, letting Isaiah drive away his ghosts. He kisses the side of my head but keeps my hand as he steps back. "How's Eli giving me the motorcycle going to help Oz's situation?"

I breathe out in relief because that means he's going to do it—he's going to accept the gift. It also means Isaiah is ready to fully accept them as family.

"Take the motorcycle," I say, "then invite Eli up to Louisville. Tell him you'd like to repaint his bike."

"So, Eli's going to find out about his bike being painted by a baby tonight? I don't see how that's going to help."

"Eli's going to be so happy that his daughter is engaged and that his nephew is accepting him as family that he won't care about his motorcycle."

Isaiah looks at me like I'm insane. "He loves that bike."

"He loves the two of you more."

CHAPTER 41

OZ

The diamond ring is out of the box, hiding in my front pocket, and I lost Emily to Cyrus and Eli. I can't blame them. After all, Emily is Cyrus's granddaughter and Eli is her father. They love spending time with her, and she loves spending time with them. She sits with them at the kitchen table of Cyrus's house.

Standing in the doorway, I think of the summer I spent watching over Emily and all the mornings I came in to find Emily and her grandmother, Olivia, sitting at this same table bickering with one another.

Emily's quick-witted. Olivia was, too. Even before Emily understood that she was loved by this family, the two of them cared for each other almost instantly—even while they got under each other's skin.

Back then, old feuds between the Reign of Terror and a rival club had placed Emily in danger. It was my job to keep her safe. The threat is over from the rival club, but my mission isn't complete. Never will be. I love Emily, and I want to spend the rest of my life keeping her safe and making her happy.

In the living room, Breanna and Razor are catching up with Nina, my parents, and Razor's dad and step-mom. On the front porch, through the open screen door, I can hear Chevy, Isaiah, Rachel, and Violet swapping stories. There's multiple conversations happening. Laughter and smiles all around. It's the way Olivia would have wanted her family to be—together.

Emily glances up, as if she can feel me watching her, and she gives me that gorgeous smile. I tilt my head toward the front door. It's a question. *Can we steal a few minutes alone?*

My original idea was to take her to the overlook to propose, but we've lost too much time. Tonight's party is already under way. Once Emily hits the clubhouse, I'll be lucky to see her again until she's dead on her feet and ready for bed.

Emily nods and I can inhale again. We'll have a few minutes alone, I'll propose to her and she'll have the rest of the night with our family.

She scoots back from the table, tells Eli and Cyrus she's going to spend a few minutes with me and Eli stands along with her.

"I'm going to give Isaiah James' motorcycle tonight," he says low enough I can barely hear it.

Emily brightens. "Tonight?"

"Yeah." He looks as giddy as she is.

"When?"

Eli looks over at Cyrus. "I don't know. We haven't thought about that yet. It's inside the clubhouse now. We had Pigpen bring it in after Isaiah came into the cabin."

"Eli," I interrupt. "Emily and I are going to take a walk."

Eli meets my eyes and the understanding is clear: I'm about to propose and I'd appreciate it if he didn't get in the way...again.

"But you and Oz take some time—" Eli starts.

"We will, but you have to give Isaiah the bike now or he'll see it when he goes into the clubhouse."

Cyrus glances between me and Emily, also catching on. "No, we'll wait a few minutes."

"Nonsense." Emily approaches me and takes my hand. "Aren't you excited to see Isaiah receive his bike?"

Of course I am. "Yes."

"Then we'll go for a walk after." She kisses my lips in a slow way, in a promising way, but I know how this will play out. She'll be lost in all the people who will want to see her the moment we walk into the clubhouse. Then, as we catch up with our friends by the bonfire, she'll fall asleep in my arms.

I wanted this to be perfect. I had planned roses and candles and music. But perfection isn't going to happen.

"Seriously, Emily," Eli tries again, "we can wait. You and Oz haven't had two seconds together since you got here."

She cocks an eyebrow. "Since when have you been concerned about my quality time with Oz?"

She's right, and Eli shoves his hands in his pockets, fumbling for a response. But Emily doesn't notice, as she's on a mission. She wants to see her cousin receive a gift that means the world to her father.

Emily slips away from me, into the living room and out onto the porch. "Isaiah, let's head to the clubhouse."

I follow, and I hear footsteps as everyone in the house follows as well.

"Emily," I say softly as a growing sense of purpose takes hold of me.

"This is going to be such a great party," she continues.

"Emily," I say a bit louder. When she glances at me over her shoulder, her long dark hair falls all around her, and I lose the ability to breathe. I love her. More than anything. I want to spend the rest of my life with her. I want her to want to spend the rest of her life with me, as well.

The entire porch goes quiet—Razor, Breanna, Chevy, Violet, Isaiah, Rachel, Eli, Nina, Cyrus, Hook, Pigpen, Caroline, my mom and dad. I don't know why they're so silent. Maybe because everyone here knows how long I've been wanting to do this.

Emily stares at me, a question in her eyes, and I stare back, hoping and praying that she does love me as much as I love her.

Lots of people are gathered in the yard, there to keep Isaiah from going into the clubhouse so he doesn't see his gift. As the silence stretches on the porch, the loud conversation and laughter in the yard dies. Emily glances around as if searching for answers, but all anyone does is watch her.

"What's going on?" she says, and no one answers.

"Emily," I say again, and the tenderness in my voice, the pure love I have for her, causes it to be deeper than normal.

She turns to fully face me then, the confusion still there, but there's a softness in her expression. Probably because the only time she hears that tone of voice from me is when I whisper how much I love her during our private moments.

"Emily Catherine Star, from the moment you entered my life, you have been an amazing challenge."

There's a low rumble of laughter from the people who remember how Emily and I butted heads for weeks when we first met. How she called me out on my crap, how I challenged her to love this family, and how I was pissed she stood in the way of my goals. Then I think of how she learned to trust me, how I learned to trust her, and how we learned to love each other.

I think of how terror seized me when she was held by a rival motorcycle club. How I was afraid that they would harm her, how I knew then I didn't want to live without her, and how I marveled at her courage when she saved her father's life.

"But I liked the challenge. Craved it even. You have taught me how to be a better man, how to chase after what I want in life and you've taught me how to love. I wanted this moment to be perfect. I've spent months trying to create the perfect time alone with you so I could propose, but I didn't propose because it wasn't perfect enough. Because that's what I want for you Emily—I want you to have it all."

She places a hand to her heart and I'd be lying if I said I wasn't nervous. "But you and I have never been perfect. We've taken so many untraveled paths, and we're better for it. So maybe this is our perfect—this moment, on this porch, where we had our first real conversations together."

"All these people..." I glance around, "they love you. Almost as much as I do, and you love them back. I don't need time alone to do this. Me and you, we're right where we need to be—surrounded by our friends and family."

With a knot in my throat, I pull the ring out of my front pocket. This wasn't just three months of savings, but a year.

Emily watches me as I lower down to not one knee, but two. I'll beg her if I need. But with the way she's looking at me now—the same way she did when I first told her that I loved her, the same way she does when I take her into my arms—peace overflows my heart as I already know her answer. "Will you grant me the honor of being your husband?"

Emily's eyes glisten with tears, happy tears, and she nods repeatedly and holds out her shaking hand to me.

Me.

Oz—Member of the Reign of Terror Motorcycle Club and employee of the security company.

Jonathan—Special Education teacher and part-time soccer coach for the elementary school.

The man who loves her with every ounce of my being. Emily. My Emily is going to become my bride.

I slip the ring onto her finger, and the entire porch and yard descend into shouts of approval and applause. Emily laughs as someone suggests we get married tonight, and Eli fires back with, "No way. Emily's mom would kill me."

I cradle Emily's face with my hands and whisper down to her, "I hope you won't mind a big wedding."

"I'd be disappointed if it wasn't. After all, they're my family, too. But you've been right about one thing tonight, and I'd like to make that right."

My forehead furrows. "What?"

Her darks eyes spark with excitement and a sexy, sly grin touches her lips. "We do need time alone."

"Now?"

"Now."

Her wish, my command. I lean down, swoop Emily up in my arms and a new wave of cheers roars around us as I carry her off the porch and through the crowd, then place her on the seat of my motorcycle.

I slip on and nothing feels as right as her form pressed into my back, her arms wrapped around my waist, and her lips tickling my neck. I start the bike, the engine roars, and the frame rumbles beneath us. I glance back at my fiancée. "You ready?"

"For anything."

With her by my side? I'm ready for anything, too.

CHAPTER 42

ISAIAH

"It's a damn fine motorcycle," I say. I'm not that into bikes so that's saying a lot. The motorcycle is a beautiful piece of machinery, and I can tell that this one has been customized by the hands of someone who has appreciation, reverence, and love for it.

The clubhouse is packed with people, and they're nearly as silent as they were when Oz proposed to Emily. The two of them left, rightly so. If anyone needs a few minutes alone to enjoy their moment, it's them.

"It's your dad's," Eli says quietly, but there's no doubt everyone standing in the large room heard. His statement becomes an echo in the room and in my brain.

My dad.

James McKinley.

He was beloved by most of the people in this room, but I don't remember him. I was still in diapers when he died. I didn't even know he was my father until I was close to eighteen, and I didn't know that I had family who would have wanted me until after eighteen.

I cross my arms over my chest as I stare at the bike, trying to see the man who helped create me. According to Nina, my half-brother Chevy's mom, James was in love with my mom, but my mom had a hard time committing to him. Knowing Mom like I do, I can see it, and I also know Mom regrets how she treated James in the past.

My father was an undercover police officer, investigating a rival motorcycle club who was threatening his family. He laid the foundation of the case against the rival club that brought to justice people who needed to be off the streets. The current lead investigator of the rival club called my dad a hero.

The bike is shiny, the silver chrome buffed to the point I can see myself in it. They say I look like my father, and I try to imagine what he would have looked like crouched low, working on the machine. Did he find the same peace of mind I do whenever he had a tool in his hand and was working to solve a problem? Did he also take on lost-cause projects because there was a satisfaction in knowing that you were one of the few who could resurrect the dead?

"Did he ever ride it?" I ask.

"Yeah." With his hands shoved in his pockets, Eli looks at the bike like he's lost in a memory. "One of the last things he did was rebuild the engine. The frame was a mess, but James rode it. I still remember the huge smile on his face when he heard it rumble for the first time. He and I, we rode around for hours after he got it working. That's still one of the best nights of my life."

I think of Noah and all the nights he and I play basketball, shoot the breeze, sit in silence, and are there for each other. I think of Logan and how we work on cars together and still race each other at the local dragstrip. I think of Chevy and how he and I have formed a bond over the hours playing pool in smoky bars. Those have been some of the best nights of my life, too.

I glance up and standing on the other side of the motorcycle is Rachel. She's watching me with her beautiful, kind, blue eyes. I incline my head to the bike, and the right side of her mouth tips up. *Want to ride?*

"Are you asking?" she says.

"Yeah."

"Then sure."

"Hey, Eli?" I say.

"Yeah?"

"I hear you're going to need a paint job on your motorcycle. Why don't you bring it to my garage in Louisville for the work? Then I can drive you back in a real piece of a machinery—my Mustang."

Eli's eyes narrow. "What do you mean I need a paint job?"

"On a night like tonight, is it important?" I ask.

He immediately shakes his head. "Naw. I have a feeling this is also going to be one of the best nights of my life."

I gesture toward the bike. "Does this thing have keys?"

He tosses the key to me. Shouts of approval and applause come from all around us as I straddle the bike and then help Rachel hop on. I start the engine, and there's a satisfaction I wasn't expecting.

I've been on motorcycles before, but this ride feels different. Like how I felt the first time I got behind the wheel of a Mustang, the first time Noah and I laughed together, and the first time Rachel wrapped her arms around me. It feels like home.

The crowd parts as I edge the motorcycle forward and soon others are mounting their bikes, starting their engines. Then there's Eli on his bike beside me, grinning, as if the paint on his motorcycle is exactly the way he intended for it to be. He tilts his head for me to take the lead, and with my new family behind me, I do.

CHAPTER 43

RACHEL

"Rachel," Isaiah says softly. His fingers gently touch my face. I suck in a cleansing breath as I turn my head toward him and open my eyes.

I'm in the passenger seat of his Mustang. I hadn't meant to fall asleep on the ride home from the McKinleys, but it had been a fun and exhausting evening. First Emily and Oz's engagement, then the motorcycle ride with the club, dinner with the club, then hours talking with friends and family.

Eli and Cyrus invited us to stay with either of them. Usually, we do stay, but Isaiah insisted that we head home, even though dawn was going to be breaking soon. As I was hugging and saying goodbye to people, I saw Isaiah deep in conversation with Eli and Cyrus. Whatever it was Isaiah was saying, they were intent on listening and even seemed to be offering advice. The only thing I heard was that they understood why he wanted to head home.

I was curious as to what they were talking about—I'm still curious—but Isaiah will tell me when he's ready.

I blink away my exhaustion to find the morning sun reflecting against the windows of Tom's garage. The place is old and more than a little rundown, but it's well loved, and I'm one of the people who adores it. Still, I frown, confused about why we're here. I was half expecting him to take me to his apartment or my parents' house, but Tom's garage wasn't on my list.

Combing a hand through my hair, I feel the thoughts start to connect. "Did the Mustang start acting up on the way here?" I told him that the radiator hose was wearing thin, but he was all insistent that it could last a bit longer.

"No, I want to show you something."

I make a point of looking at my watch then slowly raise an eyebrow. It's seven in the morning and besides my short nap, we've both been up for over twenty-four hours. "Show me what?"

He cracks open his door. "It's inside."

Stretching my stiff and lazy muscles, I also open my door, get out then shut it. I take a step and my leg gives. My hand slams downward, toward the car to steady myself, but I come in contact with Isaiah's hand. He places his other hand on my hip to help until I find my balance.

Since the car accident when I was a teen, when I'm exhausted, the muscles in my legs sometimes decide not to work right. Isaiah knows this, and I shouldn't be surprised to find him by my side.

"I can carry you," he says.

He would, too. I test my leg and it's strong enough to hold my weight, so I shake my head. I keep his hand though, and we walk at my slow pace for the garage. Inside, I glance around, wondering if there's some car he's taken on he wanted to show me, but there's nothing parked in or around the garage and there's nothing on the lift.

In fact, besides some of Isaiah's tools and all of Mack and Tom's tools, there's nothing here. After Tom's death, Mack and Isaiah cleaned out the place so the realtor could show it.

There're no filing cabinets full of papers, no desk scattered with notes. Tom's coffee mug is gone, and so is Mack's whiskey bottle. The trash can that was typically filled with old take-out containers is no longer in the corner, and the tiny bathroom no longer has the single, ancient plug-in.

What I do see are memories. So many of them. The first time I walked in to find Isaiah with his shirt off, sweating over the open hood of his Mustang. The hours we've spent laughing and talking and working on cars together. Then the kissing—oh, the many kisses that have happened here. Then there was the night that Isaiah pulled the blanket out of the trunk of his car and we—

"You okay?" Isaiah asks.

"Tired, but I'm okay. I'm going to miss this place."

"What if you don't have to miss it?"

I lean against the wall next to the empty office and try to wake my groggy brain. "I don't understand."

Isaiah surveys the room like he also sees the same memories I do. I bet he sees a lot more. This place was one of the first that ever felt like a home to him. He finally hitches his thumbs in his jeans and leans on the opposite wall from me. "The Plan."

"We have one." Five more years and counting.

"What if I wanted to change some things up?" He shrugs. "Like I move out of the shithole I live in and get a new apartment?"

I visibly sag with relief. I hate to see him living in that rat-and-drug-infested, violence ridden, poor excuse for a building. I know Isaiah grew up tough, that he can take care of himself, and that the rent there means he has been able to save a ton of money for our Plans, but I've been begging him for years to move.

"I would say that's the best 'give' you've ever given me. Can you please get a place where you feel comfortable with me staying the night? Or…" I look away, feeling as insecure as I did when Isaiah and I started dating, "maybe a place where you'd be comfortable with me moving in."

He smiles a little, not as much as I hoped he would, but it's still there. "I was thinking we could get a place in those new apartments that they're building down on Lockwood Ave. The rent is more than what I pay now, but we'll be able to handle it easily together."

Surprise washes over me. That's a nice little area of town, a couple of miles from here. It used to be a dump, but the city has been trying to revitalize the area. But then I focus on the important word—we. We as in he wants me to move in with him. Butterflies take flight in my chest. "Those are super cute. I'd like that."

"What if—" Isaiah starts and then has to clear his throat. "What if I wanted to make a few more changes to the Plan?"

"Like?" I say slowly.

He rubs his neck, his go-to movement when he's stressed, then lowers his hands. "What if we don't wait five more years until we have enough money to build a garage? What if we buy this place?"

My heart stops beating and I'm unable to breathe.

Isaiah starts towards me, his gaze roaming my face as if he's concerned about me. "We don't have enough to buy it outright—but we have enough to make a huge down payment and I've been watching my credit and I know you've been watching yours, too. Together, we can get a loan for the rest. I'm not going to lie, the building has a ton of problems, but it would be ours. I talked to Eli and Cyrus about it last night, and there are people in the club who are good at construction. I've done enough work for the club that I bet they'll do most of the work at a discount rate."

"Probably for free," I say. "They'd never take a dime from you."

And as for the loan, there's no doubt my father would co-sign for us if we asked. He'd buy the garage for us, but he respects that Isaiah and I want to create our business on our own so instead he's given us advice on how to invest the money we've saved—to make our money work for us.

"I know this isn't the best part of town," Isaiah continues, "but people around here know you and me. They trust us. We'd have business—plenty of it. Plus, this neighborhood needs good businesses. It needs people who care and aren't going to rip customers off. There are good people who live around here, and in order for things to change, people who care, people like us, need to dig into the community instead of leaving. Besides, this is my—"

"Home," I finish for him. "This place is your home."

Isaiah's eyes soften as he closes the gap between us and rests his hands on my waist. My heart flutters with his caress. "Anywhere you are is my home."

"Same."

"Rachel, talking to Eli yesterday about perfection, seeing Oz propose to Emily, receiving my father's bike...if there's anything I know about life it's that it can change, fast. In good ways, in bad ways....I don't regret the plans we've made and I don't regret sticking to them like we have. And if you want to wait five more years, we can, and we will if that's what you want because your happiness is all that matters to me. But if you're on board, I'd like to do this. I'd like to buy this garage, open it with you, move in with you...marry you."

Joy spreads through me, so quickly, so furiously, that I go weak in the knees. Isaiah wraps an arm around me, steadies me and keeps me close to him.

"I didn't plan this right. I don't have an engagement ring to give you. I don't have flowers or dinner or anything fancy. If you want, I'll go buy you a ring the moment a store opens and—"

"This is my ring," I cut him off.

"What?"

I scan the garage. "This place is my engagement ring. In fact, I'm pretty sure other women are going to be jealous when they hear my fiancé didn't buy me a frivolous piece of jewelry but instead invested with me in our business."

Overcome with emotion, Isaiah closes his eyes and rests his forehead onto mine. "Is that a yes?"

I weave my arms around his neck. "It's a yes."

"I love you, Rachel." His voice breaks with emotion.

"I love you more." Forever.

A MOMENT TOGETHER:

AN ONLY A BREATH APART PREQUEL NOVELLA

The last evening Scarlett and Jesse spent together before everything changed. This moment is referenced several times in the novel.

This story starts three years before the start of Only a Breath Apart.

CHAPTER 44

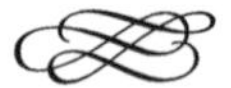

SCARLETT

It's weird being at Glory's place. Jesse and I used to hang out here all the time when we were little. From where I'm sitting on the front porch stairs of Glory's tiny cabin, and even in the moonlight, I can see the oak tree Jesse and I would climb, the garden we used to swipe fresh strawberries and blueberries, and the poplar tree where Glory once hung an old tire for us to swing on. We repaid her by stealing cookies from her kitchen. Oddly enough, as I look back at seven through the eyes of fourteen, I think Glory left the cookies out for us—as if she knew we were coming.

Glory has always been cordial to me, but we've never been close. She might flash a quick smile and wave our way before calling Jesse over to say something to him. Beyond that, I haven't had many interactions. To be honest, she scares me a little. She talks to dead people and spirits beyond the grave for a living. That is, sort of, creepy. Dad calls her a fraud, girls at school call her a witch, and Jesse calls her his distant cousin. I've said as little to her as possible.

But tonight, she invited me, Jesse, and Jesse's grandmother, Suzanne, over for ice cream cake to celebrate Jesse's and my eighth-grade graduation. My mother has taught me to always be polite, to accept invitations unless absolutely, completely unable to attend—as in the zombie apocalypse has happened—and how could I say no to ice cream cake?

The ironic part of it all is that my mother doesn't even know I'm here. Nor does my dad. It's after midnight, and about an hour ago, I snuck out from my bedroom window and climbed down the nearby tree so I could meet Jesse for the walk across his farm to here. While my mom and dad are sound asleep, Suzanne sits in a rocker on her porch and Glory sits on the porch swing. They're debating their family tree and how they know everyone in association with either school or church—a tradition that almost all families in this tiny town partake in. It's a confusing and senseless game that people over thirty entertain themselves with.

"Tink—" Jesse whispers his nickname for me "—if I start having serious conversations like that with you, I need you to shove me off a cliff."

"I'd never shove you off a cliff," I whisper back.

"Traitor." He smiles—the pirate one. The smile that makes me smile in return.

"What are you two grinning about over there?" Suzanne clicks her tongue at us as if catching us doing something embarrassing. "You look as smug as someone about to start a revolution."

"Nothing, Gran." Jesse turns his smile in her direction. "I was asking Scarlett to push me off a cliff to keep me from getting old."

Suzanne turns her playful gaze on me. "And you said?"

"I'm afraid Jesse is going to have to deal with growing up."

She laughs, long and loud. Suzanne is one of the most amazing people I know. She owns one of the largest farms in the county, if not the largest, yet lives like a pauper. Every couple of months, Dad tells Mom he doesn't understand why she won't sell her property, that she would be rich if she did. But Dad doesn't understand Suzanne and Jesse Lachlin—how they love their land as if it were flesh-and-blood family.

Suzanne is one of those people who ages beautifully. Somehow her green eyes are sharper, her mind quicker than when she was younger, but within the past few months, she seems to get winded faster and her endurance is shot. Though Jesse won't outright admit it, the way he looks at her when she's glancing away from him tells me that he's worried.

"I can't believe you two are going into high school," she says. "Time flies."

I suppress a sigh, because to sigh at a party, no matter how quietly, is rude. Time hasn't gone by fast enough. I can't wait to be older—to move out of my house, to be on my own, to have a job, an apartment, to be in love...Twenty something feels forever away, especially when, this year, turning from thirteen to fourteen felt like ten lifetimes.

Jesse looks at me, as if he can sense the shift in my mood, and bumps his knee into mine.

I return his glance and shrug with a small smile. A nonverbal, *I'm okay, and, no, I don't want to go home yet.* He raises his eyebrows in a *Should you?*

I shake my head and turn my wrist to check an imaginary watch. *I have time.*

Jesse inclines his head toward the woods that lead to his farm. *We can leave and go hiking across the fields whenever you're ready.*

A slight nod from me. *Okay, but in a few.* I move the plate, which has a small puddle of melted chocolate ice cream, a fraction to let him know that I have no idea what to do with it. He nods like he understands, then takes my plate from me as he stands.

His jeans don't reach his ankles. Instead, they stop about an inch short. Jesse has been doing nothing but growing over the last month. For a while, I think he was concerned he wouldn't hit a hundred and ten pounds before high school. Now, at his current rate of growth, I'm concerned he's going to run out of skin and his bones are going to pop out of his body. He wears his favorite T-shirt, the one that has a T-Rex trying to clap his hands, and there is a silent countdown to how many more times he'll be able to stretch that material over his head and squeeze it over his shoulders. The blue University of Kentucky baseball cap his gran bought him in fifth grade, the one that was too big, is starting to settle nicely upon his red hair, and his voice, within the past month, has dramatically deepened.

Jesse's changing, and it's awkward, because I'm not. I'm still the shortest of our graduating eighth-grade class, and my body is still like it was in fifth grade. Mom's threatening to take me to the dermatologist for acne medication, and I swear there is enough steel in my mouth from braces to stock a small manufacturing company.

Glory offers her plate to Jesse, and as he takes Suzanne's, she grips the arms of the chair and edges forward as if she's going to stand. Jesse shifts all the plates to his left hand and offers his gran his right. She accepts it and slowly rises to her feet. "I need to use the little girl's room."

Suzanne releases Jesse once she's steady on her feet. Jesse moves ahead of her, opens the screen door, then follows Suzanne into the house, leaving Glory and me alone.

I link my fingers together and rest them on my knees. I glance at Glory out of the corner of my eye, feeling like it's proper to start some sort of conversation with my hostess, but I don't know what to say other than the obvious. "Thank you for having me this evening. The cake was delicious."

"What did you dream about last night?" Glory asks.

"Um..." What type of question is that? "Nothing."

"You did." Glory tilts her head in this very airy way. Somehow, she appears cool in the humid night. "Did you know dreams are messages from the universe?"

I look over my shoulder toward the inside of Glory's house, and I'm disappointed when Jesse doesn't walk back out to save me from this strange conversation.

"My angels told me you dreamed of the moment that will set a series of life-altering events into motion."

I dreamed of a cat. There is nothing life-altering about a lost cat in a field. I think her "angels" are wrong, but I don't want to be rude. I just want the conversation over, so I lie, "I don't dream. Or at least I don't remember them."

It's not a lie, so much as a stretch of the truth. I typically don't recall my dreams, but I do remember the cat—how haunting it looked and how its cries were lonely and sad.

"You dreamed, but it's okay if you don't want to share. And just so you know, down the road, even when you think I've forgotten you, I haven't. You have always been and always will be at the forefront of my mind."

My brows slowly rise. I have a hard time believing she even knows my last name. Glory stares straight into my eyes, unwavering, and my brain works overtime to find something coherent to say in return. The screen door squeaks open, and I exhale with relief when Jesse and Suzanne walk back out.

"You two run along," Suzanne says with a wave of her hand as she sits in the rocking chair. "Have your fun. Glory will take me home after a bit."

Jesse grins at me, and I don't need another incentive to leave Glory's cottage for the safety of Jesse's land.

CHAPTER 45

JESSE

Scarlett's laughter echoes in the open field, and the sound is one of my favorites in the world. Right up there with the sound of the leaves rustling with a light breeze, creek water lapping over rocks, and my gran telling me she made oatmeal cookies.

It's three in the morning, late May, and thanks to the full moon, there's a dull light guiding our way. We're racing and she's in the lead. Not by much. A foot or two. My heart is pumping as fast as my arms as I try to catch up with her. She's fast, faster than me, and I can tell by the glint in her eye as she glances back at me that she will win.

I'd like to win. It's a great feeling to come in first, especially since she's won the last few times, but we're coming up to Gran's trailer—close to the end of a great night with the best person in the world. A night I don't want to end.

With a chuckle, I slow up. "You win, Tink! I give up!"

She eases to a walk, and when she turns to face me, she wears a brilliant smile. "You're slow, Lachlin."

No, she's just that fast.

We graduated from the eighth grade together today. She wore a blue dress she and her mother had bought in Louisville last month. Scarlett had whispered to me before the ceremony that she hated how tight the dress was, making her feel like she couldn't breathe, and that the material against her skin made her itch and fidget. She despised the dress so much that I kept it to myself how beautiful she looked—with the way the deep blue of the dress matched her eyes.

But how she looked then was nothing compared to how she looks now—pieces of her black hair falling from a sloppy ponytail, freckles showing on her shoulders from a tank top, and mud on her favorite pair of ripped jeans.

"What time do you want to head home?" I ask.

"Soon." There's sorrow in her tone, as if she's also sad this night has to end. "Dad's been waking up around five the past couple of weeks. Sometimes he cracks open my door to check on me before going downstairs."

Scarlett's dad hates me. Always has. It's because I'm a Lachlin and everyone in our town believes that means I'm trash and trouble. Also, the whole town thinks I'm cursed. Her dad doesn't want her anywhere around me. Has even said so to my face. He can't keep us away from each other at school, but he's told Scarlett, any other time, I'm off limits.

But Scarlett and I are friends, best friends, so she sneaks out her window and climbs down to hang out with me. Most nights, I toss rocks at her window to let her know I'm ready, but tonight she was out her window and dangling from a tree branch as I crossed the street from my trailer to her house.

"I think Glory and I talked once about caterpillars when I was younger," Scarlett says out of nowhere. "At least I think we did. Maybe we didn't. Maybe it was a dream."

Glory is my older cousin. She lives on the other side of my family's farm and makes money working as a "psychic."

"You're saying you had caterpillar and Glory dreams when you were younger?"

"You make it sound strange." Scarlett rolls her eyes.

"Anything with Glory is strange," I say. "You want to climb a tree before you go home? The one in the east field is calling our name."

Her gaze goes straight to the deep cut on my chin that I got when we fell during a recent climb gone bad. Concern flickers through her eyes, and before I can tell her I'm okay, she steps forward and traces my wound. Scarlett's touch causes my heart to stop and then start at a rate that makes it almost hard to breathe—reactions I don't understand.

Stop it. She's my best friend. I'm her best friend. Friends. That's what we are. That's what she needs us to be, but... there's something in her touch....something inside me that feels...different.

Different from when we were six.

Different from when we were ten.

Different from even yesterday.

"Does it hurt?" she whispers.

Yes. "No."

I see her replaying the accident in her head and she shivers. I know because the same cold chill runs through me as I think of her falling.

"I'm okay," I say softly.

I wait for her to draw her hand back, but instead she touches me one more time, and my skin burns with her caress. She meets my eyes and it's all there—the snap of the branch, her scream, the fall...and then there was me jumping from the safety of the tree to catch her.

She steps back and clears her throat. "I should go home."

"Yeah." She should. There will be other nights to climb trees.

Scarlett starts for her house, and I join her, right by her

side. Around us, the crickets chirp and frogs croak. I shove my hands in the pockets of my jeans as I consider telling Scarlett that my mom's back in town. She's been staying with some guy for the past few months. Mom's been quiet about this one—who he is, what, if anything, he does for a living. But she did tell me that she wants me to meet him next weekend.

I don't want to go. Meeting Mom's boyfriends never ends well, but I can't say no to Mom when she looks at me all hopeful—that maybe this is the one that will work out.

"Do you think high school will be different?" Scarlett breaks the silence and drags me out of my head.

"Different how?"

"I don't know." She pulls at the low branch of the tree in front of Gran's trailer and peels off a large green leaf. "Do you think people will be...friendlier?"

Probably not. The group of kids we've gone to kindergarten with will be in our first period class of high school. Can't imagine being handed an eighth-grade graduation diploma is going to help with their small-minded attitudes. "Maybe."

"It's okay if they aren't," she says, like she's honestly fine that people will continue to talk crap about her because she hangs with me. "We have each other. I only hope that we'll have lunch together. I heard they have two-to-three different lunches and that they divide it up based on where you are in the building around lunch time. It'll suck if we don't have lunch together."

"We'll have lunch together," I say as we cross the street. Scarlett and I live in the only two houses at the end of a long gravel road in the middle of nowhere.

"You don't know that," she says.

"Yeah, I do."

"How can you possibly know that? Are you psychic like Glory now?"

I wink at her and grin. "I'll skip class to have lunch with you."

She purses her lips. "You can't do that."

"I will."

"You can't. Skipping will get you into trouble, and even if you could skip one day, you couldn't skip all year."

That's what she doesn't understand, I would—for her. "You're my best friend."

"So?"

"We'll have lunch together."

We stop under the tree next to her house, the one that leads to her second-floor room. She looks at me, that incredulous expression she has when she's aware I'm up to no good—which is often. I hitch my thumbs in the pockets of my jeans and good-naturedly wait for Scarlett's stern reprimand, but as she goes to open her mouth her head darts to the right, toward her house.

Adrenaline hits my bloodstream—is it her parents? Is she busted?

"Do you hear that?" Scarlett asks.

We go silent, and I strain to hear what she's hearing.

She steps forward. "There it was again."

Once again, I got nothing.

She takes off to the land beside her house, and I'm quick to follow. Scarlett pauses by the trees and places her hands out in a signal for me to stop and stay silent. I do, and then I finally hear it. A soft meow.

My head snaps toward the sound. "This way."

We're methodical in our movements—slow and apprehensive. Most stray cats don't want to be found, and house cats that have lost their way can be skittish. Any wrong move will send the cat running, but Scarlett has a soft spot for all things with fur. Knowing her, the two of us will be tracking the cat past her three-in-the-morning self-imposed curfew so she can confirm that it's well-fed and safe.

I pause, my instincts telling me that we're close, and as if Scarlett senses it as well, she puts her hand out again. My gaze roams, searching.

"There," Scarlett barely whispers, and I follow her line of sight to the spot next to a bush. There, lying on its side in the undergrowth is a cat, white with black spots. In the moonlight, it watches us, its ears pulled back, its fur puffed out, and its body close to the ground—signs that it's scared. In the same position, I would be, too.

"Lower yourself," I breathe out, a reminder of how to handle frightened animals.

Towering over the animal only makes you intimidating. I crouch, so does Scarlett, and the cat thankfully stays in place. I glance over at Scarlett, and she's doing all that I've taught her through the years: don't make direct eye contact—just fleeting glimpses to assess the situation. Don't give the animal a reason to bolt.

The cat watches Scarlett more than me, which allows me to slip in for a closer look.

There're no wounds I can see, no blood gushing from anywhere, but there is a rip in its ear—a sign of at least one past fight. I pay extra attention to the rib cage to see if the cat is skin and bones, or if it has had the ability to do well on its own. My forehead furrows as parts of the cat show signs of malnourishment—it's thin and its rib cage sticks out. Then my stomach sinks as I notice its protruded belly, with several enlarged pink spots on the abdomen.

I watch the abdomen. The cat's stomach moves up and then down. I keep staring, intently, so much that my eyes start to burn as I fight the urge to blink. Then there it is—the rolling in the stomach.

"The cat's pregnant, Tink," I say softly.

Her head snaps in my direction, making the cat sit up. "Are you sure?"

"It's either that or she has one hell of a tape worm, but I'm betting pregnant."

"Can we catch her?" Scarlett asks. "Put her in one of the barns to keep her, and eventually her kittens, safe?"

I slowly extend my arm and the cat scrambles away with its back arched. I withdraw my arm to make myself smaller. It's a bonus that the cat doesn't dart. "If we go for her now, she'll probably run off. Why don't you go on home, and I'll get some food from Gran's."

"Are you going to trap her with food?"

I shake my head. "I don't want her to get hurt. I'm going to get her to trust me with food. Hopefully she'll like me and let me pick her up. If not, I'll consider using a raccoon trap. But something tells me once we start feeding her, she'll warm up."

"What if she's not here when you get back?"

"She will be."

"How do you know?"

I meet Scarlett's eyes. "I don't, but I think she will be. Plus, it's the best option we have at the moment."

She nods. We slowly ease back and are silent as we walk back toward her house. Once again, at the bottom of the tree, we look at each other.

"You promise we'll help her?" Scarlett asks, and the ache of leaving the cat behind is noticeable in her voice.

"I promise." I don't break those. She knows that. I especially would never break a promise to her.

Scarlett gives me a soft smile. Then without another

word, she jumps up to the lowest branch and starts scaling for her bedroom window.

There's a lot of things screwed up in my life, but I have Scarlett and somehow, that makes everything else okay. Once safely inside, Scarlett waves down to me. I lift a hand in goodbye and then head back to my land, to Gran's trailer, so I can find some food for our new cat.

ONLY A BREATH APART ORIGINAL OPENING

CHAPTER 46

JESSE

Wind whips through the tree outside the window. The thrashing limbs give the shadows on the wall the appearance they're alive—poltergeists, ghosts. I'm a realist, so I don't believe in spirits beyond the grave, but I do believe in memories. Some memories are so real they're overpowering. That's the black hole I'm sinking into tonight, memories come back to life.

Except for the soft light from the lamp next to my grandmother's bed, the trailer is dark. Rain taps against the tin roof, and the last song on the vinyl record that's been playing for the past twenty minutes ends. The room fills with the sound of dead air and the needle scratching on the paper label.

Gran loves listening to records, and that record player has been in her room for as long as I can remember. No matter how many times I've tried to bring her musical tastes into this century, she refuses. "Nothing sounds as good as it does playing from vinyl. Stop trying to change me, Jesse. I like who I am fine."

It's three in the morning. I rolled in at midnight, and something in the way she was dreaming kept me from going into my room across the hall. Gran had been in a wrestling match with an unseen force, and she appeared to be on the losing end. But I started playing her favorite albums on low, and she's eased into a better sense of peace.

Everything seems normal again, except for her breathing. It's shallow, labored, a wheeze. Her chest moves up and down, but I don't like the sound of it. The doctor told her in April that her heart wouldn't make it past July. It's August. I reach over, place the needle back into the groove, and Johnny Cash sings once again. His voice is deep, the lyrics heavy, and the crazy growling in my brain becomes harder to ignore. I'm slowly losing my mind.

"You can feel it, can't you, Jesse?" Like she's a damn ghost herself, Glory's pale face is the first part of her I see before she enters the light of Gran's room. Her wild, wet blond hair sticks to her face, and water drips onto the worn carpet from the hem of her long dress. "The air is different, weighted. The doors between this world and the next are converging here—ready to take another soul."

Glory is full of crap. She was born in the wrong era, wrong generation, or maybe she drank too much or smoked too much weed when she was my age of seventeen. Any way I look at it, her forty-year-old mind is shot. There isn't some magical, mystical realm full of fairies and unicorns. There's the real world and real problems. I can't help it if Glory can't deal with reality.

"I don't remember inviting you."

"I have an extended invitation," she says.

"Three in the morning is beyond visiting hours."

"Visiting hours are for conventional people, and there's nothing conventional about any of us." Glory float-walks to the other side of Gran, sits on the edge of the bed and gently takes her hand. "She's going to pass tonight."

"You don't know that," I snap.

She flips Gran's hand over, traces her fingers over Gran's palm and concentrates as she silently does a "reading." I don't bother to hide the roll of my eyes as I cross my arms. I lean back in the wooden chair as if I'm cool and calm instead of seconds away from losing my temper. If Gran didn't love Glory so much, I'd kick her out.

Glory is family in the eighteenth-cousin-twice-removed way, and because of that, Gran has permitted Glory to live rent-free in the rundown cottage at the other side of the six hundred acres Gran owns. There, Glory-the-Con-Artist runs her tarot-card/palm-reading business. People pay her money so she can scam them and tell them lies.

There are three Lachlins left in this world: me, Glory, and Gran. Glory possesses a hint of the Lachlin bloodline, but Gran and I are the last full-blood heirs. This meant so much to Gran and my mom that they refused to give me my father's last name. Instead, I have my grandmother's maiden name: Lachlin.

According to my great-grandfather's last will and testament, the land can be passed down only to a direct Lachlin descendant. Gran and I are the last of a dying breed. After me, the Lachlins will be extinct.

Glory's shoulders drop with a long exhale, as if holding the palm of a weak woman is exhausting. She then lovingly rolls Gran's fingers into a fist. "Yes, she'll be crossing over soon."

A muscle in my jaw twitches, and as I open my mouth to tell Glory she's no longer welcome, Gran's eyes flutter open. "I want her here."

I can't figure out if I'm annoyed that Gran's been lying

there listening or relieved she's still coherent. Gran looks frail tonight, and if my grandmother has been known for anything, it's for not being weak. She has a reputation as a kick-ass type of woman. She's also known as eccentric. That's a nice word for weird. Kick-ass, eccentric, and weird. Describes her well and it hurts bad in the chest that her body hasn't kept up with her mind.

Glory leans over the bed, and with a gentle hand, brushes Gran's short, white hair away from her forehead. "I brought saffron to make tea. It will help clear your centers and connect you better with the universe. Would you like some?"

Gran agrees, and I'm grateful Glory leaves the room. Once she's down the hall, I scoot to the edge of my seat and readjust Gran's favorite crocheted blanket so it covers her better. "Are you doing okay?"

She rolls her head in my direction, and I hate how much effort it takes. This isn't my grandmother. My gran is a woman who laughs too loud, speaks even louder, and who loves me when no one else does. She took me in when I was thrown away, and she's the only person over the past couple of years I have allowed myself to love.

My throat thickens, and I clear it. Crying's not my thing, but this is my gran, and without her, I'm nothing. A storm rumbles in the distance.

"Don't be scared, Jesse." Her voice cracks on my name.

"I'm too old to be scared of the dark." I'm teasing her, a reminder of when I was younger and how she would sit up with me on nights when the thunder and lightning felt too close and too dangerous.

"There are different types of fear."

That I know.

"I was a child when your great-grandma died," she says. "She died in her bed, in our house, and it scared me, but

Daddy told me to not be frightened, because her dying in the house meant I wasn't alone."

Good thing we don't live in her childhood home, the condemned and falling-apart building next to our trailer. Otherwise, I would have grown up with one more ghost rattling around in my mind. There're enough annoying spirits there already, and the ones that do haunt me have loud voices and strong opinions. Most of them telling me when I look in the mirror how I'm doing everything wrong.

"Don't be scared of death."

Death doesn't bother me. Her dying does.

"I love this land. Almost as much as I love you." Gran reaches out, a silent request for me to take her hand, and without thought, I do. Her skin is cold and translucent, her grip too weak, and I hold on for more than what I'm worth. "Scatter my ashes next to where your mom is buried."

Gran doesn't understand how I'm walking the line of crazy. I can't comprehend a world where she isn't here when I return home. A click of her tongue when I show past curfew, a knowing and proud smile when I come in covered in mud after working on our land, a hot oatmeal cookie after a long, hard day...

"Your uncle doesn't think you're responsible enough to own the land," she continues.

My non-blood, married-into-the-family uncle and I share an unusual amount of hate. He doesn't trust me, I don't trust him, and he's made it his full-time job to make my life a living hell. We have to deal with each other because he has power of attorney for Gran.

"He's wrong," I say.

"He says you're more interested in the money than in the legacy."

"He's wrong again." And he needs to keep his mouth shut.

"I know he is," she says softly, then gasps for air. It's such a tight wheeze that I breathe in for her and wish that her lungs would fully fill the way mine do. "He doesn't understand how you love this land. I doubt even I fully understand. There's a connection between it and you. I see it in your eyes every time you come in from walking through the fields. But I want you to be happy."

"I am happy," I say, and the sad flash in her eyes tells me she thinks that's a lie. "You know this land brings me peace." And that's the truth.

When everything in my life has gone to hell, I've had this land and Gran. When she passes, the land is all I'll have left. People look at this ground and see trees, grass, and fields. They see what they think is nothing. They see a backwards life in a technology-driven future.

They don't see what I see, and what I see is my only shot at happiness. I see something that's alive, that breathes, and is as much a part of me as my arms and legs. The land doesn't judge. It doesn't put expectations upon me I'll never meet. It accepts. My soul and the land's soul are intertwined. What happens to it, happens to me. We aren't separate. We're one.

"Don't talk, Gran. You'll feel better after some sleep, and in the morning, I'll make you a hot breakfast."

She studies me, and I'm afraid of what she sees. "I know what the people in town say. I know what some people in our family have said. I've told you this for years, but I need you to hear it again: there's no curse."

She squeezes my hand, but I can't speak. Gran being so feeble is already bringing up too many memories of Mom, and the pain in my chest is so intense that a part of me wishes I was the one dying.

"If there was a curse," she says, "then you wouldn't be here. You've brought me more joy than I should have ever been allowed."

I lightly chuckle. "You weren't saying that when Uncle Marshall bailed me out of jail a couple of months ago."

She laughs and squeezes my hand again. "You're a challenge, but most things worth loving are." Her smile fades. "That's what I want for you. I don't want you to be scared to love."

Footsteps approach from the hallway and Glory enters with a steaming teacup. I move to help prop up Gran so she can drink, but she shakes her head. "Let Glory read your palm."

I tip back the wooden chair I'm in so that it leans against the wall. "You don't believe there's a curse, yet you believe she can talk to dead people and see the future?"

"Yes," Gran says without blinking. "So, give her your hand. I want to know your future."

"I don't." I have no interest in knowing anything beyond today.

"That sounds like you believe I have the gift." Glory sets the teacup on the bedside table, then peels a lock of her wet hair off her face. "And you're scared of what I'll tell you."

"I believe you're a hustler who makes a buck off people who are easy reads."

"Nothing about you is easy. In fact, everything about you is very difficult."

"Let me guess, I'm a tortured soul, and next week I'm going to see a blue bird and that blue bird's going to represent a dead family member of mine who is there to tell me to be at peace with my soul."

The ends of Glory's mouth edge up—sarcastic and dry. "It'll be a black bird, actually, and the bird will not bring peace to your soul. The sight of it will trouble you."

Another keen observation based on things every person in town already knows—my soul is always troubled.

"You believe you are cursed." Glory watches me as if she sees more than what exists. "Is it so hard to stretch your belief in the Lachlin curse to thinking there are those of us who possess a supernatural gift?"

"I'm cursed," I say, "because I have to listen to you spew lies about spirits beyond the grave."

While Gran isn't paying attention, Glory has the balls to smirk at me.

"Give her your hand," Gran presses.

"Gran," I start to protest, but she holds up her hand, stopping me.

"I did something to help you," Gran whispers, and my heart stops beating. "I want to make sure I made the right decision."

I push off the wall, and the front legs of the chair hit the floor with a crack. "What did you do?"

"Let her read your palm," Gran says, and as I open my mouth to argue, she raises her voice to a tone I haven't heard in weeks. "Let her read your palm!"

I put out my hand, palm up, forcing Glory to come to me. She crosses the cramped room. I can't maneuver without ramming into a piece of furniture, but Glory breezes past it all and takes my hand in her smaller one.

"What's his future?" Gran asks.

"This is ridiculous."

"Any more ridiculous than the curse?" Glory whispers so only I can hear. "I know what you really believe, and I know how you think you can break the curse."

I go to snatch my hand back, but Glory keeps a firm grip. Gran's watching us intently, so to appease her, I stay still. Glory's fingernail, painted blood red, follows a long line at the center of my palm, then traces the dissecting smaller ones.

"He will be tested," Glory says in a far-off voice. The perfected one she does for effect.

"Yeah. I start school next week. Tests happen." Especially for a senior.

Glory ignores me, and Gran coughs, the rasping sound scraping the inside of my skull. "I know this. Tell me what I want to know."

"This is more. The universe has decided to take advantage of your plan."

A sickness sloshes in my stomach. "What did you do, Gran?"

My uncle has been here more than normal. Paperwork in his hands every time. Gran told me she was updating her will. She told me she and my uncle were protecting me. I assumed it was to close some legal loopholes involving me being a minor and inheriting the land. I silently curse, because I should have been smarter and asked for specifics.

Glory's eyebrows knit together as she narrows her gaze on my palm.

"Trying to see what I had for dinner?" I mumble.

"Jesse's future is unclear, Suzanne."

"Because you're a fake," I whisper, but I give her credit. She never loses her focus.

"Jesse is a volatile soul. You know this. Unless he has a clear understanding of who he is, I can't see what his choices will be." Her forehead furrows now, as if watching my palm is causing her pain. All of which I don't buy.

"Did I make a mistake?" Gran asks as a wheeze. "Will he lose the land?"

"I don't know. I can't tell."

My entire body jolts as if struck by electricity. I yank my hand away from Glory's grip and turn my attention to Gran. "Why are you asking about the land? Why would I lose it?"

Gran's chest rises, and then she blows out a breath. A

breath that's too long. A breath that's too final. Johnny Cash begins the chorus of her favorite song, and that craziness in my head becomes a scream in my ears as I wait for her to inhale again.

Johnny's deep voice croons about sunshine, and as if in slow motion, Gran's eyelids shut.